The Voluptuaires

Alais Escobar Henri

Haunted Doll House

BINGHAMTON, NY

Cover art by Fox Henry Frazier
Author photo by Tania Kaaz
Instagram: @tania_nofilter
Images are used by kind permission

Watercolor Garden Flowers copyright Lisima via Creative Market

Book Design: Sarah Reck
Editor: Fox Henry Frazier

Library of Congress
Cataloguing-in-Publication Data

The Voluptuaires // Alais Escobar Henri

Library of Congress Control Number 2022945340

Henri, Alais Escobar
ISBN 978-1-7364655-3-0

9 8 7 6 5 4 3 2 1
FIRST EDITION

Alais Escobar Henri's *The Voluptuaires* is a touchstone of deviance, opening the veins and echoing a similar warning to that in *House of Leaves*. Henri proves to be a practitioner of both beauty and pain, juxtaposing the ugliness of the human condition with stunning imagery. Her language prowls, then punches, and any reader may find themselves gutted within these pages.

The Voluptuaires is a grimoire of the grim and desolate, and a champion for the forgotten. Readers, be warned: who we are, when separated from that desperate grip of love, is often the shadow selves we have refused to confront. Are you ready?

— Hillary Leftwich, author of
Ghosts Are Just Strangers Who Know How to Knock and *Aura*

Readers will have to muster their courage to follow Alice, Jonathan, and Felix on their journey. It is forbidden— shameful— dangerous— and thrilling. Who is the hunter? Can you survive the past? Alais Escobar Henri writes beautifully, and cinematically. Read *The Voluptuaires*, if you dare.

—Elísabet Ronaldsdóttir

The most obvious comparison of *The Voluptuaires* would be to the work of Bret Easton Ellis, whose books and characters are often considered difficult. The essentially moralistic nature of his books, hidden like particle board under a veneer of nihilism, offers one at least the comfort of being able to despise the characters.

What is remarkable about *The Voluptuaires* is that the humanity of these characters is made so evident that one is not permitted the respite of simply hating them, even when they are behaving like monsters. There is little morality, and less comfort, in this book. Instead, there is deeply flawed humanity, laid out in exquisite detail, with the kind of unflinching compassion that is not for everyone. Reader beware.

— M. Pelin

CONTENT WARNING

This book is predicated on the extreme opinions and deviant behaviors of verily depraved characters. This novel contains depictions and/or discussions of the following: abduction, ableism and ableist language, abuse (physical, mental, and sexual), body dysmorphia, cannibalism, child abuse, classism and classist language, drug use, eating disorders, ephebophilia, gaslighting, gendered slurs, incest, mental illness, pornographic material, racism and racist language, rape, statutory rape, self-harm, sexual assault, sexual slurs, suicidal ideation, and other forms of violence.

The list of material disclosed above is by no means exhaustive of all potential triggers contained in the following pages. Let me be very clear: bad things will happen once you turn this page. Evil things.

If you're easily offended, or if any of the items on the above list might cause you to flash back to events or experiences you'd rather not re-live: please do not read this book.

This world is ugly. And so are The Voluptuaires.

Signed *avec amour* . . .

Alais

CONTENTS

ONE

"This is a good place to get fucked up. Don't you think?" Felix asked, pointing to a restaurant patio decked with gleaming mint-green metal chairs and tables. Each table had a spray of fresh daisies in teal-colored glass mini-jugs, and its own wine bottle filled with lemon water. The brunch crowd filled the air with laughter and animated conversation; plates of eggs benedict, bacon, and pancakes, along with cocktails and coffee, were being spirited to tables by sure-footed, overworked servers. The restaurant's waitlist was two hours long this morning; the spillover crowd was pre-gaming brunch with drinks at the bar.

"That establishment is filled with tourists and suburban sycophants who think they're classy," Jonathan Forrester replied. "Your fucking future wife will take you to enough of these patios on Sundays to last a lifetime. You will end up on one of these patios when you're cheating on her. Before that fucking happens, Dear Little Brother, I will, by God, start you out in a real fucking bar with some real fucking liquor."

Felix stopped walking. He lifted one of his delicate fingers and blinked rapidly. His pulse began racing and his ears rang with a tinnitus-like ring of shock.

"Wait…" he said. "Are we actually… slumming it today?"

Felix's entire life of twenty-one years had been spent cloistered in his brother's shadow. Their mother, doting and overprotective of her delicate Felix, had over the past handful of years become obsessively worried that she was going to somehow lose Felix to the vices of alcohol, or even worse, a trendy Fentanyl overdose. For his part, Felix was a rather pliable and eager-to-please young man. His brother Jonathan, however, was not above occasionally allowing Felix to imbibe or partake of illicit substances — privately, amongst Jonathan's own carefully curated circle of friends. Felix had experienced a moderate amount of alcohol use and recreational drug consumption. But today marked the first time that Jonathan had *ever* suggested he and Felix have an actual adult outing together like brothers — like grown men — having real fun, and not just in the safety of their bedrooms or at a living room party when the parents were away. The anticipation of what could possibly happen today, something other than the safe and normal, quickened Felix's pulse and sent his imagination racing as if he were a young child again anticipating the birthday cake that hadn't yet been lifted from its pale pink box.

"No!" Jonathan said. "I do not want to *slum it*." He had a deep voice that matched his Nordic height of "six foot awesome," and a clipped way of enunciating each word.

There was a joyous urgency in the air, a sort of noisy post-war, post-pandemic euphoria that could only mark a population grateful for a beautiful summer day and refusing to contemplate any disastrous world events. The state of the world, however, was bleak. Vulnerable Americans were dying of COVID-19 variants; a mysterious new illness was crashing children's livers, prompting news anchors to speculate on whether schools should perhaps not open in a few months; a mutation of HIV was spreading in Denmark; images of civilians uncovered from mass graves as the war in Europe continued to spread, collecting new potential daily to explode into a global conflict. All this and more blared from television screens across bars and restaurants; barely a soul in any of these establishments cared about pathogens, the houseless, or wars and siege that remained elsewhere. The world was on fire, but they had iced cocktails, air conditioning, and amuse-bouches.

"This is *America*," Jonathan said, his tone ironic and delighted at once. "The air is sweet, and the food is plentiful, and everyone is overcome with insatiable thirst. "

"They… they have cocktails," Felix said, helplessly. "I want to day-drink today."

"So do I," Jonathan said. "But *that* is a *restaurant*. So: fuck no!"

It was early June in Denver, Colorado. The sun was hammering into the city, although it was only 10 AM. 105-degree days in Denver were becoming alarmingly common, and that wasn't taking into account the collection of 105-degree days that had been hitting unusual places like Paris, London, and Glasgow. The pretty women sipping icy, pink Aperol spritzes and crushed-ice mimosas, who'd had the idea to soothe their heated souls at Denver restaurant patios, chatted vapidly about how badly they missed the icy ski season.

Felix glanced ahead at the Union Station entrance. The interior of the train station hub was pale and cream and ready for Instagram. There were tourists clogging the building; a transient woman hung onto her tattered boho bag and screamed at the top of her lungs as a security guard shoved her and accused her of "dirtying up Denver." A young local influencer named Kay-Zee Travyon filmed social media content in the lobby while his entourage held up portable lighting. Outside of the station a young man from Atlanta named Trapbone played popular tunes on his trombone, and twirled it in response to the tips and cheers from people passing by. There was an ice cream parlor; there were two bars, one upstairs and one down. It was as good a place as any, Felix assumed, for them to start off an old-fashioned day-drinking crawl, just like the ones talked about in romantic comedies (a guilty pleasure of Felix's).

Jonathan sighed, regarding his younger brother with pale eyes and a frown that was almost paternal. The brothers stood in front of a wall which was decorated with a mural of a beautiful green-eyed woman called Saint Cecilia. According to present-day mythology, she was a young woman who had spent time in Denver as a youth, and in young adulthood performed actual miracles—healing the sick by laying her hands upon them. Although never identifying herself as Catholic or even identifying with any Biblical views, Cecilia was claimed as a Saint by the Catholic church after she was assassinated in New York's St. Patrick's Cathedral in 2012. There was a network of fans, mostly women in the arts, who still often made murals and figurines of her, frequently in the hearts of Denver and New York City.

Just under St. Cecilia's oversized portrait, there was a set of angel wings painted with a blank space between them, designated for the Instagram junkies to take selfies. Jonathan stood in that void, and Felix stood next to him. They stood with their arms crossed over their chests. The linen that draped the brothers' bodies was certainly a better choice of clothing that went beyond fashion, and as it kept their bodies cool in the summer sun, Jonathan could only imagine the horror the denim- and synthetic-fabric-clad masses felt in this heat. St. Cecilia meant nothing to either man; her mural was unnoticed by them. They were simply two rich, young, white men, leaning against her image because it was a comfortable place to rest.

"Do you think we could plan to have a double bachelor party? Or is that weird?" Felix said.

"Why would it be?" Jonathan said. "I suppose we could have a bachelor party. We're nearly the same age, our weddings are on the same day. It makes as much sense as anything."

"I would want it to be wild!" Felix said. "Like in the movies!"

Felix's slim, diminutive manner of speaking matched the way his dainty fingers twitched like antennae. His breathy voice and stuttering sentences were endearing to some and annoying to others. Felix honestly couldn't believe his luck — Jonathan had already proposed that they have fun today, and now they were possibly looking forward to a real bachelor party!

"What?" Jonathan grinned, and his eyes crinkled. "Like *The Hangover*?"

"Yes!" Felix said, rubbing his hands together, childlike. Another personal tic that annoyed some and amused others. "Just like that!"

"Getting roofied and traumatized, and having it all documented in a series of Polaroids that could destroy us forever is something you… want? Our reputations are as fragile as the money that flies in the digital world around our ears, and the value of the fine art that keeps our family in business. The last thing we need is Dad cutting us out of the will because a thousand topless lesbians are protesting outside his galleries due to one of our fuckups. Why the fuck do I have to explain this?"

An image flashed through Jonathan's head — a memory connected to the consequences of the last time he and Felix had managed to fuck up and piss off their family. Gauzy skirts fluttering in the wind, a gauzy blouse, a mermaid's float of hair, backlit by the sun… flying… he saw Felix's face in this memory, stunned wide, green eyes, an open screaming mouth.

Traumatic memories were a rather cinematic thing, in Jonathan's dispassionate internal record of his own history. They were like scenes from arthouse films seen at an antique movie theater called The Mayan, a place their mother used to take them to when they were small boys. It was a place of so many strange movies, indie-international-arthouse-experimental treats that would leave fragments of memories in Jonathan's young mind that could turn as nightmarish as Willy Wonka's boat ride.

Felix's mind, coincidentally, was also on The Mayan movie theater, but he always thought of the theater in the heat of any summer day. He was perpetually grateful that the theater had survived the pandemic-spurred massacre of small business shutdowns.

This movie theater was nowhere near them at this time, but with the summer heat beginning to scorch, and Jonathan's mood clearly becoming sour, Felix wondered if the day couldn't be salvaged by just booking an Uber to The Mayan and sipping at a cocktail in the cubby-hole sized vaudeville stage that was the upstairs movie screen.

"Haven't you ever wanted to just to fuck everything up for no reason, Jonathan?" Felix said. "Everyone else fucks up their own lives, why can't we?"

"Why would you want that, Felix?" Jonathan asked. "Little brother, you're the only coke-head I know who complains about being bored."

"I'm not a coke-head," Felix replied, his posture straightened, and he flicked his gaze back and forth to see absolutely no one looking at them. "How often do I do coke? Not that often, only when you bring it around.

You're the addict."

"Well," Jonathan muttered with his jaw set, "I've never seen you refuse it. Speaking of…" he pulled his phone from his pocket and glanced at the screen, saw no reply to a text he had sent.

"Fucker," he whispered. He gazed across the street, his blue eyes scanning every face, every man, not seeing the only one he needed to see at that moment. Fucking ugly beasts all around. The best part of the pandemic had been the mask mandates, Jonathan realized, when he didn't have to fucking look at anyone's ugly gobs. He clenched his jaw and sighed so loudly it turned into a groan.

Jonathan's surly nature stood in stark contrast to Felix's natural, amenable friendliness; this incongruity had been evident in the brothers ever since they were small children. Their mother attributed Jonathan's innate churlish tendencies to traits inherited from his father — who was descended from a notorious gunslinger in Denver's wild-West saloon days.

Before Felix could inquire about his change in mood, Jonathan looked him straight in his green eyes. "How about worrying about a Bachelor Party. We will order strippers and pizza. Let's see some free-range tits."

"Free-range tits," Felix said. "I want to see tits so bad the incision scars are showing."

Felix thought about the dried and scarred women that his mother's foundation benefited, these women who had a brittle quality like they were going to evaporate to dust if they were ever forced to do a sex act again, and the thought nearly made him hard.

"Tits that bad came from the nineties," Jonathan scoffed. "They would be some pretty old strippers you're wanting to see."

A gasp escaped from a woman who had been checking her phone next to them. She wore a Denver Broncos tie dyed shirt and khaki shorts. She had broad, thick, feet with bulbous dried painted toes in oversize Teva sandals. "You two are disgusting!"

The brothers stared at her as someone would a caged banshee, until she walked away.

"Her?" Jonathan asked as the woman left them. "You're jealous of someone like her? Really?"

"I am," Felix said. "She has the ability to be disgusted."

"*I* am disgusted," Jonathan said, his voice edged with impatient anger. "You want to see fake old-lady tits on some woman at the end of a lifetime of disappointment and bitterness so you can feel alive. No. That isn't normal, Felix. In fact, it makes you a bad person."

"You heard about the Campbell girl's bachelorette party, right?" Felix asked, changing the subject in a way similar to their mother, who had a habit of cheerfully flipping conversation topics before their surly asshole of a dad could lose his temper.

"Who hasn't," Jonathan said, and he scoffed, a mirthless laugh that sounded like a cough and he glanced at the folk who walked by him. There was one attractive young woman in the group, but that would be a gun-to-his-head decision. It did not change the fact that she was in cheap clothes, used to cheap shit, except for the one or two times a year she could buy a Coach purse at a clearance sale.

The Campbell girl Felix had mentioned was a woman their age, a distant cousin at most. Her bachelorette party had made all gossip columns and even tabloids by virtue of having some minor celebrities in attendance. There were strippers of both sexes at the party, a drug overdose, a possible kidnapping, and a search party for the bride-to-be when she had disappeared with a female stripper. The marriage went on as planned the next week.

"You do realize that women are having better bachelor parties than we are," Felix said.

"Who the fuck cares about what kind of bachelor parties women are having," Jonathan replied. "I mean honestly who gives a shit?"

Jonathan thought of the small square of waxed paper folded up in his wallet, and how just a lick of precious white powder clung to its edges.

Felix sighed.

Two policemen passed them by. They were a classic old dog and rookie pairing. The older man had a salt and pepper mustache, and the younger man was smooth shaved with a short-buzzed haircut, like a military recruit.

The brothers didn't notice a young woman wearing a sunhat and pink dress who paused to let the policemen pass. The policeman stepped aside for her, however, and she gave them a small smile. The younger policeman gave a smile back to her that lingered. By then, the girl in the pink dress had turned her attention to the brothers. Her dark eyes flicked to them, she stopped as if to get their attention, she lifted her hand in greeting, but both brothers ignored her. Her cheeks turned pink, and she walked swiftly away. The policemen exchanged glances and chuckled before continuing their path.

The older policeman had seen how the embarrassment of being ignored had reddened that young woman's cheeks, but he could not imagine that she ever had to deal much with being ignored or passed over. Not a shiny young beauty like that.

The older policeman had two ex-wives and five children in his past and present. He had a lifetime of service as a patrolman, in which he'd never had occasion to fire his gun or receive a medal of merit, nor any incidents of gross negligence to be publicly reprimanded for. He had been assigned to stand outside Whole Foods when BLM protests wafted teargas through the city, and always seemed to have been at the other side of town whenever mass shootings and homeless sweeps happened. He had lived his entire life in blissful monotony alongside the millions of faceless middle-class nobodies just like him and he did not lose a wink of sleep over it.

"Hell," the rookie policeman said. He was a white-toothed, half-

Latino fellow with a taste for expensive cologne. "If they don't want a girl like that, I'll take her."

"Imagine the monthly cost of maintaining a girl like that, just imagine," the older man said through his teeth.

"Shee-it," the rookie cop said, "she's worth it. I'd start by buying her an ice cream."

The older cop patted his young partner warmly on the shoulder.

The mid-morning heat was not letting up — glorious Colorado blue skies, and brutal sun. Jonathan and Felix continued their journey up Wynkoop street, sunglasses on, beads of sweat gleaming at their temples. They proceeded up the street, turning onto 18th Street, strategically avoiding a path that would lead them straight to the ballpark, Coors Field. It was on 18th Street when a young, short, brown-skinned man with a Comme de Garcons backpack slung on his shoulder caught up to and flagged down Jonathan.

"Yo, brother!" the man said, "Haven't seen ya in FOREVER, 'member Reggie's party?"

Jonathan didn't miss a beat. He grabbed the man's hand in a tight grip, "Fuck! How could I forget! How ya been, dickhead?"

And the two men ducked into the wide-open alley.

Ridiculous, Felix thought. it was not as if the alley was dimly lit or even private. He stood by and clearly saw the men exchanging money and an envelope. But the quick transaction made Jonathan's step and mood considerably lighter, which, to Felix, perhaps made it worth the risk.

Jonathan rubbed his hands together vigorously after slipping his wallet back into his pocket, the smile on his face was broad. He playfully punched Felix on the shoulder, and then shoved him, making Felix stagger like they were rough-housing teenagers.

Felix laughed.

They passed by a group of women who were dressed in Colorado Rockies team crop-tops and high-waisted hot pants. They were chanting like cheerleaders and danced in unison, taking up the entire sidewalk as a weary faced young man stood in the middle of the street to record them with a mint-colored iPhone. The only reason the young man wasn't smashed down by oncoming traffic was the red light.

"Women are having more fun than us," Felix said. "How can you honestly stand for this?"

"Well," Jonathan said, "Women have been considerably oppressed by us for a long period of time. Say, like, all of history. God bless us, Felix, we have dicks. They do not. Let them scrape up all the fun they can, while they still can… and I thought *you* were the feminist in the family?"

Felix wrinkled his nose. He smelled cinnamon and vanilla in the warm air. There was an open-air ice cream shop close by. The men continued their walk, turning onto Larimer Street, weaving through the bustling summer crowd a few blocks, until the dry summer air coaxed more sweat that dampened their linen draped flesh.

Fairy lights lined the trees and the sidewalk, promising visitors the idea that they were part of the nouveau riche bohemian charm movement gentrifying the county. Art and clothing vendors lined the sidewalk at this handmade bazaar, stocked by small-beans artists.

Jonathan stopped at a cafe, looking up at the sign, and then waved his brother in.

"What?" Felix asked.

It was a simple one room coffee shop with a patio. There were a handful of couples at the patio tables. The indoor was a smattering of tables, a ceiling covered in hand painted blue birds and corvids (probably commissioned from a local artist), the floor was a checkerboard of black and white tiles, accents and fixtures gleamed gold, and the walls were hung with watercolors from the local artist of the month. Peter Sarstedt's song "Where Do You Go To, My Lovely" played from the overhead to which Jonathan thought it would be only minutes before a Jason Mraz and then a Damien Rice song would play next.

The register was run by one thin, brown skinned woman. She had styled Locs that were tied back with a ribbon and her eyes were amber. Large dark freckles spotted her cheeks. Neither brother read her name tag, which clearly said *Dahlia*.

"Hello, there," she said brightly as the men entered.

"We're going to be boring," Jonathan said, he had one hand on his hip and one hand theatrically in the air. "And we're going to do it now.

We're throwing in the towel."

"Um…" Dahlia said. She lifted one of her hands with its long thin fingers and short nails and rested it on top of the glass bakery case. She licked her lips like a nervous animal.

"Hi there," Felix said. His eyes darted to the menu, and he saw a list of cocktails. "I would like…"

"Don't even order a fucking mimosa," Jonathan said, cutting him off. He flashed a smile of white, perfect teeth at Dahlia's startled expression, his blue eyes exuding friendliness and mirth. "I want my brother to have something non-alcoholic. Sadly, a rabid drinking problem afflicts his soul."

Dahlia placed her skinny hand over her skinny throat. Felix kept his eyes on the menu, determined to ignore his brother's stupid joke.

"They have alcohol here. I want to start my day drinking!" Felix whispered loudly.

Jonathan grinned at the girl behind the counter. Her lips tightened in response.

It was too early in the day, Dahlia thought, to be dealing with rich fucking pricks in overpriced, pastel-colored clothing. She'd just quit working at a bar to avoid the crowds of drunken asshole trust-fund momma's boys she saw on a nightly basis, and was quickly beginning to realize that working in the coffee shop only introduced her to the morning version of the exact same pricks.

"No, we're not fucking day-drinking," Jonathan said. "You alcoholic idiot."

The woman at the counter crossed her thin arms over her flat chest. Her arms were roped with long and lean muscles, and one could see the muscle tone of her shoulders and her neck. She was tall and Felix imagined her as a dancer at some contemporary company.

Points of her sternum poked through the fabric of her tiny shirt. Jonathan imagined her as a starving, failed model.

"I ain't gonna lie," she said, "both y'all are creeping me out. Y'all had too many edibles today or something? New in town?"

Jason Mraz's song "You and I Both" began playing overhead.

"Cute," Jonathan replied. "No, we're just eccentric and really awesomely rich.."

Fucking momma's boys, every time, Dahlia thought, pursing her wine-colored lips.

"Whatever, Margot Tenenbaum," she shrugged at Jonathan. "Just order something."

As far as Dahlia was concerned, these weirdos probably jerked off to *Vanity Fair* ads. They probably ate weird-ass shit like herbed mayonnaise and kelp sandwiches in the middle of a moldy koi pond with girls in gossamer dresses and Gucci-clad house servants. These were the type of rich white boys that Italian film directors made pretty coming-of-age incest stories about.

Dahlia paused, remembering the time when, years ago, in an

undergraduate film class, she'd pointed out that those plotlines weren't seen as pornographic but rather as "experimental" and "pushing the envelope" because the characters were always white. No one in the class took well to that postulation.

And here were these two Wes Anderson-looking motherfuckers, standing in front of her a case study in the eternal freedoms of strange white people. Dear God, why was today even happening? Dahlia wanted to be in bed, nursing a kombucha and looking forward to the weekend, when her mom would be back home from Costa Rica and they could make rice pudding together and binge-watch torrent files of pirated French reality TV episodes.

Felix's cheeks burned. He wanted this woman to look at him and see a man that was worth talking to. He wanted to know what kind of tiny apartment she lived in and if she shared it with anyone and if she had a boyfriend or if she was a lesbian. He imagined her as simple and cunning, someone born with nothing, but craving everything.

"I'll have a loose-leaf chai masala," Jonathan said. "Felix, figure out what you want to order, and I —" Jonathan flashed his fingers out in a sarcastic jazz hand pose "— am going to powder my nose."

Dahlia smiled tightly at Jonathan and raised her eyebrows.

Well fuck, she thought, *and now I have cocaine on my list of shit to clean up in the bathroom. God, I hope that guy gets a nose full of Fentanyl.*

Felix stared at Dahlia, finally noticing the name tag pinned to her blouse. He wondered if his strategically tousled auburn hair and green eyes were endearing to her; but, by the deadpan set to her undiscovered-runway-model face, he quickly figured they were not.

"Um…" his eyes returned to the menu. He was so riddled with anxiety, he couldn't read it. Sweat sprang from his hands and underneath his armpits. Whenever he froze like this, someone always helped him. He stared at Dahlia helplessly.

"Look," the woman said to Felix, with a dazzling smile, "The coffee's fresh. I just made the pot."

"Perfect," Felix said desperately. "House blend? You're great! Thanks!"

Jesus Christ, Dahlia thought, *this poor guy probably lost the genetic lottery at birth. He's very pretty, but dumb as a rock.* She was struck by how much he reminded her of her father, also an alcoholic.

"Yeah, yeah," she said, and she glanced around as if gauging who was still in the room, then she leaned forward and met Felix's eyes. "Look, I'm two years sober. You can get through this. Your brother seems like a hardass, but he's got your back. If he's not letting you drink, then it means he cares a helluva lot more than the people who let you. Got it?"

Felix's smile tightened. *Thanks, Jonathan.*

"6.96 for the chai," Dahlia said.

Felix tapped his card against the reader which chirped to indicate a successful transaction.

"Are you drinking here?" Dahlia said, she narrowed her eyes.

"I…" a zing of betrayal through his belly, "I thought we agreed I wasn't drinking and that… that… you had my back and my brother…"

"I mean do you want your coffee here or to go," she said.

"Oh!" Felix said and he rubbed his hands together. The kinder and more patient her voice became, the surer he was that she probably just thought he was some mentally slow charity case. "Here… I'm assuming here."

"Just take a seat at the table? Your coffee is on me. Sobriety, solidarity."

"Oh!" Felix exclaimed, and he didn't say thank you because he was dumbstruck with shame. Until she'd pointed it out, he hadn't even realized that she'd not charged him for his coffee.

Poor guy, Dahlia thought. *It's not his fault he was born rich, I guess.* She was already $300 short on rent this month so extending five bucks of charity to a man wearing blue point-toe leather Stefano Ricci shoes felt kind of punk. Fuck it.

Jonathan had called him disgusting earlier, and of course, Felix thought, he'd been correct. Jonathan might be snorting coke in a public bathroom right now, but Felix was stuck fumbling his own coffee order, getting a charity drink from a waitress.

Felix took a seat at a table by the front window while Damien Rice's "The Box" played overhead. He gazed out the window and saw two tweens running down the sidewalk, one carrying a skateboard. Another man seemed to be chasing them. Yelling at them . . . both wore baseball caps at angles, they had hair in front of their eyes, one a boy, and one a girl.

Felix remembered running as a child, and he remembered a little girl, his sister, and the sound of her laughter and the feel of her body against his when they fell to the ground and then it was his turn to run. It was the endless freedom of being children at play. At one time he was her protector but as he grew older, into the anxiety that prevented him from functioning sometimes, she became stronger, his big little sister, a twee coltish girl named Alice.

It was so depressing to notice happy people, sometimes.

He turned away from the window to thank Dahlia who set down his cup of coffee, and a steeping pot of tea. An explosion of cinnamon and cardamom and all sorts of spices smacked his nostrils and then the acidic notes of the coffee. She also set down a tray of cream and sugar, and sugar substitutes, and cream substitutes.

"Thanks!" He said. He felt bright. He knew his green eyes would have an effect and she smiled back with the benevolent eyes of someone who believes they have a kindred spirit.

"Tell me if you need anything else, sweetie," she said. And she winked.

He poured some cream into his coffee and as he stirred it, he remembered he had ordered it black… but he hated black coffee. He did not like to drink sweet coffee in front of women, however. He imagined that women judged him for liking sweet things.

What did it matter if he were judged now, though, by this server named Dahlia? He was about to be married, who was he looking to impress?

He then noticed a young woman sitting at the other end of the coffee shop. Her form against the brick wall. She wore a pink dress. There was a pink, straw sun hat on her table. Her skin was olive, and her hair was dark and long but flimsy and fine with brown lights to it. She could be Italian or French or Native American, or Indian or Japanese or Hispanic, or a mixture of all. He could not tell. His eyes could not help but flicker over to her enormous breasts that sat firmly on her chest, high and round.

The young woman had a familiar tilt to the half-smile on her face. There was a delightful, familiar-looking fullness to her tits too. It was the face and body of every would-be A-list influencer he had ever seen on social media. The face of a thousand faces. The tits of a thousand hopefuls.

Jonathan sat down.

"What are the odds that two women would be wearing the same pink Kate Spade dress at opposite ends of this cafe?" Jonathan said. For such a big man as he was, 6'5, he had a talent for sneaking into rooms.

Felix glanced at the young woman he had noticed across the cafe and then saw the other woman that Jonathan must have noticed. When had she arrived?

She was older than the young woman. She had a woman's curvy

plumpness at her arms and shoulders, but her tits were much smaller than the young woman's. She was indeed wearing the same dress, just as Jonathan had noticed. The older woman had pale skin and dark eyes, and her hair was brunette and bobbed.

"I don't know," Felix said, "I didn't notice either of them before. But hell, they probably follow the same style influencers online. It is not that weird to see women wearing the same things. Isn't that style?"

"Uh… no," Jonathan said. "It just means they both fell for the same Kate Spade clearance sale at the Cherry Creek Mall. This is why Mom is still in charge of dressing you."

Felix didn't reply.

Frankie Miller's song "Darlin'" played overhead and Jonathan laughed. He pointed towards the ceiling and his voice carried loudly as he said, "I fucking knew they'd play this song!"

"Why would you know that?" Felix replied.

"Because I do," Jonathan said. To which Felix said nothing, because why bother?

Jonathan rested his arm on the table surface, and then cringed, lifting it. The table was shiny clean, but Jonathan found it necessary to wipe at his pristine skin. He turned his gaze around the room.

"What do you think of them?" Jonathan asked.

The older woman trailed her fingers over the rim of her coffee cup. Her hands were slightly gnarled; her nails were painted, but the backs of her hands had plump veins. The thickness in her arms was pleasing to Felix, as was the worn condition of her hands. It reminded him of a nanny they'd had, the first woman Felix had ever thought about while masturbating.

Her eyes flicked up and Felix resisted the urge to look down. She smiled and looked at her phone but continued to trail her fingers on the rim of her cup.

"Would you look at that," Jonathan said, "Finger germs, how disgusting is that? She was probably the Covid Mary spreading it everywhere through the pandemic."

"I think we should just be glad Covid is over and not talk about it," Felix said.

The younger woman in the pink dress did not have a phone in her hand or on the table, nor did she have a laptop, a tablet, or any reading material. She only had a small pink Hermès purse, its gold chain strap over her shoulder. Her gaze was unabashedly on both brothers, however.

"Well, it appears it's an audition," Jonathan said.

"You think?" Felix asked.

"Clearly," Jonathan replied. "Both women have officially thrown 'fuck me' eyes at us, it's up to us to choose."

"Choose? Which… which one would you pick?" Felix asked, his stomach felt empty and twisted, and he thought of his sweet fiancé Felicity. "Which one will you choose… we'll each… get one?"

"No, we both will get the same one," Jonathan said.

Felix's stomach turned. He had assumed that Jonathan would go for the young woman, and he'd happily get the older woman.

Felix gazed into his cup of coffee and woefully stirred in cream and sugar.

A family entered the coffee shop, a young couple, both leggy as fuck with long stringy blonde hair, draped in hippie tie-dye and surrounded by young children who were dripping in ethnic appropriations of at least three different cultures. Their first family vacation had probably been to Nepal, or Thailand, or India — somewhere where they could show their kids how to toss coins at beggars and come back home feeling like good people.

"Do you think that one's a hooker?" Jonathan asked.

"What?" Felix exclaimed. He was still looking at the couple's little blonde daughter, who had cornrows. "Why would she be?"

"The younger one's a daddy's girl," Jonathan said, the vitriol in his tone surprising Felix. "Look at her, the arrogant little bitch."

"What?" Felix's gaze went from the little girl with the cornrows to her older sister, who was also tiny and blonde, and draped in a traditional-looking sari.

He's talking about the women in pink dresses, you idiot, Felix realized.

The older woman in the pink dress also wore a chunky beaded necklace. She had a worldly MILF tilt to her grin. The younger girl was a case study in objects taken for granted. A girl her age could never afford the sparkling diamond tennis bracelet on her skinny wrist; someone like her daddy had clearly bought it for her.

"The older one's a hooker?" Felix said.

"Rude," Jonathan said.

Felix sighed and made eyes with Jonathan who let his serious face melt to laugh, then poured himself more chai. He ran the tip of his tongue over his lips where the sticky and sweet and spices would be lurking. Jonathan's entire demeanor was playful in an irreverent way that sent off alarm bells in Felix: he knew that he had walked into some sort of trap, but he wasn't sure yet what kind.

"Plain as a sparrow," Jonathan said, his gaze upon the younger lady. "Look at that, the young one doesn't even try putting on makeup to doll herself up, that arrogant bitch."

"How can she be both plain and arrogant?" Felix asked.

The girl put her chin on her hand and looked at them directly, lifting one of her eyebrows.

"Only fucking thing she has is a knockout set of tits," Jonathan grumbled.

Their mother was the sort who never let anyone see her without makeup. She woke up at five am to put her face in an ice bath, put on cold creams. Her hair was always perfect and her skin always polished. She was a woman of old money and old values. Felix did not know that

Jonathan had once seen their Mother without her makeup on. Jonathan had been viscerally horrified. Her eyes looked strange and shrunken, her pointed nose looked rodent-like. Her lips were pale and thin like something that would reach out in helplessness to her horrified son. Jonathan had screamed and Mother, startled and hurt, had slapped him.

Felix rather liked the plain and fresh look of no makeup. Felix even loved the sight of liver spots, freckles, and wrinkles. Things like that tickled his tummy and made him feel like he was attracted to something truly forbidden.

"She's just a kid," Felix said of the younger woman. Then, he noticed a glittery pink shine on the girl's lips and cheeks. Makeup, after all!

"With tits like that?" Jonathan said. His tone sounded a bit kinder, though his words were harsh. Felix realized that Jonathan probably noticed the lip gloss on the young woman as well.

Felix poured himself some more coffee as an excuse to fuss over something else, and it gave him the leeway to turn his attention to the older woman — someone more appropriate for them to be looking at, anyway. The older woman was playing with her phone. It had a pink jelly case and rabbit ears on it.

"Phones are more interesting than us," Felix said.

"Which is weird," Jonathan said, "Because the kiddo hasn't checked her phone once. She is so fucking arrogant that she doesn't think she needs to be connected to any of society by the one thing that connects all of society together."

"That's not so weird," Felix said. " Kids these days are even getting rid of Instagram."

"Ha!" Jonathan exclaimed and he went back to his chai. He closed his eyes in a way that indicated that the chai must be authentically good.

The older woman ordered a large pastry from Dahlia, who was checking her table.

"Big surprise," Jonathan muttered without looking up, now tapping at his phone. It was one of Jonathan's idiosyncratic talents — to be completely in-tune with the movements of the people surrounding him, yet entirely socially disconnected at the same time.

The younger woman sipped her coffee. Her gaze was firmly on the brothers.

"Have you ever had a whore before, Felix?" Jonathan asked, in a low muttered voice. His smile mimicked the gentle manner of his mother, made his generous mouth seem even wider than it happened to be.

Felix thought of the prostitutes and strippers he'd never touched. Those broken survivors. He had never seen the beautiful girls that were only sold on movie screens. Not one looked like Julia Roberts, Elisabeth Shue, or Heather Graham.

"Let me guess, Jonathan," he said. "You've had hundreds of them?"

"As a matter of fact, I haven't," Jonathan replied, "not once. You know me. I'm cheap as fuck. It's like paying to share a wank sock. But, I think we should get a whore before our bachelor party."

Felix glanced at both women. The older one was gazing at them, the phone still balanced in her hand. Her eyes were on Jonathan and she was no doubt appraising his height. Felix glanced at her curvy arms and wondered how those soft arms and small tits would look laid out on a bed.

"Every woman has a price," Jonathan said. "Take a look at the young one."

Felix's mouth dried out and he clamped onto his bottom lip with his teeth.

"Are you fellas finished or would you like to order something else?" Dahlia asked. Her good will hinged upon whatever they would pay for.

Dahlia felt a stone in her breast, the sort she would feel when her strange uncle hugged her too close as a child. Even her sympathy for the younger man was dwindled to nothing compared to her gut reaction at seeing both men staring at the clearly underage girl in the corner.

"I'll take care of it," Jonathan said, and he pulled his wallet out and flipped a large bill onto the counter. "Keep the change, gorgeous!"

Dahlia's eyebrows slid up. *A hundred bucks. Shit. Shit. Shit.* That was exactly one third of the money she needed towards her upcoming rent.

Goddamn rich men and their gifts, Dahlia thought. Dahlia took the bill into her hand and hid the ecstatic panic she was feeling for the tip. "Come in any time boys, preferably when I'm here."

Maybe I'm too hard on them, Dahlia thought. *Maybe they're just eccentric.*

Felix smiled as he watched her clean the table and he felt a surge of happiness knowing that his brother just did something amazing for this woman. He wished he'd done so as well.

"Oh, we will," Jonathan replied, "most definitely."

This lifted Felix's spirits. That meant if they did come back in and they probably would, it could be Felix's turn to leave a huge tip behind. Dahlia was really going to love them. She took the dishes into the back, and then Jonathan looked at Felix.

"Well?"

Felix flicked his frightened-horse gaze to the woman in the corner, the older one.

"Her?" Jonathan said. "She'd cost dinner and a movie. I want the young one."

Felix's belly jolted, and the word CHILD flickered in his brain.

Jonathan walked towards the young woman's table.

"Jonathan! Goddammit!" Felix muttered. "She's probably not even a…"

As they approached her, Felix glanced at Dahlia, who was squirting antibacterial gel onto her hands and vigorously rubbing them together.

"Hello, there," Jonathan said to the young woman, who had eyes on them now like a cat watching a dangling ball. "I am Jonathan and this is my brother, Felix."

The young woman looked back and forth between them. There

was a touch of florals and citrus in the air around her… oh, beautiful youth. But her smile froze, like a cold wind murdering flowers on their stems, before she spoke.

"Hi, Jonathan. Hi, Felix," she said, and her voice had all the vocal fry of a California girl. "Fancy…"

"Hi," Felix said, unwittingly cutting into her dialogue, and then he choked, literally. His throat closed as he exhaled, and felt like it was collapsing. He clenched his fist and pressed it to his lips as he coughed.

"Hi to everyone!" Jonathan said, and he took his knuckles and rapped them on the table surface. "Now that we have the 'hi's' out of the way let's get to the 'can you' and the 'do you want to'."

"All right," the girl replied, not quite making eye contact with either of them. "Can I, do I want to — what?"

"First, how much?" Jonathan said.

Jolt. Felix coughed again, a dry, intentional sound, a feeble attempt to stop this tragedy.

The young woman's lips parted, pink lip gloss sparkling.

"I'm hoping your price is negotiable?" Jonathan said in a low mutter. "You're a whore, am I correct?"

Her lips formed an "O" and she breathed out heavily, slowly.

"Goddammit, Jonathan," Felix muttered, and he held out his hand to the young woman. His thighs and belly were quivering. "I'm so sorry, I didn't mean, I mean, I know my brother didn't mean…"

"Didn't he?" The girl said, she glanced briefly at Felix, her gaze flicking up and down his frame before fixating back on Jonathan.

"Hey," Jonathan said, and he grinned fatally, "it's my brother's idea, not mine."

"Jonathan! Son of a bitch!" Felix yelped, this caught the attention of Dahlia and the older woman at the end of the cafe. They were both now staring at the brothers.

Fuck a duck, Dahlia thought, *why do I even bother giving these freaks the benefit of the doubt? Ever?*

The girl at the table sat with hyper-erect posture. Her complexion had paled considerably since the men approached her, and Dahlia could see one of her hands trembling.

"Thank you for the tip," Dahlia said from behind the counter. "That was oddly generous of you, but I am going to have to ask both of you to leave."

"Then I want my tip…" Jonathan began.

"It's fine," the girl said to Dahlia, "I'm not bothered at all. They know my father."

When Felix met Dahlia's amber eyes, he felt no affection from her. There would be no return visit when he could leave behind a glamorous tip for the boys to be proud of.

Jonathan leaned back, taking the full force of the young woman's gaze. Her eyes were those of a gunslinger. Ageless as fuck.

Jonathan enjoyed the flinty stare coming off this young thing, a stare that promised a creature who could put up a meaningful fight — at least, far more of one than Felix could ever offer. And Jonathan's smile was the smile of a gunslinger. Mirthless.

TWO

"Hey," Dahlia, called out, catching the young woman's attention, "Are you sure you're okay, honey?"

Jonathan's eyes fixed on Dahlia, a dispassionate predator's gaze upon something beneath its appetite. His jaw clenched.

Just try anything, Dahlia thought, *just try it, you enormous fucking Golden Retriever.* Her pulse was racing, her breath rapid. Sweet Jesus, she hated confrontations with men. At times like this, she yearned for the strength of her mother, a woman known for prowling her property at twilight with a machete in one hand and a bottle of banana rum in the other.

Dahlia had once taken pride in her own city-molded modern softness, the quirky manic-pixie girlishness she'd clothed her youth with. She'd found comfort in offbeat rom-com films, and Frankie Cosmos and Taylor Swift tunes; she'd built entire outfits around her collection of brightly colored boots, living for rainy days so she could utilize the enormous, clear umbrella she'd acquired on a trip to Tokyo.

She'd spent the beautiful, drunken, party-drug-and-caffeine-fueled blur of her young adulthood a free-spirited, delightful city girl — to the dismay of her assertive, bulldoggish mother, who never failed to leave a clunker of a sarcastic or dismissive comment on her Instagram posts. Her youthful party had ended, rough and sudden, when she'd awakened drunk and disoriented in an Uber driver's bedroom. She'd suffered through a lengthy sexual assault investigation — which was ultimately dropped, due to law enforcement using her cocktail-sloshed Instagram posts against her. Once it was all over, she quickly found there was nothing in her that could bear regularly dealing with the will of angry white men.

If she could only rescue one girl from that trial by fire, just one.

"I'm fine, thanks," the young woman said in a bright voice. She clicked open her small purse, counted out a few hundred-dollar bills, and dropped them on the table.

Christ… is that really three hundred dollars?

Dahlia's pulse now raced for a different reason, as she eyed the money: at this point, everything she had been stressing about for rent this month was covered. A literal trickle-down effect, the unicorn of all situations amongst anyone who has ever had to struggle for money in the face of the privileged.

Jonathan snatched the money off the table, and took it to Dahlia's counter, flicking one bill at a time at her. The server crossed her skinny arms. Jonathan made a fist and rapped on the counter three times with his knuckles.

"Now, why look at me like I'm a fucking serial killer?" he said.

Dahlia did not answer, but her expression remained fixed on him as if he were a spider in a bathtub.

A machete, she thought, *if only I had a machete.*

The trio left the café and Dahlia took the money and placed it in her pocket alongside the hundred-buck tip the tall blonde man had left her. She pressed her palm against the money and felt an ache at the base of her throat. Her skin felt cold as well, and she thought about how that girl's legs were so spindly and coltish as she walked alongside those tall men. There was no damn way that girl could be a grown woman.

And here I am, she thought, *selling the girl for four hundred dollars.*

"Shit, what was all that about," the older woman in the pink Kate Spade dress said. She put down her phone and she stood up, gazing at the trio out the window. "Was any of that even legal?"

"Shit if I know, Phyllis," Dahlia said, "Rich people shit, I guess."

"Days like this make me happy to be a lesbian, you know?" Phyllis said.

"Sometimes I wish I was," Dahlia replied.

As Dahlia wiped down the table where the girl had been she stopped and closed her eyes.

"Red hair," she whispered to herself, "green eyes, about 6 feet. The other, blonde, blue eyes, six foot five, has to be. The girl… might be fifteen years old…"

Four hundred dollars to go towards paying this month's rent… what a cute kid like that is worth in this town apparently. Dahlia covered her face with her hands and inhaled deeply. *I'm a fucking traitor.*

"Disgrace!" Jonathan said as they hit the sidewalk outside the café. "That's what you get when you go out of your way to help someone. Gets something for nothing and acts like a fucking bitch about it."

"I wouldn't trust a man who gave me a tip that large," the young woman replied. She'd put on her pink straw hat and the sun moving through it gave a pink tinge to her clear skin.

"Wouldn't you?" Jonathan said, eyeing her tits. "Of course, you wouldn't. All women think every man's backup car is a Murder Van. So, what about it, kiddo, were you actually being serious in there, or are you full of shit?"

The young woman made a small, agreeable sound. Her arm was lifted halfway to her waist where the small, pink, Hermès purse hung on her forearm. The tennis bracelet she wore twinkled in the sunlight.

Felix recognized the purse, once he properly noticed it, because he had almost bought that model as a gift for his fiancée, Felicity. It was *the* purse that all fashionable girly-girls from wealthy families wanted this season. The kind of purse you had to get onto a waiting list a year in advance for. Felix was mad at himself for not being successful in obtaining it because Felicity was not that pleased with what he had bought her—a similar-looking Brighton Collectibles bag.

"So, what is it, darling?" Jonathan asked. "Do you just accept payment in impossible-to-get Hermès bags and diamonds?"

Of course, Jonathan would have noticed the purse as well, Felix thought. *He would have clocked that purse the moment he'd laid eyes on her.*

"Sometimes," the girl replied. "Generally, I ask three hundred per man per hour, or if you want an overnight, it's a thousand a night, per man."

"You're serious?" Jonathan said. He let out a startled laugh, the first indicator to Felix that this must have been a joke that was going too far. In that case, what a fucking relief, because it meant Jonathan would be good-natured and pleased with himself once this joke ended.

She wrinkled her nose, looking as young as Felix feared her to be. He knew a million red flags when he saw them.

"I wouldn't be joking about this," the girl replied, and she patted her purse with one hand. Her fingernails were short and glossy with clear, sparkling varnish.

"Then…" Jonathan said, "let's go for the deal. Let's do an overnighter."

"Jonathan… really?" Felix asked.

That brought the girl's gunslinger gaze to him, and Felix wanted to hide.

"Felix, I swear to fucking God…" Jonathan snapped. "If you annoy me any more, I will fucking kill you myself."

"But where are we taking her?" Felix asked.

Felix could not imagine taking the girl back to the mansion

in Cherry Hills, introducing her to mother as what, a friend they were bringing in for a slumber party? Mother would take the girl aside, slip her full of pink champagne and talk with her into the wee hours about fashion and refugees. She would dig into the girl's family, seeing if she could find yet another patron for one of her fundraisers. She would braid the girl's hair, and tell her how good it was to be near a young woman again, ever since… well… Alice.

Jonathan had an apartment of his own, a spacious two-bedroom in the Santa Fe Art District, named for the street it was housed on but due to year upon year of rent hikes, it was in serious danger of no longer housing a single art gallery; his apartment was currently undergoing a complete remodel. Jonathan was back at the Forrester Family home for a month, occupied with ignoring his long-suffering fiancée's wedding planning, and their mother's input. Felix had still not escaped the family nest, a sumptuous old brick mansion that had enough space for a family of twenty but housed only a bored pair of grown-ass adults and their shy twenty-one-year-old son.

Felix and his fiance Felicity were promised a lovely apartment in the gentrified Five Points neighborhood, a gift from Felicity's parents, but they would not set foot into it until after the honeymoon. As tidy as a Jane Austen novel.

Jonathan patted Felix's arm, "Relax, dear brother, we already have a nice spot on Larimer Street. It's got a great view and it's genuinely nice for an overnight."

"Larimer Street? You mean Uncle Dan's apartment?" Felix exclaimed.

Felix thought of their uncle Daniel: so tall, so pale, so blue-eyed, and so addicted to dating multiple partners of all genders and ages that he practically wrote the book on sexual voraciousness. Their uncle was in Hawaii for a month; he had left his keys with Jonathan, asking him to stay in it a few days a week, "to keep the room fresh and lived in." Nothing worse than coming back home to a dead apartment, Uncle Dan always said. Every chamber needed electric warmth. And the apartment was always welcoming, stocked with clothes in both Jonathan and Felix's sizes, and all the booze anyone could ever want.

Uncle Dan was a tall, thin, fussy man who indulged in the latest alternative healing trends, crystals, and transcendental meditation. He was considered an eclectic meditation guru by the GOOP crowd, known for flying across the globe to "assist" his wealthiest patrons whenever they experienced "spiritual crises." Uncle Dan peddled his own peculiar brand of meditation, which he referred to as "electric energy harvesting." It was rather amusing to Felix to witness an electric energy harvesting session, which amounted to their uncle putting a buzzing, wired bicycle helmet on a person's head, having them hold a Moldavite crystal, and then charging five thousand dollars per session — and such sessions were only sold in "packages" of five, seven, or eleven. He could talk, straight-faced, for hours to complete strangers about his astral-plane visits and conversations with King Louis XIV, William S. Burroughs, and Wayne Gretzky.

"But," Felix had once protested, "Wayne Gretzky is alive!"

"Yeah, yeah, and Peter Forsberg has no spleen," Uncle Dan had replied grimly. "I'm talking about electricity! Heat! Dead or alive, all electricity is there for the harvesting. So you boys damn well make sure you fill my apartment with *heat*."

All in all, a conversation like that could make no never mind to Felix who generally felt like he had more important things to tend to, for instance his upcoming nuptials or his continued work with the pet-project foundations Mom championed. It was pretty much standard anyhow to have that ONE strange aunt or uncle in the family. Jonathan, on the other hand, would most certainly be up to taking on Uncle Dan's challenge, and had probably been mulling over the past week how he was going to fill that damn apartment with just the right electronic human frequency. This being the case, Felix now very much understood the error of his whining to Jonathan about being bored.

"Is there anything you want before we head to the apartment?" Jonathan said to the young woman, "We can stop anywhere you like. My treat."

"Aw," the girl said, and she flicked her hand up to stop her hat from blowing off. The diamonds on her skinny arm glinted in the sun. "A little candy would be nice."

This feels like a nightmare, Felix thought. The sort where sound and sight distorted as if stuck at the bottom of a swimming pool, where one knew the only way to wake from the terror was to wake frozen in bed and watch shadows dance and hover above you.

Felix thought of a recurring nightmare in which he could hear a woman's screams in a dark room, and in the dream he would see Jonathan's face, uncharacteristically pinched and worried, but still set with determination, even in extreme youth. How did one know the difference between a nightmarish memory and the memory of a nightmare? Every time he remembered the child-Jonathan in the darkened room, the screaming woman had on a different dress. Sometimes she was in something tight and slinky, something polyester and bunched around her waist, and other times she was in diaphanous petticoats and a rocket bra bustier, like Marty McFly's mom. Sometimes the woman's face was their mother's, sometimes it was a generic white woman face, sometimes there was no face at all, just a white marble disc with a black hole for a screaming mouth.

They went into a candy and novelty store that had taffy spinning in the window. Taffy was not a candy that Felix was very hung up on. It was something poor people ate, Mother always told them, and all it did was rot the teeth.

The girl filled a clear plastic bag, using the silver scoops provided, with taffy. Felix watched helplessly as she chose a bunch of flavors, muttering the names of each candy to herself as if determined to commit it to memory. As if she had never seen candy before.

Jonathan turned to Felix. "She's cute, isn't she? She really wants candy. If we're breaking you in, then we couldn't have picked a more user-friendly model."

"Lucky me," Felix muttered.

Outside of the shop there were three young adults sitting at the metal patio tables, a young woman and two young men. As they passed them by, one of the men called out, "Heya, Pretty in Pink, got any candy for me?"

"Sure!" The girl said, and she took the bag to the table, pulling off the silver twist-tie fastening and holding it open to them, "Have some candy."

"Are you kidding me?" the young woman at the table asked. She had on bug-eyed sunglasses with thick white frames, which she lifted to her forehead so she could fix her almond-shaped eyes on the girl, "Thank you!"

"No worries, bags of candy are meant to share, aren't they," the girl said. "That's what Norman Bates always said."

"Well, actually," the man who'd called out to her said, "I was meaning you, not the candy."

The man was wearing vibrant red basketball shorts and a crisp, black t-shirt. His skin was shining with summer sweat and was very dark. A strand of rose quartz beads strung on red thread circled his wrist.

He was young and handsome, with a face and physique made for either professional sports or sporty brand modeling.

The girl fixed her gaze on the man who spoke, and Felix noticed a flaky, breezy expression in her eyes, but then she grinned and spoke, "Just take another piece, okay?"

As they left the folk with a handful of candy apiece, Jonathan's strides were long, almost leaving Felix and the girl behind. His lips were tight, his fists clenched. It made Felix feel like he was eight years old again, Dad staring down at him and the stain of soda pop on the antique rug. Felix did not want the girl to notice it.

"Are you upset?" she asked Felix. The jittery movements of his lips and the trembling in his hands were painful for her to see. Nervous creatures were always sure to reach her heart.

"Actually," Jonathan said, assuming that the girl was speaking to him, "I am."

"Why?" The girl asked, turning her attention away from Felix to Jonathan. "Did you not like a Black man talking to me like that?" Her gaze fixed on Jonathan, gauging his reaction but now it was the other brother who reacted.

"What? Why would you jump to that conclusion?" Felix said. "That's an odd escalation."

"Hm," the girl said. Her eyes remained on Jonathan, expression flat.

They stopped walking, standing under a string of lights and banners advertising the upcoming chalk art festival.

"I'm going to be honest," Jonathan said, "I don't like it. Sure, he's Black, but worse than that, compared to us, he's poor as fuck. *And,* he probably feels like he's rich in cheap-ass Converse — and he thought he could just have you by asking for candy! He even SAW us clearly with you, and he still had the steel as shit balls to call you out like that!"

"Ha," The girl said. "Well, I didn't see you speak up once when he 'called me out.' What happened there, if you're so outraged and offended? And anyway, a woman is *not* the property of the men at her side, if someone wants to talk to me, they…"

"Two thousand dollars for a night sure as fuck makes you my property," Jonathan growled, one hand on his hip, and the other pointed straight in the girl's face.

She faced him down with a pert and pretty posture which accentuated the shape of her breasts; one of her hands was holding her hat in place, and the fact that Jonathan had to almost bend in half to come to her level made a somewhat amusing picture. He almost looked like he could be her angry father or exasperated older brother.

Felix tried to remember what had occurred to him initially when the man had asked for the candy; he'd seen three people of three different races, but the fact that the man who had hit on the girl was Black hadn't mattered a bit to him personally. How could it have?

The girl did not break, despite Jonathan's stare-down. She took a piece of candy from her bag and slipped it into her mouth, warming it up on her hot tongue before she spoke again. "What if *I* weren't white? Would it bother you? You follow that 'one drop' rule?"

"Being racist doesn't lock a man's dick up," Jonathan said.

He stood now with his hands sunk deep in his pockets, staring at the sidewalk, profile of a pensive American god.

Felix really thought he was going to be ill. If this were Jonathan playing a game, he had never seen him take it that far, not so far as to convincingly play Dad's specific variety of blow-hard bigot. Of course, he had never seen Jonathan straight-up offer to buy a girl like a whore, either.

The girl skittered alongside them through the marbled lobby when they arrived at Uncle Dan's apartment building. Her feet were quite small and her steps so fluttered and unmeasured it was as if she were a trespassing mouse. The icy air of the building's air conditioning enveloped their sweaty bodies and put a shiver through each of them.

The more Felix saw her the more his heart dropped with the imagination of who she could be. She seemed younger and younger with each step. Her gangly demeanor and large eyes struck a familiar chord with Felix, almost as if he had known her forever, it was the universal cookie cut-out of youth.

"So, where did you get that Hermès bag?" Jonathan asked.

"Your dad," the girl said.

"Hmph," Jonathan scoffed.

Their uncle lived with a view to the busy streets and trees below. Uncle Dan said he enjoyed whenever there was a chalk art festival or a food festival. The energy from the crowds was pure electricity. They crackled! If only one could capture, patent, and sell that energy, if only people could huff it from a can and gain all of life's nourishment from that.

On the fridge there was a list of numbers, and half of them were for various cleaning companies. There was also a list of numbers that were attached to no written name, and Jonathan had never tried dialing them to discover who would answer.

In the dining area there was original art on the walls, framed charcoal studies of couples both straight and gay in erotic positions, and an enormous oil painting of Barack Obama reclining with his naked thighs spread, a proud, bare, uncut cock on full display.

"Awesome," the girl said as they entered the apartment, staring at the painting. "Your uncle has a fetish for naked Black dudes, I see?"

Jonathan laughed loudly and pinched the bridge of his nose, inhaling with a sigh that was both fed up and amused. He exhaled, gazing towards the living room area where a shiny black Steinway piano stood.

"What?" Felix exclaimed, "No! Uncle Dan is a *patron* of the arts!"

"I dunno," she wrinkled her nose. "I mean, is this *really* respecting Obama?"

Jonathan was grinning broadly but he had stepped back, hands sunk into his pockets. Felix realized he had to be the one to speak.

"The painter, Rick Dallago, he's local, he flies solo! He's even independent of our family foundation, *the Forrester Foundation*, if you've heard of us," Felix said, and his voice was tighter, higher, more anxious than he wanted it to be. "He's a Norman Rockwell of Americana *satire!*"

"Yeah, I've heard of you," Alice replied, "I really love art. If you're with the Forrester Foundation, I know you folk *make* names for new artists and deal in world class art. Lucky me."

Felix nodded eagerly, hoping for some glimmer of respect from Alice, but only meeting with an oddly mature and patient grin.

"This painter, Mr. Dallago," Felix continued, holding his hand up to the painting, "belongs to a non-profit Denver co-op, the Denver Art Society! Have you heard of it? It is *the* most diverse gallery in Denver."

She smirked. "Oh, I see. You're apparently not *common* voluptuaries; you're wealthy ones."

"Yeah, whatever," Jonathan cut in. "The best part is he got Obama's ex so drunk she opened up about describing the cock of America's President of Hope. So in the end, we're all profligate men, aren't we? "

"Cute," the girl said, her eyes drinking in the naked Obama portrait. She twirled as her eyes appraised the rest of the surroundings, she tossed her hat like a frisbee where it landed neatly on a settee. "It's really cozy here."

She spun herself into the living room and stopped when her eyes caught sight of the lacquered, black Steinway grand piano.

"You're mixed race, raised white?" Jonathan said with the question in his tone, staring at her. "Is that why you're only *half* interested in the race-baiting conversations you abandon?"

"Quite!" She said with her smile set to sunshine. "But I won't tell you what race."

"Funny thing, you tossing out the word *voluptuary*," Jonathan said, holding up his hands foppishly. "Where did you come across that?"

"I'm well read," Alice said with a dismissive shrug, she was still staring at the grand piano, "I learned it from reading a collection of Lewis Carroll's personal letters."

"I would say I doubted that," Jonathan replied, "But there is no fucking way that word is going to appear in *Twilight*, so I'll give you that. You're probably telling the truth."

Alice wrinkled her nose and giggled. As she pulled her gaze off the piano, her eyes fell to the coffee table that was offset in the room, next to a plush sofa with claw-foot legs. Atop it lay an oversize book of paintings by Caravaggio and a glossy vinyl record sleeve.

"You gotta be kidding me." She walked over, snatched the vinyl sleeve, and held it at arm's length, squinting at it. "Your uncle listens to this shit? Do *you* guys listen to this shit?"

She flipped the square of cardboard around and on the album cover was the underfed, pinched little face of a young indie alternative singer with soft brown hair and bangs, and impossibly round sky-blue eyes. The singer in question was a young woman named Brennan Talbot who currently had a chart-topping folk-pop hit called "I F****d Your Dad."

"No wonder you boys picked me up, if you're listening to this spoiled rich kid shit," she said and she set the record back on the coffee table. "You know spoiled toxic shit when you meet spoiled toxic shit."

The girl lifted her arm and stroked the diamonds on her wrist, twirled, and held up her Hermes bag on a finger. Her long dark hair swirled around her and came to a shiny rest on her slim shoulders.

An image flashed through Jonathan's mind, a memory of a young woman spinning around their living room, her infectious laugh. His memory flickered and popped like a melting film strip and he saw white limbs, blood spatters, dents in metal and an unusually untouched face. It was a memory of a photograph and it felt like it was jammed sideways into the flesh of his brain because it did not fit.

"Uh…" Felix said, and he ran his hands through his hair, he looked up once again at the Obama painting and then at the girl. He found himself wondering what he was supposed to say.

He looked at the album cover; its color scheme of pink and green brought to mind last summer's garden party — tasty cocktails, barefoot girls playing on lush grass in frothy dresses, all of the young men dressed in ridiculously vintage suits. None of the party guests had seen each other since before the start of the Covid pandemic, and the gathering had felt especially decadent as a result. Quite a few of the guests had finished the party by hooking up amongst the trees, in the pond, and on the picnic blankets. Felix had met his fiancée Felicity that day, as well: they went into the house together, and became soulmates over strawberry lemonade and fresh-baked cookies. The young singer from the vinyl record on the coffee table, Brennan Talbot, had been there too; she'd brought a ukulele and typewriter with her, which she'd used to write fresh songs about the orgy happening in the grass.

"Yeah, we know the singer of that album," Felix mumbled. "She's —"

"I know she's a friend of yours," the girl cut in, an edge to her voice. "Everyone knows this girl got a record deal because her daddy's rich, so her daddy must be friends with your daddy, hm? It's all the same incestuous rich kids' club, isn't it?"

"Not a Brennan Talbot fan, I take it?" Felix said. He had started twisting his fingers together. "Yeah… she's actually…"

"Not that nice," the girl replied. She picked up the album again and pulled the record out; it was translucent and pale pink. She rolled her eyes and set it back onto the coffee table. She clasped her hands behind her waist and twisted back and forth, her movements mimicking the posture of a fresh Disney princess or anime girl character, the movement made her long, glossy hair sway and shimmer over her body.

"Have you ever thought of cutting your hair?" Jonathan asked.

His eyes had been watching the girl intently during this exchange between her and Felix. "Or doing something different with it?"

The girl stopped moving, her lips had a downward sulk to them, and her eyes seemed shiny like melting chocolate kisses as she met Jonathan's gaze. "Is there something wrong with it? I have amazing hair."

"You should do something different with it," Jonathan replied, "It is pretty, but you probably have worn it down your back like that for the last ten years, and girls who never change their hair tend to get sticks up their twats over stupid shit like jealousy of pretty young women with record deals."

The girl touched the base of her throat, her other arm crossing over her small waist.

"Rude," she muttered.

After a pause, she spoke again, though seemingly not to anyone in particular, but rather just setting words on an imaginary shelf in the air.

"I usually wear more makeup, a lot more. I… actually have changed my look up quite a bit. I used to always wear a tight ponytail." She gathered her hair in one hand and pulled it back, tilted her face to one side. "Like Ariana Grande."

Felix liked the look, and he imagined her with a lot more makeup. No wonder she had seemed familiar to him earlier: she did bear a resemblance to the pop star.

"What's your name?" Jonathan asked, narrowing his eyes.

Felix stood behind Jonathan, every inch the little brother: hands in his pockets, trembling, feeling like he had forgotten the English language. Seeing this young woman animated over her distaste of the vinyl, trying to justify "her look" to Jonathan, made her vibrant and real to him. It was as if she became a solid creature with definitive opinions, and independence, that he could imagine squeezing to his body during a slow song at a school dance.

"Alice," the girl said.

Electricity through his body, and through Jonathan's. Felix knew his brother could not be immune to the shock of hearing that name, the name of their dearly departed sister. He saw Jonathan's body flinch.

The girl's eyes went back and forth between the brothers. She could not possibly understand the effect of her name upon them, but in some strange way, it seemed as if she were looking upon a reaction she'd entirely expected. Perhaps it was Felix's paranoid anxiety, but the word **predator** flashed like pink neon over and through this girl's aura.

"And you're Jonathan, and you're Felix," Alice said, her gaze upon Jonathan.

"Good memory, Scrappy Doo," Jonathan muttered.

Her fingers were not delicate, but her hands were small, Felix noticed; plump at the palms and fingers.

"I actually don't have a good memory for detail," Alice replied. "I probably make up more things than I can keep track of." Her attention wandered again, and she looked towards the Steinway piano, her tongue running over her lips.

"Hey, beautiful," Jonathan said, and he cleared his throat. "Would you mind doing a little favor for us?"

"That's kind of the point," Alice said, and she set her bag down on one of the settees.

The delicate pink and gold bag looked good on the pale blue settee. Uncle Dan was all about that Louis XIV vibe and the interior of the apartment was like a white and gold candy box with pale pink and blue accents. The apartment had two bedrooms, two bathrooms, one fitted with both a shower and a bath. The sitting room had French doors that opened to a terrace view of the city, and the kitchen was a spacious wonder of stainless steel with rose quartz countertops. It was as though Sofia Coppola herself had directed an entire movie where they stood. The floors were emporio pink onyx tile, white and pink like cherry swirl ice cream. Pale blue celestite geodes; and sparkling rainbow amethyst cut bases sparkled from almost every corner in every room. Polished selenite slabs, Himalayan salt lamps, and singing bowls could also be found wherever one turned.

"Could we have a look at your ID? My skittish little brother would probably appreciate that," Jonathan said.

"I'm of age," Alice replied.

"So, can we see the ID?"

"No."

Felix noticed that the gunslinger's glint had returned to Jonathan's eyes.

Alice seemed to have noticed the change in Jonathan's demeanor, too, and she held out her hands in a gesture of supplication. "Look, guys. I'm of age. Are you really going to be a stickler about this?"

What's wrong with this girl? Who or what fucked her up to the point that she resorts to this behavior? What the fuck's wrong with us, *that we feel the need to drink from the same poisoned well she does?*

"This isn't going to work," Felix said, and he felt so fucking adult and in charge. He wanted to leave this apartment and wake tomorrow morning to sugar and cream in his coffee. He wanted to marry Felicity and live a long, fruitful life together, filling her with babies yearly for the next decade.

Bravo, Jonathan, Felix thought. *Lesson learned!* It was a game of chicken he was happy to lose. He looked at Jonathan, hoping to see his brother crack and start laughing. Any second now, Jonathan would begin to crow about how funny this joke was. Maybe he'd even hired this girl to be in on it.

Jonathan loudly cleared his throat and then tapped on the face of his Omega watch. An older model, which their father had given Jonathan on his eighteenth birthday. Felix had received no such watch from their father on his own eighteenth; he'd been given a Jackson Pollock painting, which was worth more than Jonathan's watch but had inspired no outward jealousy from Jonathan at the time.

This was our out, Felix thought, desperately. *And we are not going to take it. Absolutely everything is fucked.*

"Oh… I suppose we can work with what we have here," Jonathan said.

Felix felt the moment as sure as a guillotine's blade.

Alice's little fingers were intertwined in front of her waist, her hair slightly tangled and falling loose around her shoulders. She did not move away from Jonathan as he draped his arm over her little shoulders and turned his smartphone camera to their faces, and Felix was struck with the panicked idea that she looked so familiar. Their cheeks pressed together looked like an Instagram post from when their sister had been fifteen. *When Alice was fifteen.*

"I, Jonathan Abernathy Forrester," Jonathan said into his phone camera, recording video.

"Abernathy?" Alice exclaimed. A laugh escaped in a wet raspberry.

"Shhh, it's a family name. Just call me, Abe," Jonathan said. "Okay?"

"Fucking Forresters?" Alice said. "Really?"

And now Jonathan laughed with her. "What do you have against Forresters?"

"Who *doesn't* have a thing against Forresters," Alice replied. "All of America hates your laundering-money-through-art privileged-ass family."

"Fair enough," Jonathan said. "Our father certainly is a king amongst dicks."

Alice laughed and covered her mouth with the back of her hand, "Sorry. I'm being an ass. It's not your fault you have a shitty father."

"I, Jonathan Abe Forrester," Jonathan continued, shaking off the conversation, moving life forward, "Being of sound mind and exceptional body, am asking Alice…" he frowned and stuck his bottom lip out, "What's your full name, beautiful?"

"Just Alice," she said. "But I am of sound mind and fabulous body."

"Well…" Jonathan said, "Confirm for me right now, on the pain of excruciating death, that you are of age and consentingly available to have nasty fucking sex with my brother and me. Do you swear?"

Felix cringed, but did not say anything.

Alice giggled, "Yes. Yes!"

"On pain of death!"

"On pain of death!" Alice echoed.

Jonathan looked over the video clip, their voices haunted and tinny as they escaped the screen. Alice stood on her toes to watch as well. Jonathan slipped the phone into his pocket.

"Well, sweetie? Your phone. Let's see it."

"I never carry a personal phone to work. It's rude, and dangerous, and could compromise my clients."

"Fine, secret agent," Jonathan said. "So, where did you get that bag, really. I tried to get one for my fiancée last season. Apparently, there was one last bag that someone beat us to. Don't tell me you were the little bitch responsible for that?"

"It was probably your dad," Alice said, her voice deadpan without a hint of humor.

Jonathan rolled his eyes. "Cute."

Felix wanted to sit down, but he did not. He wanted to take a nervous piss. His mother's voice rang in his ears about getting drinks for company, about taking shoes off before they touched fine rugs. He was thoroughly well-mannered for a million different scenarios, but there remained this strange girl with a Hermès purse in front of them, and a million different wrong ways they were intending to act, and no magical, motherly figure to bail them out now.

"So…" Jonathan said. "Want to get to business?"

"Cold, hard cash," Alice replied. "Or else you can sit and watch me eat candy all day."

"How much?" Felix said. *Dear God, isn't one of them going to pull the plug on this yet?* "Two… two thousand you said?"

"Actually, I could swing a two-for-one!" Alice said, "Best deal in town."

"All night, a thousand dollars," Jonathan said. "Both of us."

Alice nodded.

"I…" Jonathan said, he scratched the side of his nose with his thumb, "Payment first?"

Felix rubbed his hands together.

"Um… credit card?" his voice floated up and out of him. *Fuck, it sounds so bad. It sounds so fucking bad.* And yet he still let it leave his lips.

"Okay there, Charlie Sheen," Jonathan said, "I don't care if hookers are using square readers these days. We're not that progressive, you infantile twat."

Felix shook his head, "I don't have the cash." He almost opened his mouth to ask if she used pay apps but at least had the presence of mind to zip that shit up. Jonathan clearly didn't want them making money transactions that would leave a digital or paper trail.

"I have about four hundred cash on me," Jonathan offered with a shrug. "Could we use it as a retainer?"

"Nope," Alice replied. "One thousand cash for the night or three hundred a piece for the hour, right now, or I walk."

"I DO have three hundred!" Felix piped in. "We can do the hour!" That felt like a better compromise: just an hour, and then they could be done with this horror.

"We're not fucking doing an hour!" Jonathan snapped. "It's all night!"

"Then get your white ass to the ATM," Alice said.

Jonathan laughed. "Okay, Missy. I'm hitting the bank. There are snacks in the kitchen, Felix can make you a drink. I'll be right back."

"Jonathan!" Felix said as Jonathan headed towards the door. "What …"

"Just babysit her, oh my God, Felix," Jonathan snarled.

His hand was on the doorknob when Alice piped in, "Of course there is a cheaper way of doing it."

Jonathan looked back at Alice. "Oh?"

"You could kill me," Alice said. "Kill me when you're done, and then you'd get the death discount. Just find a way to dispose of the body."

Felix felt like his head was going to pop. Jonathan's eyes remained fixed on Alice, his gaze that of a dog about to bite.

THREE

"It's a joke," Felix said. "Right?"

Jonathan loomed over Alice, and she faced him with her hands on her hips, her nose in the air, and he ran the tip of his tongue over his bottom lip. It could be a worrisome image, Jonathan so big and Alice twee. But Jonathan was wearing pastel-colored, hand-tailored linens, and Alice her breezy, straight-off-the-rack, Kate Spade petal-pink dress, twinkling diamond bracelet, and fresh-looking, dark pink John Fluevog leather ballet flats. The entire scene looked as if they could be posing for a magazine ad.

"You think you're a badass," Jonathan said to Alice, stabbing the air with his finger. "But you should be at home playing with toys."

"You're my toys," Alice replied without humor.

The truth of that touched Felix. Alice looked to Felix like a young girl trapped in a basic, bourgeois golden haze, drowning in her parents' nurture, trying to live weird, if just for one day, and he felt compassion for her. How different was she than he?

The stillness of this moment reminded Felix of that scene in *The Exorcist* in which the possessed little girl pisses herself in front of the dinner party. For a moment, he even thought that he could hear the urine splattering onto the carpet even though nothing of the sort was happening.

"Come on, I give you permission," she said. "I can help you set up an alibi. Hell, if you kill me first, then you wouldn't have to pay a dime. It could be so easy for you boys."

"What is *wrong* with you?" Felix moaned. His mind's eye saw skirts against the sky, sunlight floating on a dying mermaid. He felt the absence of their sister; a pain gnawing his heart into a throbbing nerve ending. He felt news cameras and interviews, and he saw his normally austere mother with badly applied red lipstick and a fresh glass of wine in her hand as she spoke to a teary-eyed gathering of family and friends about all of the wonderful things her precious little daughter would never get to experience.

"Stop worrying, Felix," Jonathan said. "She's not serious." If his words were skeptical of her posturing, the slow way he crept towards her, his eyes on her and his hands outstretched in a steadying fashion, seemed to say otherwise.

Alice licked her lips.

"She's a fake," Jonathan said through clenched teeth.

"Try me!" Alice growled.

Jonathan grabbed her. She made no noise, simply folded into his long arms like a small child to a father. A trickle of blood escaped one corner of her mouth, down to the tip of her chin.

But Jonathan had not hit her.

The room was silent except for their breathing. Felix's breath came out in jagged stutters. Jonathan's breath was slow and deep, mostly coming through his nose, and Alice's breath was quick and excited. The air was cold and heavy, the whir from the air conditioning filling their ears, and it was such a welcome breeze against all this anxious heat from their bodies.

"If," Jonathan said, and with one of his enormous hands he turned Alice around and pressed her cheek into his chest. Felix recognized that move: it was one their father had used on them when they were small children. *Let them hear your heartbeat and they will calm down.* "If I let you go: will you threaten to die again?"

One of Alice's arms was draped over Jonathan's shoulder and around his neck. Her fingers slipped into his hair and gripped. She pulled, and then slapped, but her efforts seemed limp and half-hearted.

"You're fucking crazy," Jonathan said.

Alice coughed, and when she pulled her face away from Jonathan's chest Felix could see red smears on her chin and his pale shirt. Blood mixed with pale rose-colored lip gloss.

"We should just let her leave," Felix said. His hands were shaking violently, and he squeezed them together. "This was a bad idea. Sweetie, why don't you go home and rest. We can take you home. Let's get your lip patched up."

Everything in this moment was amplified in Felix's ears: voices in the hallway, a woman loudly laughing, a man's low muffled words. It couldn't be on this floor? Car horns and traffic sounds. The world was hot, and he was a boy smothered in blankets, terrified that his older brother was never going to unwind them from his face.

Alice pressed her hands to Jonathan's cheeks and pushed against him. Futile.

"Do you want me to go home?" Alice said. She lifted her feet and pushed against Jonathan with her legs, the skirt of her dress swaying, the tops of thigh-high stockings revealed on her scrawny thighs. Her pink ballet flats were useless against the young man's body. One of the shoes fell off, and Felix stepped forward to grab it but then stopped himself.

"I think Felix is the one who wants to go home," Jonathan said. He grunted as Alice made another flailing attempt at pulling away from him, and he gripped her by the shoulders and now held her at arm's length, his eyes locked onto her. There was something more dangerous than a thread between their gazes now: it was shining piano wire.

"Come on, Jonathan," Felix said. "I've learned my lesson. You were right about everything. None of this is working out. I... believe you now. I understand."

This time Felix picked up the errant shoe, warm and slightly damp, and he folded it in his hand. He held it out to Jonathan and Alice, neither of whom acknowledged him. Felix pulled the shoe back to his body, twisting it in his hands.

"Glad you've made a life-changing discovery," Jonathan said.

Alice made another attempt to wriggle free from his hands and he twirled her in his arms. She cried out, a high, dog-like yelp; and he flipped her so that she hung under one of his arms, pressed into his waist like an uncle might carry a small child. Her arms and legs were tense and bent.

"But we can't let her go," Jonathan continued. "Not just yet. She'll go home and call the cops and tell them we did all sorts of prurient things to her, and she has corroborating witnesses. Dahlia in the café, for one, would probably be more than happy to vouch for how terrible we were."

"Well, what are we going to do?" Felix asked, and he still had the pink shoe pressed to his chest.

The girl lifted her head. She was hanging in Jonathan's arms and her long hair obscured her face. She laughed and pulled her hair from her eyes, holding it up delicately in her small hands. Her smile, with the blood on her lips, looked terrible.

"Come on, Darling," Jonathan said, and he groaned as he swung Alice and set her down onto the soft, powder-blue settee. He tapped his finger over the small cut on her lip. The girl flinched but had no fear in her eyes, which were fixated on Jonathan. They were dark and bright with animated curiosity. Jonathan ran his fingertips over the hem of her dress. The move quickened something lusty in Felix, and he felt a new rush of dizzied energy as Jonathan pushed the skirt up, revealing the tops of her knee-high nylons.

"Nice," Jonathan said.

Alice's fingers curled into fists and Felix wondered if she would try hitting Jonathan.

"Here," Felix said, offering the shoe he held to Jonathan. When Jonathan's pale eyes met Felix's and there was nothing short of contempt on his brother's face, Felix had to wonder why he even assumed Jonathan would take the shoe. Felix dropped the shoe onto the carpet.

"Relax," Jonathan said, and he rolled Alice's nylons down and slipped off her remaining shoe. There was a monogram "F" in italics stamped into the soles of the shoes, Jonathan tapped his thumb on the monogram before tossing the shoe aside. He used one of her stockings to tie her hands together. She didn't resist him, not even when he tied up her ankles with the other stocking.

"Bondage is an extra charge," Alice said.

Her voice wavered with those words, just slight, but enough to betray more than a little uncertainty coming from the girl.

Jonathan pressed his palms against her cheeks. Her face was dwarfed between his enormous hands. "I'm not going to cheat you. We had no idea you were a crazy bitch when we procured you, but that does not mean I am going to back out of any agreement that we've made thus far. The thing about me and my brother, our word is respectable. We're going to make sure you leave this apartment an extraordinarily rich and incredibly happy little girl, okay?"

Jonathan inspected the bracelet on her wrist, tapped one of the diamonds. "This is fucking real," he muttered.

The tip of Alice's tongue poked out and touched the wound on her lip that was already darkening into a scab.

She may have bitten herself when Jonathan first grabbed her, Felix realized.

Jonathan looked through his wallet.

"You are running a great scam, you crazy little girl. I will give you that. Felix, watch her while I'm out."

"Where are you going?" Felix cried out, watching his brother heading towards the door.

"To the goddamned bank," Jonathan said, he then stopped, grabbing Alice's expensive little bag. He tossed it to Felix. The leather felt so soft and smooth, it was like velvet money tickling his nerve endings.

"Hey, that's mine!" Alice exclaimed, for the first time sounding offended.

"She looks familiar," Jonathan said, "Doesn't she look familiar?"

Felix studied Alice: her large dark eyes, her little pink lips, her long hair, and large tits. She seemed generically familiar, like a teen pop idol, or catalogue model, but he felt like if he knew her already, he would at least remember. He thought of how she'd held her hair up in a ponytail fashion earlier, the comparison to Ariana Grande.

"She does, kind of," Felix replied diplomatically.

"Find out if we know this crazy bitch," Jonathan said. "Go through her bag."

"You got blood on your shirt!" Alice said.

Jonathan glanced down and whistled through his teeth. "I'm deducting for that!"

He then shook his head, discarding the dark mood that was threatening to descend on his temper. He grinned, a small, rather private laugh escaping his lips and then he met eyes with Felix, pointing at him. "You're getting your wish."

"My wish?" Felix said, at this point in such a state of panic that he was relieved he could even remember how to speak.

"Today's gone weird," Jonathan said. "Isn't that what you wanted?"

Jonathan opened the door to leave.

"Weird?" Felix gasped.

"Stop fucking repeating everything I say," Jonathan said. "You sound like a fucking mentally handicapped sixth grader."

"That's ABLEIST!" Alice shouted, with a burst of cheerful vigor.

Jonathan grit his teeth and pointed at Alice, saying nothing. When he left, he locked the door from the outside. That annoyed Felix because it was as if he were telling his brother that he did not trust him to lock the door like a normal fucking adult.

"I'm… sorry," Felix said to Alice.

Her eyes were on the door. Her dainty ankles bound together like her wrists, her breasts rising and falling with her nervous breathing. The allure of bondage beckoned.

"I must go through your bag. I… promise I won't steal anything."

"Of course," Alice said, her eyes still on the door. "Whatever."

Felix opened her Hermès bag, the click as he opened the clasp both solid and satisfying. The scent of roses and oranges escaped the bag and his fingers tingled. He glanced shyly at Alice, who regarded him with the unblinking calm of a lizard.

In her bag, he found a new box of condoms, still shrink-wrapped. It was a pack of twenty-four. He found a coin purse stuffed with cash, mostly tens and twenties, nothing like that impressive trio of hundreds she had used to tip Dahlia. There was no wallet, no phone, not even credit cards. There was not a single picture ID in her bag. Some Arbonne hand cream, earbuds, and a bullet vibrator.

"What's your full name?" He asked.

"Alice."

There was a practiced tone about her voice, calm and light. *Would it matter what she said? Was any of this the truth?*

Alice wiggled a little in her seat.

Felix cleared his throat, catching Alice's attention, and meeting her dispassionate, brown-eyed gaze unsettled him. She seemed to have a great ease for absorbing high-stress situations.

"Um," Felix said. "Let me get… uh… would you want something to drink?"

"Yeah, please," Alice nodded, and her voice sounded dry, almost husky. "I'd like something with alcohol and ice… but something sweet."

"Heh," Felix said, and he smiled and nodded. "Refreshing and boozy? Got it!"

Alice did not return his grin, and Felix felt like a failure.

Is she even old enough to have alcohol? Of course she isn't, but I won't even say it out loud at this point because she's already tied to a chair in Uncle Dan's apartment. What's the point?

He looked away from her, his eyes half-closed, not wanting to focus on this. Felix fell into a sudden daydream of a different life for himself where he indulged the freedom of having a precious two hours being poor, napping on a couch in a studio apartment, a pile of bills in paper envelopes on the coffee table, checking a miniscule nest egg of crypto and meme stocks on an app before running down to meet someone for drinks. It would be a life lived normally, cleanly, honestly, and certainly not one that would involve dealing with young ladies tied to chairs.

"Poor thing," Alice, the girl with her legs and hands bound to a chair, said in a soft and friendly manner. "You must be so stressed out."

This startled Felix from his reverie. Tears filled his eyes and his throat tightened.

"I!" Felix said and he dropped a tear. Then, wiping both eyes quickly with the back of his hand, he tried to cover his emotion with a forced laugh. "I was going to ask *you* that!"

"My throat is dry," Alice replied, effectively reminding Felix that she had asked for something to drink, "and I admit, my nerves are shot."

"Ah," Felix said, and he laughed nervously, but to his delight Alice laughed with him. "Well, then, the most merciful thing I can do is… is… let you ha-have a little bit of alcohol?"

Alice closed her eyes, and inhaled slowly, exhaled through her lips.

Of course her nerves are shot! Felix thought, *She's human. She's a young girl. She's not a fucking Minotaur like Jonathan!*

Felix made her a mimosa using a half-empty bottle of Veuve Clicquot that was languishing in the refrigerator. The refrigerator itself was filled to the brim with fresh and half-opened groceries: vegetables, milks, sparkling water, meats, free-range chicken, duck and goose eggs. Uncle Dan always left a full refrigerator for the benefit of anyone who might be taking care of his apartment. The orange juice was full pulp and probably acquired at a farmer's market. The sound of the ice cubes cracking as he poured the champagne in the glass was a comfort to Felix.

"Let's… let's get you cleaned up first!" Felix said, and he took one of the fine linen napkins his uncle had stored in the kitchen and trickled some water onto it. He used it to gently wipe the blood from Alice's face. Her eyes were closed as he did it, and Felix was glad of this because this simple act of touching her — the first time he was *really* touching her — was sending all manner of electricity through Felix's heart. It was like picking the gravel from his little sister's knees, back when he knew what it was like to be a big brother.

Alice sat, unflinching. Fortunately, her lip showed no signs of serious swelling.

Felix brought the mimosa to her lips and the girl took a long, cold draw, swallowing noisily and she inhaled deeply when Felix pulled the glass back.

"God, that's good!" she muttered, closing her eyes.

Felix opened his mouth to speak but the sound of the door unlocking, and Jonathan swooping in, stopped him.

"Are you really an escort?" Jonathan asked Alice, and he slammed the door behind him.

"Mm," Alice replied, and she kept her eyes on Felix who was nervously sneaking a drink from the mimosa. "I like fucking, so why not get paid for it?"

Jonathan's blue eyes rested on Alice but his gaze did not seem particularly interested in her or her reply.

"I fucking go out," Jonathan said, "and instantly attract the attention of some pint-sized, Eponine-from-Les-Miz little bitch who asks me for a buck. So I give her a goddamn fucking twenty to get rid of her. Does that get rid of her?"

Jonathan's hands were on his hips, leaning forward and glaring at Alice.

"No, it doesn't get rid of her," Jonathan continued. "Why WOULD it? I come out of the bank, and the little bitch is waiting for me! And starts begging for more money!

"I tell her to fuck off, and she has the fucking gall to start waving her arms in the air like a crazy bitch! And she's screaming that I *stole her cigarettes*, and she wants me to *give them back*!"

"Oh?" Alice said politely, her tongue worrying the scab on her lip.

"Right?" Jonathan grumbled. "So I crumpled up another twenty, and threw it on the ground. She picked it up — *of course* — but this doesn't end the situation. Fucking *no* it doesn't!

"Another woman sees me do this, and now *she* starts following me! Screaming at me about being an elitist asshole!! Me, while all I'm trying to do is mind my own business and leave the fucking bank!

"I walked an entire block up the street, making like I'm ignoring that fucking hag!" Jonathan's rant continued at the same decibel, but his tone had lost a bit of vitriol; he was winding down. He shrugged with both arms as he spoke, his palms upturned as if to emphasize how empty they were. "Is this *Crazy Fucking Bitch Day*, or what? I want to be very clear on this: you *better* be a legit escort, because this was *a lot* of trouble for me to go through, getting your damn cash!"

Jonathan pulled a thick envelope from his pocket. He shook it at Alice, before putting it back into his pocket.

Alice closed her eyes.

"There's nothing in her bag," Felix said. After tending to Alice's lip, and giving her the mimosa, he now felt like he was in charge of and protective of her. He knew he needed to distract Jonathan from yelling at her any more.

Before today, Felix had never seen Jonathan *this* angry at a young woman. True, he spoke crassly and dismissively; and he was, as a rule, belittling or sarcastic about women in general; but he'd never before sunk to the degree of screaming into a woman's face while she was tied down.

The Forrester brothers had been raised with an unfortunate exposure to their hot-tempered, long-limbed father: a man with little patience and much disdain for women he did not find attractive, and a habit of love-bombing, harassing, or assaulting the ones that he did. Their mother had always put a great effort into cultivating kindness and empathy toward women in both of her sons. Felix happily responded well to these teachings; Jonathan always seemed ambivalent at best. But their parents had never separated, never divorced, and their mother never directly complained about their father's views or treatment of women.

Well, here it is, Felix thought, and he felt disloyal to their mother for thinking that she could have made a mistake in never being more forceful in calling out their father's crimes. *Jonathan is turning into Dad. Well, that's something I won't ever be!*

"I looked at everything. No phone. No ID," Felix said, carefully avoiding mention to Jonathan of the bullet vibrator and the condoms, and in fact he found himself wishing that he'd disposed of those items.

Jonathan grunted, snatched the drink from Felix, and swallowed down the rest of it, tossing the glass over his shoulder. The glass did not shatter; it landed on a plush white rabbit-fur throw rug, bounced once, and lay unharmed.

"Unbelievable," Jonathan muttered, rolling his eyes. He brought his foot above the champagne flute and smashed it under his shoe. The snap of the crunching glass brought a startled flinch from both Felix and Alice.

"What... what are we going to do?" Felix asked.

"I'm fucking exhausted and too fucking freaked out right now to make the call on that," Jonathan said. "Felix, do whatever you fucking want. The girl is yours."

FOUR

Felix licked his lips.

"I'm not going to hurt you," he whispered, moving towards Alice. Blood swelled the veins in his temples as his heart raced. He had to hold his breath to keep from panting, and he almost prayed that his tone didn't betray his nerves.

"I'm not a horse you need to hush," Alice whispered back in the tone of a conspiratorial child, her eyes locked with his.

A scoffing grunt escaped Jonathan, who stood watch behind Alice, but otherwise he said nothing. His fingers were in his pockets, the thumbs hanging out, his elbows bent.

Her skin! The electric zing of it went through to Felix's elbows as he touched the knot on her tiny wrists and pulled it loose. She smelled like oranges and roses, like pink if pink had its own unique scent. There was a sweet, powdery smell that wafted from her shining hair.

Did she wrinkle her nose? Were her eyes on his soaked clothes? Did she know what it was like to be so wet and uncomfortable after the warm flush of sweat had passed?

Her hands came alive as the knot loosened. She flapped them. The fluttering movements panicked Felix's nerves. He could not imagine going for the binds around her ankles: just the glimpse of her bony knees and the edible fucking caramel flesh just below that pink hem…

Alice untied her ankles. Instead of screaming and running for the door like any normal girl being held captive might do, she circled her fingers around her wrists, rubbing the feel of the bind off them.

"Want to play cards?" she asked sunnily. "I'm feeling generous!"

"Generous?!" Jonathan exclaimed. "Fuck you."

"Shut up," Alice said, without turning around. "And yes, I'm feeling generous. I like playing Go Fish."

Jonathan growled, running both hands through his hair. The alpha male was standing immobile, letting this girl annoy him; far more than this girl could understand, Felix knew, it meant she was way ahead of Jonathan in the game. For now.

Ah, for once, Felix thought, *someone has Jonathan on the ropes.*

Felix remembered the smile of his sister's little white teeth as they played Gin Rummy.

Alice giggled, her eyes wide and dark like the eyes of a Bohemian girl in an antique cabinet card.

"You look young, so very young," Felix said. He noticed her dainty little knees again, and remembered an Agatha Christie novel in which a dissembling woman's age was discovered because she had the knees of a woman and not a child. Felix had never understood what difference that could be. He had spent a good deal of his teenage years staring at knees, sometimes with incredibly awkward results, and he now found himself staring at Alice's knees.

Alice placed her hands on the bulging kneecaps and drummed her fingers in a spidery rhythm.

Felix looked away from her, to the cream and gold-leaf papered wall; he had no fucking idea what to do with any of this.

"My brother, the eternal pussy," Jonathan said.

Jonathan leaned his tall frame over Alice, almost doubled in half to do so. His large hands encircled Alice's throat and then slid down to her chest and pressed over her breasts. Alice leaned into his hands. This girl melted into his touch with practiced ease and Jonathan kept his hands on those tits, pressing them so that her cleavage pushed together and swelled, her back arched up. He kissed her, their mouths meeting urgently, picturesque as a movie. She whimpered in a coquettish way.

Felix noticed her hands were against the cushion of the chair and her fingers were curled in tiny fists. Jonathan's hand, the one still on her breast squeezed hard, and then harder, his knuckles turning white and finally Alice cracked, her face twisting with pain. She cried out and pushed him off, cradling her offended breast with her hands. "Fucker!" she said.

The cut on her lip had reopened; a small trickle of blood darted down her chin.

"You smell like Girl Scout Cookies," Jonathan said, and he wiped the back of his hand against his lip, wiping off Alice's blood. "Like delicious citrusy Girl Scout Cookies."

One of her hands was still on her tit, her little legs were folded underneath her body and her back was still arched. Her face was so clean and pure; Felix kept hearing the words **younger than you think** over and over in his head.

"You know," Jonathan said, and he circled the chair, putting his hands in his pockets like he always did when he was in the mind that he was talking about profound things. "I remember seeing this animal program once, about a cheetah that stumbles across a baby gazelle. The baby cries out and stands up, and the cheetah and the baby stand face to face. It's crazy, because the cheetah holds up its paw and touches the baby gazelle, like, what the fuck was it supposed to do in this awkward clusterfuck of a situation? It's supposed to kill the baby gazelle and eat it, but without the chase or the initial intent it's just… weird."

"So, I'm the baby gazelle?" Alice asked, she held the meaty base of her palm against her lip, pressing it to stop the fresh flow of blood.

"Or my brother is, I'm not sure," Jonathan replied, squinting as he looked at Felix. "Talk about clusterfucks. Fucking hell, Felix, go take a shower and get in some fresh clothes; you look like you've been wrestling in gelatin, you're sweating so goddamned much."

"I…" Felix said.

Alice snorted, blowing air out through her nostrils, one hand on her lip, the other hand cradling her abused tit.

"Look, Felix," Jonathan said, "be content with the novelty of renting out another human being and if you don't want us to be perverts about it, then we're not going to be perverts."

"How genteel!" Alice said and she smoothed her hands over her tummy and then over her dress, leaving tiny specks and streaks of blood over the pale pink fabric as she did so..

"And you," Jonathan said, "Missy."

"Hm?" Alice replied without looking at him, she was worrying her thumb over one of the blood spots on her dress.

"Earn your fucking keep. If you are getting a shitload of money off us, you better start by getting in that kitchen and making us the best goddamn cookies we've ever had. And I don't care if you don't know how to cook. Figure something out. As for me, I'm taking a nap!"

Jonathan went down the hallway to the apartment's master bedroom and slammed the door. Felix's fingers were sore from wringing them together and he looked at Alice.

Alice stood up.

"All right," Alice said with a groan. She tenderly touched the breast Jonathan had grabbed, and wrinkled her nose. "Time to make some cookies." She walked with a smooth, tip-toe stride into the kitchen and Felix followed.

Once on the creamy tiled floor, she spun around to face Felix, she held out her hands, made eye contact, and lifted one eyebrow. Her face was a shock of drying blood and she'd adjusted her smile to a cocky half-grin so as not to reopen the scab. "Tadah!"

Felix laughed. It felt good to finally laugh. He didn't know why he was laughing, but Alice laughed as well. Their nervous energy expelled.

"You are actually going to make thousand-dollar cookies just because my brother told you to?" Felix said.

"That's the sum of it," Alice replied. She ran around the rose-quartz-topped kitchen island, trailing her fingertips over the smooth surface. She picked up a fresh linen napkin and ran it under water, dabbing at her chin with it, watching blood stain the cloth.

"You could just leave," Felix said. "Right now. Just… actually, please," and Felix felt relief and weight leave his shoulders and a pain leave his throat as he spoke. "I *want* you to go. This is just so messed up, and you're bleeding! I really do apologize, and if you… I mean you can leave me some contact info, I'll… I'll compensate you or something? For this trauma?"

Jonathan will probably laugh at me if I let her go now, but it doesn't matter! Felix thought, *It would be better for all of us if she's gone.*

Alice's expression did not change. She blinked twice, quick, deliberate blinks. "And miss out on the chance to frolic in this apartment? That's not how this story plays out."

"I don't understand," Felix said, flinching. "Who is writing this story?"

Alice shrugged, "Dunno. Someone is. You'd be surprised at all the folk pulling strings in our lives. Come on, go rinse off your sweet, sweaty face, and help me with these cookies!"

Felix was shocked at how sweaty his auburn hair really looked, once he saw himself in the bathroom mirror. The stress of the past hour had paled his skin and made his green eyes seem feral and bright; sweat sparkled on his brow and throat. Felix splashed water on his face and ran his fingers through his hair, using a spray-on dry shampoo and then a Himalayan salt spray from the cabinet to re-style it. He took off his shirt and washed with soap and water under his armpits, using the deodorant from the medicine cabinet to freshen up.

When he re-emerged from the bathroom to see that Alice was in the process of rummaging through the kitchen cabinets and had not taken the opportunity to leave the apartment, Felix felt warmth and swelling pleasure through his entire skin. Her gaze on him, the way she regarded his freshly cleaned face and hair, and the nod of approval, also tickled his senses. He found himself wanting to be completely endeared to this girl.

She's actually serious about baking cookies! Felix thought with some elation.

Their mother was handy enough in the kitchen — she could prepare things like French toast, basic snacks. Jonathan, on the other hand, was a very accomplished cook. Their friends made recipes from cooking blogs, and apps, whereas Felix had always been happy enough to just let anyone cook for him or to order out for food rather than cook a thing for himself.

Alice recited the recipe for Felix when he asked. He forgot the recipe as soon as she spoke it, but he found delight that she had it in her head. She crawled onto the counters searching for ingredients in the cupboard, and he looked up at her little legs, her tiny smooth feet..

Alice's brain was both spinning and sparse. *God, my tit hurts,* she thought, but the throbbing pain also brought to her mind a wordless image: pulling down her bra in the morning, perhaps, facing herself in the bathroom mirror to reveal fingerprint bruises.

What could her fate be by this time tomorrow or even in five hours?

Everything now as it should, she thought, but she couldn't remember what she had awoken that morning expecting, or needing, or wanting. *If I push this too far off track, I spoil today.*

Her lips still tingled from Jonathan's kiss, the cut freshly tightened and dry, her tongue held the warmth, her pulse trembled with adrenaline titillation, the sort a girl will always get when a handsome man kisses her. She retained the scent of his cologne in her nostrils, Tom Ford Tobacco Blend Oud, and his hot breath had exchanged with hers.

I want to fuck! She thought, uncomfortably aware of how sore and wet her pussy was. *But, if I want that money he pulled from his bank, I need to get these cookies baked! I don't think they're really going to get me fucked. They'd have done by now if they were going to.*

And the thought of baking sent her to a blissful memory of being a babysitter, of a boy watching her with adoring eyes as she let him eat raw cookie dough, of knowing the boy had a crush on her, and the sad joy of being his confidante, knowing that at some point his desperate longing gazes would turn cold and hateful once he realized she would never be his girl.

Strangely, the gaze touching her from Felix's kitty-cat eyes was very similar to that boy she used to babysit.

Dear fuck, she thought, *I'm already sad. I'm going to hurt Felix the same way, aren't I?*

All the ingredients and utensils were piled together on the counter. Felix helped gather them, he was humming along to the music, whistling at intervals, his steps light and the way he set utensils down, without making an appreciable sound against the stone countertops, so gentle. She asked for music, and he picked a playlist marked as "Sunday Afternoon" on his streaming service, connected his phone to the bluetooth speakers his uncle had installed in the kitchen walls. It was a mix of Lana Del Rey, Billie Holliday, Nina Simone, Carla Bruni and every throaty sad vocal one could ever desire, and yes, even songs from some more modern voices like Phoebe Bridgers, Frankie Cosmos, and the girl from the vinyl record currently on the coffee table, Felix and Jonathan's acquaintance, Brennan Talbot.

"Is this day even real?" Alice said, when Talbot's song purred from the speaker. She looked up as if the voice and the lyrics were tangible objects she could swat from the air.

Felix offered to skip the song, but Alice waved him off and proceeded to sing along to Talbot's song, her voice high and warbling, but somehow a smooth compliment to the throaty, smoky, power coming from the song. And then, just as the moment seemed so picturesque, pure, and dreamy, Alice tilted her nose up and she howled. Like a basset hound, holding her long hair up at the sides to mimic a dog's ears. Felix could not help but howl alongside her.

She rolled the cookie dough, her tiny hands and wrists and fleshy fingers covered in flour, her long hair pulled back with a sliced string of kitchen twine. The sunlight captured the flour floating on the air, sprinkles of light. Her profile was kissed by light, and it was just so golden that Felix felt a strangle of desire and happiness rolled into one. The girl was as sweet as family, with only the now slightly swollen spot on her lip and the spots of red on the neckline of her dress to mar the perfection.

This was the type of moment a magazine photo shoot or a fashion ad would try to capture, something to tell the lower classes that this was how the blessed and privileged beautiful youth of America lived. Felix had participated in a few of those types of photo shoots. Ever since more than a few of the wealthy peers he'd grown up with, and had gone to school with, had become dedicated artists, singers and writers of great

American novels, he'd become hyper aware of the pressure upon his age group and class to become meat and treacle for the masses to consume in magazines, novels, "indie" albums, and on social media. Yet, he knew that all of those photo shoots and faux interviews done for social media and entertainment platforms were artificial environments that never existed, even on the most fey of golden afternoons and yet, here he was right now, actually experiencing one.

It left Felix feeling dizzied, and he had to press his hands into his belly to calm himself back to reality. He snuck a ball off the dough to taste and Alice laughed, "Sneaky!"

His tongue was blessed with sweet deliciousness that had a fresher quality than store bought and refrigerated dough.

There was rosewater on the countertop. And she'd found lavender and orange essential oil in the cupboard — stuff that she could use in the dough, she said.

He let the girl work her magic with the ingredients and he prepared the oven and the pans to her specifications. She showed him how to roll the dough into balls and they did it quickly, filling all the pans and then slipping the first two into the oven.

There had been a socialite fantasy magazine article he and Jonathan had participated in the year before in which the young adults involved shared their favorite recipes. All the recipes in the group were quickly googled shortly before the interview, and there was a "ghost chef" on hand to make the recipes that were photographed with each participant. Jonathan had actually assisted the chef, due to his hobby of being as good as anyone doing anything.

The first batch of cookies were on the cooling rack when Jonathan joined them. The smell of the cookies was probably more than enough to wake him. It was a magical vanilla and rosewater scent.

"Jesus Christ, those smell good," Jonathan said as he staggered out of the room, he ran one hand through his hair. His buttoned shirt was loosened at the top, golden hair tousled, eyes blue as fuck. "Let's get some fucking Moet on ice!"

Felix saw the happiness that glittered on Alice's face, and it was so like the face of Jonathan's fiancée whenever she saw him. It was the expression of a young woman being struck by a young man's beauty. More than a few women and girls on this planet had gazed upon Jonathan in that manner.

Jonathan selected a champagne from their uncle's fabulous collection, and he was pleased to find a Moet & Chandon Espirit du Siecle, and he packed it in ice. They ate the first of the cookies off the cooling rack. They were so sweet it was as if they could taste every individual grain of sugar, and the salty butter made them even better. Felix ate three right away and Jonathan ate twice as many. Felix noticed that Alice nibbled very slowly at one.

"You're a fucking psycho, Little Girl, which means you might be a compulsive liar, which would make you an excellent storyteller," Jonathan said, and he pointed at Alice with half a cookie, chewing at the same time while he was doing so, "So entertain us with a half-truth while we're eating these fucking expensive cookies."

"What kind of story?"

"Any kind," Jonathan said, "Do you have a poet's soul? Are you a poet?"

Alice shook her head. "Nah, nah I don't, and I'm not, but I could fashion something passable if you gave me a seed to work with."

"Well," Jonathan said, then his eyes flicked to the nibbled cookie Alice put down, "Finish the rest of that cookie, you're not going to get away with poisoning us you little bitch."

"Ha!" Alice said, "I'd rather not finish that. I'm a great cook but…"

"You puke it up all the time," Jonathan finished. "Well, that explains your horrible fucking teeth."

Finally struck, Alice pressed her lips together and dropped her gaze. Felix did not like seeing her dejected like that, especially since he did not think her teeth looked horrible at all; he found himself wishing that Jonathan would put himself back to bed for the next twelve hours.

Felix grabbed another cookie. "I watched her bake them," he said, "there's no poison."

Felix cleared the cooling rack and plated the rest of the cookies, basically making a show of being helpful to Alice, sliding the fresh cookies onto the rack.

"How about tell us about the time you lost your virginity," Jonathan said, "and I'll tell you if I believe you."

Alice's cheeks pinked and Jonathan narrowed his eyes.

"Ah," Jonathan said, "Why would an actual whore be so shy?"

"Come on, Jonathan," Felix said…

Jonathan held up his finger at Felix. His eyes directly on Alice he said, "You're giving us my money's worth. Here, I'll pour the champagne!"

Alice's cheeks paled, she looked at him with a flash of annoyance, perhaps, but then her lips parted. There was a glassy look about her eyes that Felix recognized on the face of someone who liked their booze.

"You want the truth or a sexy story?" Alice said.

"I want the truth," Jonathan said, as he made good on his word and poured only the finest champagne to be found in Uncle Dan's kitchen.

"Well," Alice said, "You're paying me for my time, so it seems better if I just gave you the sexy story, gave you your money's worth. Otherwise…"

"I'm paying for the best," Jonathan said, "If your daddy stuck it up your ass when you were five while mommy slept in the bed next to you, I want to hear it."

Visibly, she showed no acknowledgment of Jonathan's comment, but she mulled the words over in her mind. In truth she had a childhood blessedly free of any adult tampering with her, much less someone so close as a parent. Every year before the advent of her teens was an unfurling blossom of happiness, a winking Morning Glory on a fencepost, and she truly had nothing to offer Jonathan's eagerness for her trauma for those years, lest he sniff out the lie. Alice thought of other things, the first bloom of her blood in the toilet, the first embarrassing whiff of an armpit that needed deodorant and having a teacher in class bring notice to it. She thought of her virginity which had withstood countless nights of compulsive masturbation, the times she'd tried inserting her fingers to do it, the pain of it, the addiction to stroking her clit before the night IT finally happened to her…

Alice didn't start speaking until she was served more champagne. It was ice cold, and she nibbled the rest of her cookie and took a long swig until the glass was empty. They took the cookies and drinks to the living room. Alice chose the couch to sit on, a cookie in one hand, a champagne flute in the other.

"It was on the beach," Alice said, and she belched, trying to stifle it unsuccessfully with the back of her hand.

"Liiiiesss…" Jonathan said, his tone a playful growl, one of someone warning their child to behave. He seated himself on a powder blue chair, the one Alice had been tied up on earlier.

"It was on the beach," she repeated. "It was a party on the beach, a bunch of socialites during The Season. At that time, I hated parties. Now I love them. Back then I thought if I stood away from the party and pretended, then it meant I was better than the pretentious fucks boring the hell out of me. I thought it meant the perfect boy would find me in the shadows and sweep me away. I believed in love then."

"Awww…" Jonathan said, a bite to his voice.

Alice grabbed another cookie, this time eating the entire cookie almost immediately.

Condescending fuckface… she thought.

"Hey, everyone is allowed to believe in love," Alice said, and she washed her cookie down with the rest of her champagne before continuing to talk. "This won't be a romantic story. And how about some more champagne." She lifted the glass and jiggled it and Jonathan jumped right to it.

This is too much alcohol, Felix thought. His erstwhile dreams of day-drinking now seemed nightmarish. He paced the living room and sipped his drink.

"I was avoiding the party at the beach," Alice said, droplets of fizz tickled her hand as Jonathan finished pouring into her glass, and then he set the bottle down, gave her space as he sat back on the powder blue chair, "and it was dark, and I had a new green dress and I loved it. That dress was satin and felt like cool water against my skin, I still had small tits because it was before the first summer that my breasts swelled. I used to be so cute and flat-chested in my early teens and then it felt like overnight I swelled into this," she pointed at her chest with both thumbs, bringing both men's attentions to her tits. "Wearing that dress for the first time, I felt so grown up and sexy; it was soft against my legs, I didn't have pantyhose on, so it just… it felt so good."

"I bet," Jonathan said with the hint of a purr to it, and he rested his chin on his palm, his eyes were half closed, not narrowed in an intimidating way but the eyes of someone listening. "How old were you? No tits yet?"

"Like I said, late bloomer," Alice muttered, lips above the rim of her glass, "I was on the beach under the dark sky, there wasn't a moon. I felt so hot, so I started masturbating."

Felix choked on a bite of cookie and coughed it back into the champagne flute.

Jonathan smiled.

"You dirty little whore," Jonathan said.

"Well, someone found me. A man three times my age, one of my dad's friends."

Felix looked at that cute little face of hers. He understood the men he knew and how they would look at her, a young girl diddling in the sand.

"Like a cheetah finding a baby gazelle," Felix said aloud.

"Astute," Jonathan muttered.

Felix poured himself some more champagne, his hand was unsteady and it sloshed on his fingers and the floor.

"That champagne is amazing," Alice said, and she held out her glass, which Felix topped off. "Anyway, one of my dad's friends found me.

He was watching me, and I heard him breathing so I stopped, and it was so awkward. For a moment I didn't… I mean at that point, had he really done anything wrong?"

"Understandable," Jonathan said.

"I held my hand out," Alice said, "Towards him and I don't know… to this day I don't know if I was asking him to help me up or if I was just offering myself to him."

"Was it your wank hand?" Jonathan asked.

Alice looked towards the ceiling. Her lips tightened, and she swallowed hard.

"You know you were offering yourself," Jonathan said.

"He almost… he fell over getting to me," Alice said, "He had to step over a few things. He grabbed my hand and before I knew it, he'd pushed my skirt up and he was just… licking me!"

"You… you didn't consent to that," Felix said. "There was no real consent, you do know that?"

The evening's magic was officially dampened for Felix. The golden sunshine of the afternoon, the smell of baking cookies, the fun of the chilling champagne, all erased. Now they were sitting there, exposed like worms when the rock was flipped. The good little social worker their mother had raised in Felix could not be held back: he locked his caring gaze upon Alice so hard that she couldn't help but notice and meet it.

Alice rolled her eyes, "Whatever, it was weird. I mean, I *like* oral nowadays, but at the time . . . it was just his tongue, and it felt like a finger, I don't know. I didn't even realize guys liked doing that. I didn't… I was worried that I wouldn't smell or taste good or…"

"You're telling the truth," Jonathan said, he picked up a cookie and pointed it to her as he spoke, "I can tell. Because this should ideally be a sexy story and your entire voice sounds like some twelve-year-old fucking up the retelling of her first porno. I swear to God you better not start crying."

Alice shrugged.

She didn't look at Jonathan. Her nostrils were filled with the memory of ocean, and thick air. Her mind was filled with the memory of jet-black hair with crunchy gel in it, the top of the man's head between her open thighs, the sight of it had caused her entire body to tremble….

"Please go on, I love it," Jonathan said with his mouth full. He closed his eyes and puckered his crumb covered lips.

"I grabbed the guy's ears," Alice said, "I lifted his face because I wanted him to stop and I wanted to at least talk to him, I don't think I felt particularly scared, I just wanted it to slow down. But the very act of me touching his ears, I gripped them real good like…"

She made fists of her hands, wrinkled her nose.

"Like that! And he moved so fast, he grabbed me around the hips and pulled me under him and he didn't even take off my panties, he just sorta pushed them aside."

Felix was red-faced, his breath came short, fresh sweat was starting to seep over his body, "That's… that's rape! Who was the guy who did it?"

This is it! This could be the reason for this entire terrible day, Felix thought. A scene flashed through his mind: him, swooping Alice up, carrying her through the night to the Forrester family mansion. There, he could introduce her to Mother, and together they could figure out some sort of real fix for her situation. *This is the type of story that could move mountains: a privileged, upper-class rapist taking advantage yet again of another young lady — and us, exposing him. Named and shamed, destroying the abuser could become a victory for this girl…*

"I was wet as fuck when he pushed it inside me, it hurt so bad, but he slipped in like balls deep," Alice said, "It felt like… it felt like paper ripping inside me, and he held onto me, holding me down, not even playing with my tits or anything, he just held me down…"

Her eyes lost fire at this point. The spark that illuminated that girl's face and was responsible for the bulk of her beauty, vanished.

"I remember his weight, and his skin, his cologne, he smelled like leather and violets, he breathed hard, and he moved so quick, his hips, in and out of me, and I was very excited, thinking… this is it… but… his hand covered my eyes, suddenly, like… I didn't know if he didn't want to see my face, or if my expression was ugly or…. I don't know.

"I didn't have an orgasm, nothing close to it, I just… the sound of his moan when he came, he pressed his cheek into my chest and at that point he was too heavy and warm, and I knew my dress was ruined that there would be sand stuck to everything. I didn't want him to cuddle me or love me. I pushed him off me and stood up, and I remember the sight of my blood running down the inside of my leg."

"Did you cry? Did you scream and run to daddy?" Jonathan asked. He poured himself another glass of champagne.

"Bitch, please," Alice said, and the wobble of champagne sparkled in her voice. "Do I look like someone who is going to run to daddy the moment her virginity is gone?"

Beautiful creature, Felix thought. His pulse was racing, thinking of her raped and standing on the beach, sand stuck to the blood on her skinny leg. All thoughts of helping her evaporated as he was caught up in the shining, razor-blade brutality of that situation. It was that predator's need to see a public execution, a viral video of a suicide, or a deflowered young woman staggering over the sand.

"I asked him to commit suicide with me," Alice said.

"Oh," Jonathan said, "there's a surprise."

Alice smiled, "I wanted him to walk into the ocean with me. Like the way Scientology people kill themselves. I thought it would be amazing to float and die like a fucked-up mermaid. But he didn't want to. He was like you two. He just… didn't take me seriously. So, I walked into the ocean by myself, and the water was so warm, and it washed the sand and blood off my skin and before I could get too far, he'd run into the waves and grabbed me, and he dragged me back to shore. And that's when people saw us, and it was a good moment for him because then everyone thought he'd just run in to rescue me from drowning, the blood was washed from my skin, and just like that he was a hero."

Alice blinked back tears, perhaps remembering Jonathan's warning about crying, and so no tear fell, she half grinned, wispy and wistful. "I really liked that part, him carrying me out of the water, and everyone doted on me. They wrapped me in towels and let me have some red wine. It paid off, I guess."

"Did he come inside you?" Jonathan asked.

"I didn't need an abortion."

"How old were you?" Felix enunciated each word, the same way Jonathan usually did when he was putting himself in charge.

Alice took note of Felix at that point; she tilted her head in a puppy-like fashion, blinking a couple times. She looked at this younger brother and she saw someone who could possibly be twenty times more dangerous than his elder. She held it as common knowledge that the quiet, less dominant male of any pairing was the one most likely to take a high-powered rifle to the sorority of the girl who rejected him.

"Guess," Alice said.

Felix sighed.

He thought of her tiny feet… he looked at her hands. They were plump and smooth, and they seemed childlike. He was so glad that they hadn't fucked her.

"What was the motherfucker's name?" Jonathan said, suddenly irate. "Old son of a bitch fucking girls on the beach who are just trying to have a good time by themselves."

"His name was Stephen," Alice replied, and she thanked Felix who poured her another glass of champagne. "And he wasn't such a bad guy. He was stuck in a boring marriage with a dried-up socialite. I used to babysit his nephew."

"I take that to mean you kept fucking him after that?"

Alice nodded, "For… a year or so, maybe longer than that. The guy's nephew found out and… it got a bit messy."

Jonathan smirked. "I bet."

How many glasses of champagne deep are we in, so far? Felix knew he should stop because even if they were not fucking her, they were contributing to her delinquency. *There's no way in hell she's old enough to drink.*

Alice tried to pour another glass herself, but the bottle was empty; she placed it on its side.

Alice asked for a glass of water, Felix gave it to her, she guzzled it, and then went for a piss. Once on the toilet, the girl stared at the bathroom door which wasn't completely closed. She wondered if one of the brothers would push it open or peek inside, but neither brother did. She washed her hands dutifully, pumped a squirt of Scottish Lichen scented Buly 1803 lotion that was resting on the sink.

She squinted at her reflection in the mirror but closed her eyes before she could really look at herself. Her lips were beginning to go slack; one glass of champagne makes a girl seem loose and charming, but half a bottle of champagne makes her expression look like a mugshot. She tapped the blackened scab on her bottom lip. It was mostly on the inside of her mouth, but the edge of it was visible. It was fucking annoying that it was marring her face, but there wasn't much she could do except smile crooked.

Not drunk. Don't get drunk, she thought, and she turned the cold tap on, stuck her lips under it and drank deeply. The water filled her belly and she felt grateful for it, but then she had to pee again. *Already drunk.*

Felix went into full-on domestic mode, tidying the counters and finding a container to put the rest of the cookies into. This was a habit he had from hanging around the kitchen at home since he was a tiny child, tagging at the heels of chefs, housekeepers, and his mother whenever she had the whim to cook.

"How about them thousand-dollar cookies," Felix said, "Not too bad, huh?"

Jonathan smiled. "Not bad, I agree. I ate ten of them, or more, I don't fucking know. Anyway, having the girl who made them talk about losing her virginity to some pedo on the beach is worth it."

Felix smiled back. "This is actually kind of fun. I mean, not the pedo stuff… I mean it started off weird and it has escalated badly, but it could be worse."

"Well, that's what you wanted, isn't it, weirdness?" Jonathan asked, stretching his legs out, resting his feet on the coffee table.

"Sure," Felix said. He rubbed his knuckles under his chin, his gaze seemingly on nothing. "I promise I won't ever want that again."

Jonathan laughed.

And Jonathan thought about the blood on that girl's lip. The little spot of red and how light her body was when it flew in his arms. He had to stop himself from crushing Alice in his arms when he'd held her, overcome with a predator's urge in that moment. And she smelled like oranges and roses, and he wanted something about her, but he was so confused about what it was exactly.

Imagine, Jonathan thought, *eating her kidneys right out of her…*

"Felix," Jonathan said, "get some more tumblers out."

"What… for water?" Felix stood up quickly, dramatically so, the sure mark of an over-eager beaver.

"For booze, idiot," Jonathan said.

"Jonathan she's clearly not old enough to…"

"And you've been pouring champagne for her all afternoon, don't give me that bullshit," Jonathan said.

Alice came back into the room, her step so light over the carpet she barely made a sound.

What a quiet little vampire, Jonathan thought.

"Do you like Scotch?" Jonathan asked.

"If you mean whisky without an 'e', then yes, I love it very much," Alice said, and she skittered on her toes to join Felix in the kitchen, her little face gleaming with the anticipation of delicious booze. "Whisky was the first drink I ever had."

"Excellent. Are we going to get a weepy story about how you lost your whisky-without-an-e virginity?" Jonathan asked.

"Fuck you," Alice replied, pointing finger pistols at Jonathan. "No. I don't have a good story about it other than it was delicious, and I love it."

Felix poured a tumbler for Alice, who took it eagerly.

"This is Chivas," she commented airily, eyeing Jonathan. "It's really a *blend*, you know."

"I didn't promise you single malt," Jonathan muttered, rolling his eyes. *Arrogant little bitch.* She was probably showing off, in the way that underage pick-me girls were wont to do.

But Alice lifted the tumbler to her lips and downed that motherfucker. Her face didn't flinch. Finally finished, she closed her eyes and sighed.

Felix poured her another finger; she took a sip.

And Jonathan watched her lips on the glass, he inhaled long and deep as she exhaled the whisky's fumes.

FIVE

Alice was on the powder blue couch and the color of it against her pale pink dress made Felix think of a still from a perfume ad. He imagined a dreamy, soft filter over her as she sat with her back arched, her shoulders straight and pulled back, her tits straining against the light fabric of her dress. There was a time when she was flat-chested? It was hard for either brother to look at her now without thinking of her story, trying to piece together the truth of it, imagining a time when she had tiny tits, imagining her fingers diddling her slit, and imagining the blood down her spindly calf, sand sticking to her legs.

Jonathan carried three freshly filled whisky tumblers as deftly as a waiter. He'd sidelined the Chivas and moved to a 14-year Caribbean cask Balvenie that Uncle Daniel would never notice had been pilfered, despite the price tag attached to it. He delivered Alice her tumbler of gloriously pristine whisky, and then extended one to dear Felix.

A toast was not had, and they drank with delight.

Alice licked the flavor of the whisky from her lips. "Oh God. That is delicious. Holy shit."

"You only lost your virginity not too long ago, but… you're already a whore?" Jonathan asked.

"A guy accidentally paid me once for sex," Alice said. She held the tumbler under her nose and inhaled the bouquet of single malt fumes, which had a buttery, dessert-like aroma. "And it was good money. I started charging after that."

"Is that how you came across that tennis bracelet?" Jonathan laughed. "How do you accidentally pay someone for sex, how does that happen?"

Alice took an earnest drink from her whisky and licked her lips again. Jonathan wondered at how the alcohol must burn that cut on her mouth.

"Okay. He was trying to humiliate me. He fucked me, then he threw the money at me. I kept it and spent it, and I wanted more. It seemed like a good idea. And I stole this bracelet." She lifted her wrist and gazed down at her twinkling diamond bracelet. Somehow, it didn't feel like the truth: the bracelet seemed like a casual accessory on her, as if she'd been wearing it for quite a while.

"I suppose," Jonathan said, and he downed the rest of his drink. "Stop fucking sipping that Balvenie, it's a pussy's whisky anyhow, down it like you did the Chivas, be a man."

Alice grinned, "Well, this pussy wants to savor the shit out of this."

"You'll be getting more booze," Jonathan grumbled.

He huffed down the rest of his tumbler, letting the caramel

smoothness of the spirits fire his belly.

Felix did not want to gulp his down, either; like all single malt Scotches, he felt, it should be savored. Yet he downed his whisky in the same manner as Jonathan. What a delicious burn it caused, annihilating the cookies and the champagne in his belly.

Alice slumped into the couch, closed her eyes, and pressed her hand over her tummy. Her head had bobbed, as one does when sleepy, she stifled a yawn. Her legs stretched and Felix noticed that her feet did not touch the carpet.

"Little shark," Jonathan said, sitting on the couch next to Alice. She looked at him with a contented cat's sleepy gaze. No part of his body touched her, however; he respected at least six inches of her personal space.

"Big shark," she said.

Jonathan chuckled.

Alice ran her finger along the inside of her glass. Jonathan took the empty glass from her hands and set it on the coffee table.

"I lost my virginity when I was fifteen, to my violin teacher," Jonathan said. His voice was conversational, light, a tone purely reserved for women and children. He turned his palms upwards, remembering the blisters on his fingers from that adolescent flirtation with stringed instruments.

He turned his hand back over, clenched a fist and then let it go.

Fine, blonde hairs could be seen on the backs of his hands, if one looked close enough.

"To MISS CAMPION?!" Felix exclaimed, and he thought of blonde Miss Campion. She was a Juilliard trained violin tutor who earned money teaching the children of the privileged. Felix remembered her powdery lavender scent and how Jonathan barely paid attention to her when she spoke. Oh, he practiced often enough by himself and sounded proficient at it, playing the odd Bach etude or two to the delight of their mother, but Felix never once remembered Jonathan showing Miss Campion an ounce of respect.

Alice laughed.

"Just once, but it was good," Jonathan said, "It's not too different from your story. I was having a wank in the bathroom, thinking about how angry she was at me for calling her a glorified house servant. She walked in on me, pushed me onto the toilet, sat on my cock and finished me off in less than a minute. Good times."

"I bet!" Alice said, a champagne bottle's worth of giggles in her voice. She met Felix's gaze. "What about you? When did you lose yours?"

Felix thought of the two hand jobs he had received from his fiancee, Felicity. She was a small blonde with soft lips and skin. Her bones poked him when they held each other. He had trembled at the Dior smell of her pulse-points, and almost passed out the first time she'd squeezed her soft hand around his cock, pumping it to spill on their laps. The sight of his sperm soaking her pink skirt felt awkward and slightly embarrassing. Memories of wetting the bed as a youth were still keen for Felix.

The idea of sex, to Felix, was fraught with their father's depictions: a world filled with landmines of blackmail, violent allegations, and secret babies born out of wedlock. And so Felix had only ever allowed Felicity to give him a hand job. She had been quite sweet when he'd admitted to her that he was a virgin; she told him it meant she didn't have to be jealous about some woman from his past.

"Felix hasn't done it yet," Jonathan said, "have you, my dear brother?"

Felix couldn't reply. He stared at the floor, matte pink and white swirl colored stone tiles, a lush rose-colored Persian rug on top.

"Really?" Alice exclaimed, she leaned forward, resting her palms on her knees. "Felix, you're a virgin? Honestly?"

Of course he is, Alice thought. *Clean and cream*. She could imagine Felix barefoot and draped in sackcloth, his hair long and to his shoulders, benevolently turning his green eyes onto the penitent yet lusting whores on their knees around him, mouths open and waiting for his virgin cock to fill them.

Hot blood flushed Felix's cheeks, but he still couldn't speak, or look at Alice. He hated always being at the mercy of someone's smug betrayal of his privacy.

"Well, there's nothing wrong with that," Alice said. Her voice rose with the instinctive, practiced kindness any popular high-school girl uses on widows, nerds, and orphans. Her eyes rested on Felix's crotch, imagining how quickly it would spit seed between her legs. Would it even make it into her cunt before voiding itself?

"No, there isn't, baby brother. I say that with all honesty," Jonathan said in a voice that could calm kittens. Hell, Jonathan was not half the dick he often pretended to be most of the time, in Felix's experience. "Fucking pity, though."

"Is that why you hired me?" Alice said. "To break in the colt?"

"Yeah, partly," Jonathan replied. One of his legs was bobbing rhythmically. The air conditioning clicked on again, blasting all of them with a refrigerated breeze. "He's getting married soon, we need to make a man of him, hm?"

Felix leaned forward and pressed his hands to his burning, reddened cheeks.

"Well fuck, congratulations to you and your lucky bride," Alice said, "Now I feel bad for freaking out and scaring the shit out of you both earlier. I ruined your gift to him!" She was sitting forward so that her feet touched the rug. Her fingers were interlaced, and she nodded sagely to Jonathan who nodded back.

If awkward is, Alice thought, *and life is… if drunk is good as fuck…*

She wanted a pen, and she wanted paper. She'd lied earlier to Jonathan about not being a poet. Words and phrases were addictive to her:

she wrote them on scraps of paper, and urged them to sprout in the wee hours when she was finally alone and in charge of her privacy. *If drunk is good as… if good as… fuck…* and it didn't matter, because this phrase she wanted to sprout would be forgotten within the hour if she didn't write it down now. And she wasn't going to write it down now.

The only thing worse than being pitied is having two people discuss you as if you are not even in the room, Felix sat brooding. He knew too well the world of sympathetic gazes, solemn nods, and being toted around by more capable family members like a shelter dog. He slapped his hands against his thighs so loudly it startled Alice into fumbling her champagne flute.

"Would you have acted differently if you'd known that before?" Felix asked Alice, a bite to his voice. He wanted to be angry, but was not quite sure how to go about it without sounding hurt; and, he wasn't sure who to be angry at.

"Nah," Alice replied, looking at no one in particular. "If I'm being honest."

If fuck is… she thought *…as good as drunk…*

If awkward is as… good?

Her body swayed on the couch; her eyelids drooped, and she stifled a hiccup. She curled her toes into the carpet, her feet pointed like a ballet dancer.

"You really knew I was a virgin?" Felix asked Jonathan, turning his vitriol to him. "How did you know?" Again, he wanted to be angry, and could not navigate how to accomplish this.

"If you'd have done anything except get those handjobs Felicity told her sister about — so of course she told me — I would have heard about it from you," Jonathan said.

"Well… a hand job is sex," Alice said.

"Is it?" Felix asked, sounding far more hopeful than he had ever wanted to betray.

Jonathan leaned back and rested one of his ankles over his knee, the wide spread of his limbs crowding Alice on the couch. She wiggled away from the touch of his knee, and wrinkled her nose, crossing her legs away from him. The moment was not lost on Jonathan, whose gaze remained on the girl's legs.

"No, it isn't sex," Jonathan said. "There is a huge difference, and there'd be far more happy marriages out there if women just fucking learned to understand that."

"Oh…" Alice said with a cough, "Oh! So, if you come home and your wife has Gaetano the pool boy's cock in her hand…"

Jonathan snatched one of Alice's skinny thighs and pulled it so that her legs opened. Alice, nonplussed, lifted her hands and pivoted to face him. Jonathan then pressed his left hand against Alice's crotch. "Shutting you up," he growled.

The girl did not react the way Felix would imagine she would and should have. Instead of protesting, she moved into Jonathan's touch, her legs fairly spread. Lacy pink panties were visible.

"Good girl," Jonathan said, and he slid his hand to her thigh. His hand could wrap around it. There was a bit of muscle tone to her calves, but her thighs looked tiny and soft.

His hands were so hot and strong and big, Alice's blood quickened at the touch. It was like the thrill of pressing against the pelt of a caged lion: no, it can't bite — not yet — no, she wasn't in the cage — not yet — no… no…

Alice closed her eyes and remembered her first orgasm that had awakened her womb… the thrill of seeing fireflies for the first time, the sugary sparkle of a fresh dessert, the echoes of an event horizon caught in a time loop, and the caramel burn of Caribbean cask still on her lips…

Felix's hands shook as Jonathan took the hem of Alice's dress and slid it up until the skirt bunched around her waist.

Fuck, Felix thought, *we are not supposed to be doing this.*

"Look at that. You little slut," Jonathan breathed, " that's a thong." He slid his hands under Alice's bottom, feeling her smooth, bare butt cheeks, his finger teasing over the lace.

There was a large damp circle on her panties and Jonathan gently pressed down upon it and moved his fingers in a slow, circular motion and the girl gasped, tightened, and then draped one arm over Jonathan's shoulder. Her lips parted, her tongue visible against her teeth.

"You like it?" Jonathan whispered. "Years of clitoral stimulation before getting that cherry popped? Yeah, you like it."

And he kissed the side of her neck, gently.

And Alice soaked in the feel of his lips against her throat, and oh how she loved a man's skin, and his warm scent that was a mix of smoky Oud resin and heat. She thought of the first man she could have loved, and how she preferred when he had fucked her with his clothes on, because she was still very young and intimidated by the sight of a man's bare flesh.

"Fuck you," she gasped.

She could come right now, but it would be a tragedy; she'd never allowed a man's hand to bring her to her *petite mort*. And so she breathed out slowly to stop herself. *Not this soon... not this close... and awkward is as fuck as...*

"*Drunk!*" Alice gasped.

"Fucking dirty," Jonathan murmured. He wanted to slide his fingers under the cloth, to see if she were shaved or trimmed, he wanted to pull her legs apart and push into her…

"Do you play any instruments?" Felix squawked.

That stopped both Jonathan and Alice, his hand still on her crotch, and she let go of him. They both looked at Felix who was standing, his arms limp at his sides, and his green eyes were wide.

"Felix, no wonder you're a virgin," Jonathan said.

"I do play piano," Alice said, her voice wavering. Her legs were trembling.

"I saw…" Felix's voice started strong but then faltered a little bit as he spoke. He paused, then tried again, "I mean, I saw you look at the piano when you came in. It's just… only people who play the piano are the ones who stare at a piano first when they enter a room. It's like a spiritual thing."

"I play the piano," Jonathan said in a rather sulky tone, "and you don't catch me staring at a piano first thing when I enter a room."

"Actually, you do," Felix said.

Jonathan raised his eyebrows and grimaced. "Oh?"

Both Felix and Jonathan had started taking piano lessons at a young age, but only Jonathan had stuck with it alongside his violin lessons. He was not a great pianist, but he did play a lot on his own time. It amused Felix to know something about Jonathan that Jonathan either didn't want to share or didn't know was there.

"I do? Really?"

Felix nodded.

"Aw," Alice said, "that's sweet."

She closed her legs, her voice regaining cheerful composure. She slid her feet under her bottom on the couch cushions as she looked at Felix.

This one, she thought. *Felix is a beautiful boy; even when he's seventy, he'll be a beautiful boy.*

"What the fuck ever," Jonathan said. "If you play the piano, little girl, make my brother happy. And it better be something fucking better than the stuff I play."

Alice wrinkled her nose and hopped off the couch, smoothing her dress with a quick slide of her hands to become a modest young woman once more. She went straight to the piano, touching the black, lacquered sides of it as if stroking an animal. The beguiled joy on her face was beyond something she could ever share with a man; Felix could already see that.

She flipped through the music books on the instrument.

"That's shitty, looking at books," Jonathan said. "I can at least play music by heart."

"Whatever," Alice said as she lifted a music book and set it up. "You probably know that ONE sonatina movement that you play at parties to impress people. Am I right?"

Felix laughed.

"Fuck you," Jonathan said.

"Is it that piece by Clementi?" Alice said with a sarcastic twang. "I bet it's Clementi, first movement." Standing next to the piano, her arms were crossed, and her voice full of confidence.

Jonathan clapped his hands slowly, loudly, sarcastically.

Alice was not a particularly amazing player, but she was proficient enough to be entertaining. She played classical music and cherry-picked through a couple of the song books, played a longer piece by Beethoven and then played a famous piece by Chopin. When she finished playing the Chopin, Jonathan filled some fresh tumblers of whisky.

She played small tunes for a little over an hour, and not at any point did she ask if they wanted her to stop. Every now and then her fingers slipped on the keys, but she never seemed embarrassed about her mistakes.

Jonathan contented himself with futzing with his phone. He leaned back and crossed his legs. He was the sort of person who would tear walls down in search of a socket to plug his phone in if the battery were fading. There was even an incident that made papers in New York where Jonathan had dashed onto a live theatre performance stage to plug his phone into the wall. If there were absolutely no charge available, he was not above simply taking someone else's phone to tinker with.

But eventually, Jonathan's attention span — notoriously short as it might be — was won over by Alice's piano playing. Over the course of the hour, he checked his phone less and less frequently; finally, he put his chin on his steepled fingers, listening to her music, and closed his eyes completely.

Alice abruptly stopped playing in the middle of a piece by Erik Satie and went to the kitchen, where she poured herself a large glass of water and chugged it.

Not dry, Alice thought, *not drunk*.

She found a cold bottle of Perrier in the refrigerator and took some large swigs from the bottle. She stifled her belch with the back of her hand.

"I really liked it!" Felix called out to her.

"Thanks," Alice said. And she grabbed a cookie from the tub on the counter and scarfed it down.

"You're not very good. Even with sheet music, you're prone to fucking mistakes," Jonathan said.

Fucking asshole, Alice thought, she pinched the bridge of her nose. *No more alcohol. Give it an hour and then you can have some more, pace yourself… pace…* She took a deep breath in, exhaled slowly.

"Play some Clementi for me," Alice said loudly, as she took herself to the bathroom for another piss. When she returned, she went back to the kitchen to guzzle some more Perrier.

"Bring that fucking Chivas over here," Jonathan replied.

Alice did. She carried that big fucking bottle of Chivas, walking on the balls of her feet.

She could have been a ballerina but for those goddamn tits. Felix imagined her spinning on her pedestal leg and then tottering. He smirked. She had probably never tried ballet; if she had, she would have better muscle tone, and probably better overall personal discipline.

She poured for Jonathan, and the liquid sloshed into the glass.

"Whoa, hey!" Jonathan exclaimed. "Slow it down, beautiful, don't you know how to measure your pours?"

Jonathan's tumbler was half full and Alice brought the bottle over to Felix, who eagerly held up his glass to receive.

"I'm not complaining about your pours," Felix said, oblivious to how desperate the tone in his voice was, and Alice winked.

The girl's dark eyes meeting his — it thrilled him to his belly, warm as the whisky touching his lips.

Felix found himself transfixed on Alice's bare feet as he gulped the entirety of his glass down. It filled his belly and turned his brain into a million golden bells. *Oh, my, god.*

"Jesus Christ, Felix," Jonathan said, "That's a lot of fucking booze you just swallowed. What do you think you are, a sorority pledge?!"

"I can…" Felix said, and he felt his brain spinning. He leaned back into his seat and dropped the glass onto the rug where it rolled onto the tiled part of the floor, making a scraping sound as it did. The world felt churning, rocking underneath his body as if he were on a boat during a storm.

"Do you sing?" Jonathan asked.

"I like to sing but I'm shit at it," Alice replied. Her eyes were on Felix.

"Well… you may as well sing us something, while Felix recovers from what he just did."

"Ha!" Alice said.

She took a swig from her tumbler and sat at the piano. Her movements were long and flourishing, her hair spilling over her shoulders and down her back. It seemed to Felix that she was moving under water, in slow motion. He wanted to belch, but he didn't … at least, he hoped he didn't. He made fists and rubbed his eyes.

Alice did not need sheet music for her songs. She played three of them and sang. Her voice could, very charitably, be called soprano; but she obviously had no talent for it.

Felix didn't recognize any of the songs; when she stopped playing, he stood up, wobbled and clapped. "You're fucking adorable. That's cute. That's really cute."

"Cute?" Jonathan said and he smirked. "*Cute* is right: she sounds like a cartoon mouse."

Alice laughed.

"Our sister did!" Felix said. "Our sister used to sing like Minnie Mouse! Remember, Jonathan, you used to call her Minnie?"

Jonathan's mirth disappeared. He set his tumbler down on the side table next to the couch. He pointed at Felix wordlessly, his lips disappearing into an angry slash across his face.

"You have a sister?" Alice said, "Did you mention that before?" She took a sip from her tumbler and ran her tongue over her lips; this time, she winced. Her eyes narrowed.

"Yes!" Felix said, "But Jonathan doesn't want us to talk about her!" At the back of his mind, he could hear the words from his brain coming out slurred and jagged just like the movements of the people he was seeing in front of him.

"Why not?" Alice asked. "I have a couple of sisters. They annoy the fuck out of me."

"Well, our sister can't annoy us," Felix said, "because…"

"Shut the fuck, shut the goddamn fuck *up*, Felix!" Jonathan said. "Goddammit, I hate you when you're drunk."

They were quiet for a spell, the hum of the air conditioning filling the silence.

"No one is likable when they're drunk," Alice said, "I try not to get too inebriated myself." She hiccupped. "Why can't Felix talk about your sister? Is she dead or something?"

Jonathan whirled around, pointing at Alice now as if his finger had the power to silence her. There was more than anger on his face now, there was grief: his lips trembled, his eyes sparkled. And of course his finger held no power at all.

"She's dead, I know," Alice said. Her eyes were round and shining and the tip of her tongue poked in and out over her lips. "Look, you guys are Forresters — everyone knows what happened to your sister."

She felt like something soft, amorphous, and alien was pulsing under her hands; something she needed to be careful not to burst.

"*Don't!*" Jonathan barked.

"Dude! I'm sorry, okay? I shoulda said something earlier in the conversation. I was playing dumb. I fucked up," Alice said, and she lifted her hands. Devoid of smile and mirth, her face seemed just a little bit older now; shades of the woman she could grow into, perhaps. Someone similar to what her mother must look like.

"I get it," she offered. "I won't bring her up again. I am so very sorry I even said anything. Sacred is sacred."

Jonathan's jaw worked back and forth, his eyes narrowed and then he lowered his hand. "Good. That's good. Thank you."

"We're all a bag of cunts," Alice said, "But we're not fucking cunts. Can we drink to that?"

Jonathan lifted his glass and took a long drink, as did Alice.

"I want more!" Felix groaned. He rolled off the couch and crawled after his dropped tumbler. It rolled away from his fingers, and he watched it with glassy, helpless eyes.

"You're taking a break for a few hours," Jonathan said. "I don't want to deal with you being a drunk useless piece of shit."

Alice went into the kitchen again to get a fresh bottle of Perrier.

"Does my singing voice really sound like your sister's?" she called out to them. Clearly, she had already forgotten her vow not to bring up the brothers' dead sister.

Felix wanted to say something productive, but he swallowed it down into booze and spit and whatever it else was to make a drunk useless. He stared at the rug and his Stefano Ricci shoes. He stared at them against the floor. They were so uncomfortable in this summer weather. Jonathan had opted for a respectably expensive, yet completely comfortable pair of Christian Dior tennis shoes and Felix hoped to all of high heaven he'd gone with that option.

Felix had an annoying habit of always feeling sick before he'd even got to feeling drunk. Now he wanted to belch; but he knew that if he belched, he would vomit.

"You sound like our sister when you sing, yes," Jonathan said, and he stood up and straightened his shirt, picking up his glass to join Alice in the kitchen. "She sounded like a cartoon mouse, like you."

"One of my sisters makes money singing, but her voice is shit," Alice crossed her arms over her flat tummy, her expression drained, her eyes focusing on the swirling gray flecks she could sometimes see in her vision when the light was just right. .

"Do I look like her, your sister, even just a little bit?" she persisted. Inebriation had made the muscles in her cheeks a little slack, her eyes a little sleepy, shadows under them as well. Her bottom lip hung as she breathed through her mouth.

Jonathan raised his eyebrows.

Alice picked up the Brennan Talbot vinyl album which had found its way into the kitchen. She held it up next to her face, so that the face on the album cover and hers were posed together like teenagers taking selfies. "Imagine if I got famous with my piece of shit cartoon mouse voice?"

"Our sister was paler than you," Jonathan said, "Skin like milk, what do you have in you? Romani, Italian, Mexican, Native American? All of the above?"

Alice nodded.

"Fucking mutt," Jonathan said, but with a grin. "That's pure American, you know. A pure American mutt. Are you a fucking Jewess as well? A bit of Ashkenazi?"

"I dont know."

"Our sister was willowy, she took dance lessons, she had poise and grace, she never cursed, she was gentle and kind. You are nothing like her," Jonathan said.

"Except when I sing?"

"Yes," Jonathan said, "But that's not creepy, is it? You do sing like her. It's cute, but nothing special. Like a mutant Joanna Newsom."

"You know, I like Joanna Newsom!" Alice said. "I begged for harp lessons because of her. But Dad bought my sister a guitar and the piano was supposed to be enough for me… and then my sister got a harp… we got into a fight once and I slashed the harp strings with a scalpel. She tried protecting the harp, and we both got cut. It was awesome."

"You tried killing her, didn't you?" Jonathan said, squinting at Alice as if trying to record her face to memory for the first time.

Alice did not make eye contact with Jonathan, she stared at the floor and then she nodded. "I guess she wasn't protecting the harp, she used it to protect herself from me. My chin got cut when one of the strings popped back. You can see the scar if the light is exactly right."

Alice put the album down and lifted her chin, tapping at a spot where no one could see a scar.

"See, now," Jonathan said, "that tidbit just made you nine hundred times sexier."

Alice felt stung in a way she did not expect, in a way she did not care to share. She remembered the blood on her chin from the snapped harp string, and she felt it in the same way as when she snapped a guitar string trying to tune the damn thing.

"You probably have whisky dick by now," Alice said, and she picked up a phone, one with a reef teal and bubblegum pink case, Felix's phone, and then handed it to Jonathan. "Order us some food."

"Fuck that," Jonathan said. "Cook something for us."

"I begin and end at my amazing cookies," Alice replied. "And I want Chinese food."

Felix was asleep, legs hanging over the side of the settee, snoring the universal snore of the drunk. Jonathan ordered Chinese food delivery while Alice let herself onto the balcony, pacing the railing, gazing down at the city, gazing up at the sky. It had crept past late-afternoon, not a cloud visible, the summer heat feeling blissful after being trapped in the air conditioning for hours. A murder of crows circled above, their raucous caws echoing.

The smell of the Chinese food, the crinkling of the paper bags, the room filling with the scents of food — none of it served to wake Felix. The young man continued to snore. In the kitchen, Alice climbed onto the counter to pull the plates down; Jonathan saw the bottoms of her bare feet, tinged with dirt from the balcony, and he shook his head.

The little brat could at least wash her fucking feet more often. The sight of them stuck in Jonathan's mind and annoyed him as he sat at the dinner table Alice had set.

"Hey," Jonathan called from the table to Felix, "Shithead. Chinese food is here. I'll eat all your egg rolls if you don't wake up."

Nothing.

Alice grinned; she was crunching down an egg roll.

"So, the bulimic is hungry, huh?"

"Mmmm," Alice replied. Still chewing, she grabbed some lo mein noodles with her fingers and slurped them down.

"But you're gonna throw them up later?" Jonathan said.

"Mmhmm," Alice replied, not looking at Jonathan, and she washed her food down with a gulp of whisky. "I might, but if I keep drinking into tonight, I'm going to puke anyway."

Alice thought about the first time she had intentionally puked; it was as easy as leaning over a toilet and letting her stomach contents spill out. She had not even needed to shove her fingers down her throat like girls did in the movies.

It was a habit she had picked up the first morning she'd stared at

134

the budding breasts on her chest and pinched her puppy-soft thighs. In a losing battle to stave off her growing curves, she'd taken up vomiting. For three precious years, she'd kept her breasts at bay; she still remembered the rage she'd felt, the summer she couldn't hold them back anymore. How her mom had held her arms at her sides, staring at the bulging cleavage, terrified that her beautifully blossoming daughter would be pawed at by every man in America.

"You're picking at your food like a little Capuchin Monkey, at least use your goddamned chopsticks," Jonathan said.

Alice wiped her fingers on a napkin and fiddled with her chopsticks, picking up a piece of broccoli and popping it into her mouth. The broccoli was steamed and crunchy, and snapped in her teeth.

"Only skinny girls like you think you can get away with eating like peasants," Jonathan said. "It's never cute, it's just straight-up rude."

He did not say out loud that he remembered how his sister used to like eating steamed rice with her fingers, plucking entire clumps of it to eat. Somehow it always looked sweet, cute, and clean when she had done it.

"Whatever," Alice replied, drinking more whisky.

Jonathan shook his head. He wanted to be angry with her, but he could not dredge up the energy to do so. Instead, he watched Alice enjoying her food, and he dug into his. He left an egg roll for Felix and dug into a pineapple curry and then some noodles, and then some vegetables. Alice made a pot of tea and served it to them both.

"Our sister was fifteen when she committed suicide," Jonathan said suddenly, apropos of nothing, despite his earlier demands for silence on the subject. "It was in the summer."

"I remember that, seeing it on the news. I mean, I'm sorry," Alice said, "That's horrible." She held her tea just at her lips, then slowly set it down without drinking. Her eyes were red, exhausted, and drunk; but she seemed committed to showing Jonathan proper attention on this subject. "Summer? That means the anniversary is, what, now?"

Jonathan shrugged, a yes or a no answer; Alice could not tell which.

"She threw herself off the top floor of one of our penthouse apartments. Felix and I both saw it. We had just had a very delayed high school graduation for Felix via Zoom; Mother was in the kitchen, she had no clue what was going on at first. We had some vinyls going, and she was dancing, danced herself all the way onto the balcony and then without warning," Jonathan whistled, held up a finger, "she jumped. Neither of us could even react, or process what we saw. My baby sister took flight, her skirts and blouse floating with the wind, in the sun, her hair flying. It was a beautiful sight." Jonathan lifted his hand and fluttered his fingers.

Alice pushed her plate away, her forehead wrinkled, and she pinched her lips together in a way that indicated that she did not quite know what to say. Jonathan waited for either a crass or syrupy response; but Alice, to her credit, did not wander into that forest.

"She was pregnant," Jonathan said, and he was a bit amused to see

Alice's expression as she fumbled the whisky tumbler in her hand, as if she'd just witnessed a plot twist to her favorite television show. "They did an autopsy. Mother wanted to know if she had an illness or was on drugs, or anything that could have contributed to her suicide, and they found that she was eleven weeks pregnant."

"Jesus!" Alice said, she sat up straight, her fingers clenched. "She feared being stuck with the baby? Who was the father?"

"Don't know," Jonathan replied. "We never found out who it was. We thought it could be one of our peers, a secret boyfriend. But nothing turned up. We even went through her teachers and mentors. Hell, maybe she was raped by some stranger or bum, but I don't think if that happened, she would have been so ashamed of her pregnancy as to commit suicide."

"I'm so sorry," Alice repeated. "I… family shit always burns, doesn't it?"

And we burn, Alice thought. She envisioned her own mother's face, eyes wide and dancing like those of a distressed horse, her high voice, and the violent way she could grab Alice sometimes during a fit of temper, the burning feeling it left on her arms. Alice thought of her father's dark eyes, olive skin, and firm voice as he would pull mom away, hugging her close to calm her during manic episodes.

Your mother isn't well, Dad would say. And Alice understood it, left her alone, sometimes ventured to peek into the darkened bedroom where her mother's body lay, pale as a drowned Ophelia, a lavender eye mask on her face, a garden quartz tumble balanced on her forehead, healing and opening that pineal gland and third eye. Dad would come up behind little Alice, hug her, lead her away and take her to the movies, or for ice cream, where he would explain to her gently about how sometimes people are sad and they can't help it, but that they would both work hard to let mom know that they loved her, and that she loved them.

"Yeah, it does burn," Jonathan replied, "Do you know, because of that, our father…" He ran his hands through his hair. "Yeah, Dad, he blamed Felix and me. He felt that we had somehow fucked up, and that if we weren't so obsessed with higher education, maybe we would have noticed something going wrong with her. So he had me pulled from DU, and made Felix reject all his college acceptances."

"Is that why…ugh… your father can't *ban* you from going to college, come *on*!" Alice exclaimed, grateful to be shocked from her self-pitying reverie. Her hands were clasped together, completely invested in this sad tale. "This is *AMERICA*! You're fucking *wealthy*!"

"Yeah, well," Jonathan replied, "The old man threatened to disinherit us if we disobeyed him and figured we'd end up running the family business anyhow, so why did we need anything that could possibly induce us to move into another vocation?"

"Nepo-babies of the art world, huh?" Alice breathed out loudly through her lips, and she shook her head. She didn't want to look at Jonathan anymore, and in fact, felt quite unsure what to say now, "Man, that sucks."

Jonathan nodded, he felt sleepy, slow, and stupid, his belly was full of food and his brain was swirling with whisky. He was in that heavy warm stage where he did not mind unloading any manner of secrets to a stranger. "You know what the real bitch of that situation was?"

Alice shook her head and took a sip of tea.

"Mother said to me at her funeral that she didn't understand why our Alice would have killed herself over a goddamned pregnancy because she would have happily made sure to terminate it for her. All she had to do was ask. It was completely pointless."

Alice's lips parted, her breathing quickened and deepened, she looked as if she wanted to speak a thousand words she wasn't letting escape. She closed one of her eyes, "Ah, so Felix is getting married, what about you?"

Jonathan nodded, and felt a surge of warmth within himself, pleased that Alice had taken the initiative to change the subject, "Yeah, I'm getting married as well. My lady is the sister of Felix's fiancée , in fact."

"Cuuuuute!" Alice said, she had a knuckle pressed to the scab on her lip. "You boys actually in love? Or is it benefitting the family somehow, marrying these gals?"

"Well, they're good girls, not bad to be around; and yes, it is benefitting our family, and theirs as well," Jonathan replied. He rather liked the way Alice was sitting, with a child-like expression, as if she were a kid listening to a teacher discuss American history. "Their family controls the other half of the art world, — playhouses, ballet companies, auction houses. After our weddings, my new wife is set to take over as the main operator for the Forrester family galleries."

"Damn," Alice said, "She's set. You're set. Is your Dad retiring from running the galleries or something?"

Jonathan smiled with a paternal glow, reached over, and patted Alice's cheek. She closed her eyes, leaning into his touch. The gesture suddenly felt too intimate to Jonathan, and he pulled his hand away.

"No," Jonathan said. "My dad only owns the galleries. Proper curators runs them — and our current head of operations is soon to be out of the job and fucked over, despite the fact that he's an old friend of our father's."

Alice bared her teeth and wrinkled her nose, "Cold blooded."

Jonathan scooped more food up with his chopsticks, shoveled it into his mouth, and talked with the food mashed into his cheek. "Great gains never were accomplished without at least one head rolling at the guillotine. Anyway, our curator's name is Richard Talbot — the *father* of Brennan Talbot. Seeing as you hate her music so much, I thought you'd appreciate that detail."

Alice sighed and looked away briefly; when she spoke again, her voice was deflated and low. "Look, I gotta…"

"Is that food?" Felix was awake now. He rolled off the settee, landing on his hands and feet and then stood up, running his hands down the front of his crumpled clothes. His eyes were the sort of glassy one sees in mugshots. He arrived at the table and grabbed a plate and started scooping food.

"Egg roll!" Felix said, pulling it out of the carton and crunching into it. "Oh my god, I'm so drunk! This is so good!"

Alice picked up the empty teapot, taking it to the kitchen where she put the kettle on.

"Can you sing more?" Felix called out to Alice, his voice raised as though calling to her from a great distance although she was just across the table from him. "I want you to sing more."

"What do you want me to sing?" Alice asked. She leaned against the counter, her arms crossed over her tummy. Tears filled her eyes, and she used a napkin to wipe them away before either brother saw. She opened a fresh bottle of Perrier and took a long swig from it. Her emotions were twisted; she wanted to vomit the food in her belly, certain that she was swollen, filled with salt and fat and sugar.

A deep breath in, another long drink of sparkling water, and Alice felt sorted enough to at least not be sad. She returned to the dining table, where Jonathan snatched the Perrier bottle from her hand and began to drink it. Alice half-grinned at that. Clearly, Jonathan had that tall man's habit of never being satiated: always hungry, always thirsty, always lusting. *Voluptuaire.*

"That song our sister used to sing, our sister," Felix muttered, and he began to eat his lo mein noodles with his hands, in an even sloppier manner than Alice had, slurping them and sucking the sauce off his fingers. Alice cringed and met eyes with Jonathan.

"Do I look like that when I eat?" she asked.

"Yes," Jonathan said, without looking up.

"Our sister," Felix muttered, with his cheeks stuffed. "Our sister killed herself. Cos… she was cos…"

"Yes," Alice interrupted, "Jonathan already explained it to me. She was pregnant and scared. I am so sorry."

"Tragedy," Felix said as he munched. "Mm, I watched her…I mean I … I wonder who… get pregnant. I watched… Maybe I dreamed… it was a dream…"

Alice's eyes widened, and she looked at Jonathan, who was staring at Felix. She realized she had to feel this situation carefully because there are landmines and then there are *landmines*, and she was not willing yet to step on something this devastating so soon.

The electric kettle beeped urgently and clicked, so Alice went to it, steeped the fresh pot, and poured some tea for everybody. She didn't sit down; she cradled her glazed clay teacup in her fingers, looking at Jonathan. He met her gaze directly. Alice could tell he never felt the compulsion to camouflage his gaze. He was the type of man who looked straight at someone, wanting them to see it and know he was beholding them. He could get away with it as well because he had such a pretty face.

"Will you have a bachelor party?" Alice said.

"This is it, I think," Jonathan replied.

"What do you think Dad's bachelor party was like?" Felix asked, lifting his head from his food. There was a tremor to one of his hands, and a noodle hung from the corner of his mouth.

"Dad's?" Jonathan replied, his gaze firmly on Alice as he spoke. "What do you think that would have been… knowing Dad, it probably began with some massive Illuminati-level bullshit and a bunch of expensive strippers, then he probably raped a cleaning lady."

Alice half-grinned. Her lip was now a bit swollen at the scabbed part, but it only succeeded in giving her mouth a trendy, collagen-injected sort of plumpness.

"If it is the dirty element that gives pleasure to the act of lust," Jonathan said in his deep, booming voice, ready to deliver a literary quote to the admiration of all around —

"Then the dirtier it is, the more pleasurable it is bound to be," Alice interrupted.

The fucker! Jonathan thought. Alice's placid countenance reinvigorated for him. *She just fucking quoted Marquis de Sade back at me!*

"We'll have to talk novels," Jonathan said to Alice, resisting the urge to reach out and caress her, somehow feeling he'd already given her too much regard.

"Well I don't want to talk books!" Felix snapped, emboldened by inebriation, "I want her to sing more! Like our sister used to!"

"Our sister used to sing that 'Over the Rainbow' song on the ukulele that the fat dead guy used to sing," Jonathan said, "But there's no ukulele here."

"I know that song, I can probably play it on piano," Alice offered.

"Eh, don't bother," Jonathan said.

Alice realized that Jonathan was the only one of the two brothers still dialed in at this point. His eyes were glassy with booze, just as Felix's were, but he was not smashed.

"Go on," Jonathan finally said. "Play us something, but not *that*. Help us digest what we got going on here."

Alice sat at the piano and announced that she was going to play a song she'd written. And instead of being treated to something whimsical and charming, the brothers were introduced to strange lyrics about watching a woman rip linen off wooden planks. There was blood dripping off the linen, and something about a man being crucified; and something about cocaine and a hand job, too, all sung in their dead sister's voice.

When she finished, Jonathan clapped, his large hands giving the full force of applause.

"Fucking Joanna Newsom," he said. "And you wrote this?"

Alice nodded primly. Her cheeks were red.

"Then why are you sitting around fucking complaining about

Brennan Talbot? Go find some rich daddy to cut you a record deal. It's what hookers do isn't it?" Jonathan said.

Alice cast her gaze downwards, sucking on her bottom lip.

"S'pretty," Felix replied. He was drinking tea now and had managed to find the presence of mind to wipe his mouth and cheeks. He dipped his napkin into his teacup to wash his fingers. "You kinda sound like Bjork."

"Jesus Christ, you need to wash up," Jonathan said. "You stink like sweat and Chinese food and whisky. It's *repulsive*."

Felix hiccupped.

Alice rejoined them at the table and tucked into her tea. Her steps were light and quick, her eyes darting back and forth.

"So tell us, what's your weird little song about?" Jonathan asked.

"It's about a man I haven't met yet," Alice said. "You're the first people to hear it, because if my sister heard it, she'd just steal it and record it as her own. She's a real asshole like that. She took some of my poems and…"

"And earlier you were telling me you weren't a poet. I don't care about your sister," Jonathan said, "All girls hate their sisters. I'm more interested in your lyrics. Tell me about that man you haven't met."

"Yeah?" Alice smiled, straightened her posture, everything about her demeanor blossomed with youthful eagerness, "He… he teaches me the worst things and I see him on a crucifix but he ain't Jesus. And he's always there, with this massive hard-on and cocaine."

"S'based on a dream?" Felix asked.

Alice poured some more tea. "Do you remember your dreams, Felix?" she asked.

"Sometimes," Felix said, and he belched.

She flicked her eyes to Jonathan, and he shrugged. "Who has time for that shit? I remember my dreams, but they're not worth dwelling on."

"I had a dream last night," Alice said, "that I lived in the '70s and I was wearing this fabulously horrible macramé two-piece outfit that was orange, white, and brown colored. And I was living in a high-rise apartment and there was a man, some dude in a seersucker suit, and then another man broke in and someone's limbs were amputated. A TV got thrown out the window. It was *amazing!*"

"It could make sense, I guess," Jonathan said. He grabbed a fortune cookie and tossed it to Alice, who caught it, cracked it, slipped the paper out, showing off that it was blank. She then turned and walked back to the piano.

She pulled a sheet of Chopin out and started playing it, lost in it. Felix sat next to the piano, on the floor, looking up at her.

Jonathan had made the mistake of drinking more of that Scotch. Drunk as fuck, he wandered out of the room and to the master bedroom. He pulled off his shoes, his pants, his shirt, and fell on top of the covers, sinking his head into the goose-down pillow and listening to the deep tones of that grand piano his uncle always kept in tune.

The music, the way the girl played it, it sounded deep and rich, sort of hopeful. There was light tenderness to it, there were flaws. Chopin in the hands of a feral young creature.

Jonathan tugged at his cock, feeling some arousal, but he did not get very far; he closed his eyes and then pressed his fingers over them. He thought about the tidbit Alice had shared about having sisters, including one she hated. He imagined that the one she did not like was prettier than she, that sister had a beautiful voice and was better on the piano. He already knew he wanted to meet that sister and see Alice's face when she learned he was fucking the shit out of her. That sister was probably older, of age, and far more worth a man's time.

He wanted more whisky, but instead he fell asleep.

And in the living room, Alice felt Felix's fingers on her calf. Alice finished playing the piece and looked down at him. When they met eyes, he slid his hand up her leg and onto the inner thigh. She placed her hand over his.

"Can I touch you?" Felix asked.

"You can," Alice replied.

"I mean… it's ok. You're not forced? You want to do this?" Felix asked, sweat beaded his upper lip and his hairline. He smelled like whisky and onions and failed deodorant.

The beautiful creamy young man, melted into this sweating creature, gave her a slimy feel in her brain. It was a slippery tickle, like a tongue over every crease and wrinkle.

Felix was breathing so heavily. Alice wanted to take his head off with her bare hands. She wanted to crawl out of a pit holding it aloft and screaming at everyone who saw her. She wanted to slice his face open.

Whisky was making her surly.

Instead of assaulting him, she pressed her palms against his soggy cheeks and then slid them up into his soaked hair and over his slick scalp. Trembling, he touched her cheek and even though she worried that his greasy palm, which smelled like an overflow of Chinese food, could cause an acne breakout on her cheek, she did not flinch.

"I want to kiss you," he whispered. "Is it true that whores don't kiss?"

"You can kiss me," Alice whispered.

Felix thought of his childhood nanny, an older, well-fed woman who had cuddled him into her body, and pressed her palm against his crotch and told him that warm was good, warm was safe… and he'd burned with curiosity about what more she could do with her hand, and she'd never gone farther than that. Something that felt like it should be a crime, and a secret, but nothing much more.

And Felix fell away from her without kissing her, staggering, and ran into the bathroom. Alice could hear him throwing up what could only be a seriously putrid mix of Chinese food, whisky, champagne, and cookies.

"Fuck," she muttered.

Alice grabbed a full bottle of Reyka vodka and held it by the neck as she crossed the living room and the hallway, past the bathroom where Felix was puking, and into the master bedroom Jonathan had gone into.

He was snoring with one arm tossed over his face, his Omega watch pressed against his forehead in a way that Alice knew would leave a mark. A Himalayan salt lamp on the nightstand glowed, warm and orange as a campfire.

The vodka bottle felt cool and tempting in her hand. She could still hear Felix gagging into the toilet. She caught the bedroom door with her foot and swung it shut.

It smelled like a drunk sleeping man, spiced with sweaty cologne, whisky fumes, and sulphur. The carpet was soft and plump under her toes, giving the floor a delicious spring. The room was cavernous and the air felt cool and clean. Twinkling specimens of rocks and minerals lined the room: quartz, fluorite, rainbow amethyst cut bases, celestite, and more. A clock ticked. One of the bookshelves was dedicated to antique books, and it added a dusty tobacco scent to the room. She saw clothing on the floor.

Jonathan continued to snore as she approached the bed. She reached out with her free hand and trailed her finger up his long shin, which was covered in soft, golden fur. His skin shuddered like a horse when a fly is crawling over its flesh. The snoring stopped and she could see his eye, peeking from underneath the arm.

"What do you think you're doing?" Jonathan said, his voice low and manly.

Gripping the bottle, Alice climbed onto the bed, and she swung her leg over Jonathan's waist, pressing her crotch down onto his, feeling the large soft mound against her. With her free hand, she slid her fingers up the side of his hard thigh until it touched the edge of his silk black boxers.

"Do you want another drink?"

With her thumb she finished loosening the cap on the vodka; when she flicked it off, it flew across the room, hit the wall, and bounced onto the ground, where it spun.

Jonathan moved his arm off his face at the sound.

"No," he said. "I don't want that shit mixing with my Scotch. Vodka is a woman's drink."

"Oh," Alice said, and she took a swig from it. It burned, the taste of Icelandic lava, and she had the fleeting, panicked thought that it would make her stomach bloated. "Like, a million Russian and Ukrainian soldiers who are pulping each other right now would probably disagree with you on that."

"Shut up," Jonathan said. "I'm drunk."

"Do you want to fuck?" Alice asked. She wiggled her hips slightly, but she felt nothing harden underneath her. "Don't you want your money's worth?"

"You can't fool me," Jonathan said. "You're too young. Your scam worked, little girl; you're getting a lot of cash off me. But I am not stupid enough to go to prison for fucking you. Where's my brother?"

"Your brother is puking right now," Alice muttered, feeling the delightful squish of their soft genitals against each other. She rocked on him gently, rhythmically, but he did not get hard.

"He's a pussy," Jonathan said.

"I'm a pussy," Alice replied.

Alice gathered her skirt around her waist and pulled it up slightly, just enough to flash the panties over her mound to him. "I have a nice pussy."

"I'm sure you do," Jonathan said. But still, he made no move.

Alice sighed and then rolled off, lying down next to him. She had to sit up, however, to take another swig from the vodka bottle. She sloshed it as she drank, and it splattered down her chin. She frowned, setting the bottle aside with an unsteady hand.

"Heh, booze getting to you?" Jonathan asked.

Alice rolled to her side and tapped Jonathan's chest. "Give me some cocaine."

"What do you know about cocaine, little girl?" Jonathan asked, mirth in his voice. He decided he liked her, in the way someone gets used to a stray cat. He let out a sigh, a long exhale that collapsed his belly, and ran his finger along her arm.

"Go to sleep," he said, and he pulled her body into his, holding her like she was a doll. The orange and rose scent filled his nostrils, and he inhaled, cupping his hand over her soft little ass. Within moments, they were both asleep, the lamp light still on.

SIX

Felix opened his eyes to the sound of someone gagging vomit into a toilet bowl. He saw the dirty bottoms of Alice's bare feet facing him on the bathroom floor, as she kneeled at the toilet. The cobwebs drifted as he felt the throbbing headache of a hangover and he peeled his sticky tongue from the roof of his mouth.

He squinted and saw Alice; her hair tied back with what looked to be a shoe lace. Her hands gripped the side of the toilet bowl, her knuckles white from the strain, and he saw Jonathan's shirt buttoned around her body. She grunted, and stood up, flushed the toilet, and then rinsed her face in the sink. Felix watched as she peered into the mirror, her face was ashen and puffy, she grabbed a toothbrush, clearly not caring who it belonged to, and she brushed her teeth.

Watching her now, with the crimes of alcohol pounding in his brain, the morning light unforgiving and bright, Felix could see how plain Alice was. Her skin looked dull. Her eyes surrounded by dark, baggy shadow. A few pimples dotted her face.

"Good morning," Alice said, toothpaste still on her lips as she rinsed the toothbrush, "I think your brother is making breakfast. Lucky us?"

The smell of coffee and bacon hit Felix's nostrils and he groaned and sat up, rubbing the sore parts of his limbs. His mouth was like sandpaper, and he gripped the cold edge of the sink and pulled himself up.

Alice stepped away from him. "You slept there all night, you weirdo," she said.

Once at the sink he folded his body over it, and then he felt an intense wash of shame because his nostrils flared, and he could smell how much he stank like rank sweat and anxiety. He turned on the faucet and began to gulp water, swallowing down deeply.

During that time, Alice hobbled to the toilet and peed, and the sound of it churned his guts and he staggered towards her. She stood up from the toilet when he approached, not quite finished peeing, urine splattering onto her legs and the floor. Felix kneeled in it so he could puke into the pee-water swirling in the toilet bowl. It was just bile at this point. He could not even feel embarrassed about it because he felt like he'd be dead soon anyway.

He finished puking, staring at the long line of mucous hanging out of his mouth before he spat it all out. As he bent over, wheezing through his lips, he felt something cold and refreshing against the back of his neck. Alice had soaked a towel in chilly water and had placed it on him.

Oh, God. It felt so good.

He closed his eyes and sighed.

Her hand rubbed in circles over his sore back and spine and shoulders. She did not say anything comforting or anything flippant or anything at all. It was just her touch.

She filled the glass on the sink with water and he drank long and deeply from it and then took another glass. He watched as she used a fresh towel to mop up the urine from her legs and then the floor and she tossed that to the side. She slipped her arm into the crook of his when they left the bathroom, and arm and arm they wobbled down the hall and towards the delicious smell of breakfast from the kitchen.

We're touching! Felix thought. He had a vague memory of wanting to kiss her last night; he wasn't sure if he had. And he did not want to know, because he knew that he'd probably fucked it up. But at the moment, this electric thrill of their arms locked together was enough.

Bright daylight poured into the frosty apartment, another hot and cloudless day ahead. They were safe and cool inside. The sounds of Chet Baker filled the air; Jonathan was in control of the music now, and his brunch playlist included selections of John Lurie, Frankie Miller, Tom Waits and Leonard Cohen.

Alice delivered Felix straight to the table and as he sat down, they were met by Jonathan, he was holding out a cloche, silver and shining. He balanced it with both hands, holding it out to Alice, who had set herself down.

"For you."

"Do you even know what I like for breakfast?" Alice said. Her elbows were on the table. Shadows under her eyes, lines around her mouth, a ghoul of a young woman.

"I'm good at educated guesses," Jonathan said.

Alice lifted the silver lid revealing a pile of cash, stacks of fifty-dollar bills fastened with rubber bands.

"Whaaat?" Alice exclaimed, and the glory of joyful youth shone once again upon her face as she dug her hands into the cash. Her smile was toothy and vibrant. "What the hell. You want me for a week or something? Did you go back to the bank?"

"Yup," Jonathan replied. "I just want to make extra sure that you shut the fuck up about this interlude with us. I don't want you making some goddamn TikTok where you go on and on about how we debauched you with cash and plied you with alcohol."

"But you *have* debauched me with cash and plied me with alcohol," Alice replied. She picked up her glass, and helped herself to the clear, fat-belly pitcher of sparkling water on the table.

"I think I'm being more than fair on this. This is good money; I even made the bills small enough so you can spend it readily and get small change back. See, I am an exceedingly nice man, and this proves we're all good people here." Jonathan said.

"It proves we're all shitty people," Alice replied, stifling a sparkling-water belch. She flipped through one of the fifty-dollar bill packs and then set it back onto the super neat stack. "But I won't complain."

Alice's euphoria did not last long; immediately upon finishing the sentence, she gagged, pressed the back of her hand to her mouth, and dashed out of the room to vomit.

Felix watched how tiny she looked in Jonathan's long shirt as she ran away, and he felt a pang of jealousy. He'd drunk so much alcohol last night and essentially puked himself into a stupor in front of this girl, leaving her to Jonathan to show her what a golden boy could really be. *Fuck.*

As soon as she was out of the room, Felix leaned forward and whispered, "Did you guys fuck?"

"Nope," Jonathan replied with a popping emphasis on the "P" sound.

"Oh?"

"I'm not a fucking moron," Jonathan muttered. "Who the hell fucks drunk kids? Besides our dad?"

Jonathan pulled out his phone, started scrolling. There were twenty ignored text messages and twice that many ignored DMs. There were three voicemails, all of them from his fiancée; Jonathan listened to a quick snippet from each. The content was the same: she needed him to fucking answer his phone, Felicity was looking for Felix, and they better not be off on some stupid bachelor trip to Vegas like the stupid fucking "Hangover" movies.

Shut the fuck up, he now texted in reply.

Just don't fuck this up, she replied immediately, *for your mom's sake, at least.*

Fuck her, Jonathan texted back, grinning. *Fuck all of you soulless mongrels.*

Her response was an emoji of a man wearing a turban, and a heart.

The fuck? Jonathan frowned, squinting at the emoji response. He really enjoyed the cryptic nature of his hot-tempered fiancée's emotions, sometimes. He silenced his phone as another call came in from Felicity.

I'll tell Felix you called, he texted quickly. That should hold her off for a while. Felicity was much more manageable than his own fiancée.

And Felicity at least had dignity: she didn't lower herself to respond to his text message. At least there was a bitch who could understand the importance of silence.

Alice returned with apologies, a hand to the back of her mouth, one eye closed.

"It's going to take more than cold, hard cash to cure this hangover," she mumbled.

Jonathan could not help but smile at the sight of her: mystery girl, stranger playmate. This morning marked Day 2 of whatever this endeavor was, and he was eager to keep it going.

Jonathan served bacon, eggs, pancakes, and Bloody Marys. For Felix, it was a lifesaver. His gut, his brain, his chest, everything felt so much better as he mopped up the runny yolks with buttered toast, and then chased it down with bacon and maple syrup. He gulped everything down, except for the Bloody Mary. Alice and Jonathan drank theirs heartily enough; instead, Felix treated himself to extra helpings of orange juice and coffee.

"Do you get hangovers?" Alice asked.

"Never," Jonathan replied, and it sounded oddly like a boast.

"Only alcoholics never get hangovers," Alice said.

Jonathan's eyes stayed on Alice, but he said nothing.

Alice nibbled on her breakfast, a couple strips of bacon, an egg, and half a pancake drowned in syrup. She asked for a mimosa, which Jonathan made for her. She took it with her onto the balcony, stepped out the open French doors and gazed at the city below, crossing one leg behind the other.

There was a perfection to that sight of the girl at the balcony. Felix could not help it; he snapped a picture of her with his phone. He felt guilty as soon as he did, and he met eyes with Jonathan who tilted his head. Felix gazed at the photograph on his screen, already thinking of three different Instagram filters that would really make it pop, he couldn't imagine a way of posting it with an explanation Felicity would accept. He knew he should delete it.

But he didn't.

He posted it to his Finsta instead, one that not even Jonathan followed.

Jonathan's phone chirped out a notification and he picked it up. Squinted.

"Delete that, you moron," Jonathan said.

Felix's mouth gaped, "Wait, how did you…"

"I have a Finsta too, you idiot."

Felix deleted the picture. He did not delete the original snapshot from the gallery on his phone.

Jonathan finished off a buttery stack of pancakes and washed it down with black coffee. He was wearing a gleaming white Bruno Cucinelli t-Shirt and black silk boxers. Still barefoot, he carried his coffee to the balcony and stood next to Alice.

Felix took another picture. This one looked just as good as the first one, Alice and Jonathan like a still from a romantic movie. There was nothing one could do with a picture like this except to keep it. Felix thought he could print it up sometime later and keep it privately in a secret envelope. It could collect dust at the bottom of a desk drawer for decades, until the day their grandchildren dig it up and pass it around the family with questions.

Felix poured himself a half cup of coffee and poured heavy cream and a copious amount of sugar into it, and took it with him. He had to regain his standing with the group.

Denver was already well on its way. Scores of people filled the sidewalks, the smell of onions and red meat on restaurant griddles filling the air, music. Voices and laughter clattered up to their ears. Cars honked, belching smoke. The sea of humans below ebbed and flowed in a chaotic blend of disparate colors and styles: tie dye, denim, sports jerseys, Crocs.

Felix's attention focused on the people of color. He wanted to know what their lives were like and what languages and accents they spoke. He wanted to give them things and give them opportunities and get home-cooked meals from their mothers.

Felix was self-aware enough to understand that these thoughts were racist. Mother had been calling him out on these things his entire life. *Even if you think it 's "benevolent," that's a degrading way to think of someone*, she would say. And then Jonathan would chime in, in a smarmy tone, saying like, *Yeah, it's better to just be violently racist, don't you think?*

That's not the point, Mother would say. Felix was replaying a thousand interactions in his mind now, if he was replaying a single one. *The way Felix is thinking reduces people of color to zoo animals and that is degrading. It is beyond degrading. It is looking at people as if they were shelter dogs and cats and wanting to adopt them in that style.*

And of course, so it was. Felix knew that.

It was a roasting dry heat, yet another day when it would break a hundred degrees, the only dampness in the air came off the sweat from their skin.

Even though there had not been any sex to speak of aside from the Ingmar Bergman-esque monologues about losing virginity the night before, Felix decided that it would still be an awesomely bizarre tale to harbor in memory. They could always say that they had once picked up some crazy young woman who begged them to kill her, got stupid drunk with her, and played music with. Hell, they might not even need to tell the part where Jonathan had tied her down with her own socks, tied her right to a chair in Uncle Dan's apartment, though it *was* a pretty choice detail.

The sun, hot and strong, caused fresh sweat to creep around the back of Felix's neck. He immediately became aware of how fucking badly he still needed a shower. He smelled like a dying body, one particularly worse for wear: scents of vomit and hangover sweat, emanated from him, plus he had Alice's pee from the bathroom floor still staining his knees, adding to the olfactory cacophony. No one had commented on it that morning, but he knew it was only a matter of time before Jonathan started letting really cutting remarks fly. Anxious at the idea, Felix downed his coffee.

In truth, Felix didn't want to shower because that meant Jonathan and Alice were going to continue this interesting morning without him. They were going to say life-changing things, get to know each other better, and he was going to be left out. All of this was because he had to be an actual human being who sweats and gets hangovers and stinks and needs showers.

Jonathan looked pristine and so did Alice, annoyingly so. Breakfast, booze, and coffee had returned her demeanor and skin to a flawless sheen. She held her head high, looking to Felix like a Native American maiden, something he could never say aloud to her because that would be racist, but he just… well…

"You're so pretty," Felix said, and his cheeks burned. His eyes, however, lingered on the small pimples on her chin, just three.

Alice smiled and crinkled her nose.

She sipped from her drink, and they looked down on the street that was crowded with flat American voices; no one down there was interesting or special. This was a street and time of day for vapid tourists and their families.

What does our uncle like about this place? Jonathan thought. Uncle Dan was supposed to be a classy, elegant, bisexual man with a lot of fucking taste. *Or does he just pretend at that? Hell, everyone's always pretending about everything, aren't they?*

Across from them was another row of buildings, bottom-level businesses and top-floor lofts. Felix looked at the row of windows, most of them open; he saw people moving around, and wondered if anyone across the way had looked in on them. It was the sort of thing someone with binoculars might be interested in. Not that he particularly wanted to peep in on anyone.

"I'm… I'm going to shower," Felix said, his voice far meeker than he would have wanted it to sound.

Alice said nothing.

"Yes, you go do that," Jonathan said in that older-brother voice, echoing the tone their mother took whenever one of them announced they were going to do something they should have done hours ago.

Felix discarded his reeking clothes in a pile as he disrobed, wondering if he should just burn them. A spare bathrobe lay folded on a shelf, pristine, white, and waiting. The hot water against his flesh stripped all the filth from him. He used up every fragrant bottle of expensive, herbal, floral, organic-coconut-milk-creamy product that Uncle Dan's guest shower had to offer.

On the balcony, Alice continued to stare down at the people. Children and teens and young adults were the only attractive things in this city. The adults all seemed odd or lumpy or dry, or just old before their time. She watched the crowns of heads and saw thinning spots on men and women. She saw women with mullets, she saw men with their hair twirled into top knots. Dreadlocks, curls, cornrows and buzz cuts, pink hair, blue hair, and girls who chose to dye their hair granny-gray. Alice imagined her own hair chopped off, the very idea of it being so short that it floated above her shoulders sparkled in her mind like a waking dream. Sprinkled amongst the unenlightened hordes were the stylish leftovers of the pandemic: men and women choosing to maintain N95 and handmade masks in public.

"All a bunch of shitheads," Jonathan said, "Leftover mask wearers."

"Yup," Alice said.

"Did you get vaccinated?" Jonathan asked, "Felix did."

"Yup," Alice said.

"Weak," Jonathan said, "You don't really want to die, then."

Alice's heart skipped; her throat tightened in a way familiar to someone who actually dreads the replies in the argument they started. She thought of the relief on her mother's face when she showed her the crisp, fresh vaxx-card in her hands, and the band-aid on her arm. She thought of her own feelings which were annoyance at the sound of a woman who began crying loud tears of relief when she had received her vaccination. It was like being caught in a salty riptide she'd wanted no part in.

"Would it be different if Saint Cecilia were still alive, though?" Alice said.

"Saint Cecilia happened fifteen years ago," Jonathan said, laughing drily and looking at Alice with fresh eyes, perusing her face for an indicator of age. "She only died ten years ago. Do you remember her?"

"Nah," Alice said. "You probably don't remember her, either."

"I don't," Jonathan said, "It's true, I don't. I would have been eleven or twelve. How old would *you* have been, hmm?"

Jonathan leaned back in his memories, trying to access the time in his childhood when the world had been gripped by the international Saint Cecilia craze. When evidence and testimonials of her ability to cure the incurable with the slightest touch of her bare hands was on every news channel, every social media post, on the tips of everyone's tongues. Saint Cecilia ultimately died in New York City, gunned down in Saint Patrick's Cathedral by a man who believed she was a heretical womb on legs, daring to challenge the Word of God as the last daughter in a lineage of women with healing powers. There had never been any real evidence, Jonathan remembered, that any of her miracles had been authentic; after she'd been declared a proper saint by the Vatican, a scandal had erupted, revealing a paper (and digital) trail of murky half-truths and unanswered questions that threw Saint Cecilia's identity into a new light — including doubt that she'd ever been Catholic at all. To this day, controversy surrounded the story in his memories.

Despite evidence of the hoax, however, there had been a worldwide malaise at the young Saint's death, something Jonathan remembered his mother describing.

What a shame, Mother had said. *What a shame that Saint Cecilia, who was such a positive force for women, is dead. She had been a bright spot on a dark planet.* And Jonathan knew the Saint's face, because she was pop culture these days, her big green eyes and raven black hair an image as iconic as the green-eyed Afghan girl who'd graced the June 1985 cover of *National Geographic*. But he only recalled her image, not a feeling of sharing a universal plane with her. Trying to bring up these memories only brought other things to the surface: the sound of a woman's screams, the feel of ankles in his hands, the thought that he was too young for any of this…

too young…

"We're both too young," Alice said.

Jonathan patted her back warmly, rubbed between her shoulder blades, feeling her warmth and her little bones beneath the skin. Small girl, little girl, tiny woman in the making. She made a small noise of acknowledgment, but did not look at him.

"She could have cured Covid," Jonathan said, "Imagine. She could have pissed in the water supply and healed us all with her magic ovaries."

"Amen," Alice replied. "But what do you think she really was? The Saint?"

"Psy-ops," Jonathan said, "testing all of us shitheads to see how gullible we are, and how quick we are to forget a trauma, how quick we are to forget a hoax. And we do love to forget."

"Imagine if we could forget trauma," Alice said. "It would be so useful to," and she whistled to emphasize her point, "erase it from some people's brains so we don't have to deal with their bullshit and fallout."

"What fun would there be in that?" Jonathan said, and he happened to be thinking of his Uncle Bertrand.

Jonathan and Felix had another uncle, apart from their Uncle Daniel. Dr. Bertrand Forrester was a bland, milquetoast, bespectacled stereotype of a man, dark hair and dark eyes, a neuroscientist who never lost his temper. There was a safe prettiness about him that one could imagine their dead sister Alice took after; perhaps her prim and polite way of existing, also favored Uncle Bertrand. He was working on new medical technology, funded in large part by the family's foundation; a biotech project with the goal of creating new techniques for treating — and *removing* — psychiatric trauma. Uncle Daniel, he knew, had contributed some research regarding his brand of meditation techniques. But by and large, as with most competitive, high-stakes biotech projects, virtually all information was considered proprietary. He'd heard some whispers about experimental therapies on human patients, and had dismissed him, though personally he didn't care one way or another if they were true. But why was this girl suddenly broaching the topic?

Ah, it's just paranoia, Jonathan thought, but still he decided that it was safer not to reply. He met her dark-eyed gaze, and he imagined what possible traumas she could be speaking of, other than a fevered tumble on a beach.

Alice was thinking of one of her father's friends who'd catch her in his arms, once she'd turned thirteen years old; he would take deep inhales of her hair. He'd never done anything more to her than that, but she remembered keenly the oily feel that lingered in her flesh even days after he would hug her. She thought of reading a *National Geographic* magazine that had an article on her favorite author Lewis Carroll's unusual adoration of young girls.

Alice thought of her sister, the one she had tried to kill as they fought over a harp, and how that sister had started the laughter at her expense when Alice tried singing for the school talent show. Alice's sister had also frequently mocked Alice over her habit of finishing a classic novel every week. Alice's love of literature, to her sister, was something geeky, alien, something ugly losers and folk obsessed with dead white people did. Where was the fallout for that? It was all bullshit. Alice couldn't forget any of it, but she could deal with it by not talking about it. It was good as trauma erased, at that point.

"'And yet and yet! That strained look on her face!'" Jonathan said. He tapped Alice's chin, and her expression blossomed with delight. "'A gnawing sorrow is there all the time. Her very soul is in her eyes, and she would give worlds to be in the privacy of her own familiar chamber where, giving way to tears, she could have a good cry and relieve her pent-up feelings.'"

"That's so pretty," Alice said. And tears did sparkle in her eyes.

Jonathan was quoting from one of Alice's favorite novels by James Joyce. She couldn't tell if he were trying to take credit for the words and wanted her to feign belief that the poem was his, or whether he might respect her more if she acknowledged the novel.

She finished her drink, and she held the glass to Jonathan.

"'Though not too much,'" Jonathan continued, "'because she knew how to cry nicely before the mirror. You are lovely, Alice, it said.'"

Because he had swapped her name into the quote, Alice concluded that Jonathan was taking credit for the novel's words, and she let the moment pass in silence.

Jonathan had not used Shakespeare on her, but she wished he had: if it had been a sonnet, then she could have laughed it off as many a modern girl who is immune to Shakespeare. No, he had quoted a novel to her, and one she knew well. She must have endeared herself enough to him that he shared the passage with her, and the tenderness of that gesture… it rested on her emotions like an itchy, thin membrane.

She scratched the base of her throat.

It feels cruel when he's kind, she thought. She set the empty glass down on the small terrace table. She sighed, composed herself, and met Jonathan's inquisitive gaze.

He raised his eyebrows; his cornflower-blue eyes were so pretty in this light, against his golden hair and eyebrows, his golden-boy skin. He was the paragon of beautiful American whiteness. He grinned, and Alice felt her womb stir with longing. This man was entirely pleasing to her in every way. She thought of his golden-furred thighs and how they tickled against her skin, and she found herself wondering what it would really be like to ride that cock of his. She had not seen it yet, but it was a considerable thought to lie between a maid's legs.

Jonathan took the glass from the table and carried it away.

Alice put her chin on her hands and continued to watch the people down below. The smells of the cafes were drifting up towards them and she could see people gathered on tables, drinking, and eating and laughing, ladies meeting up to brunch with each other, everyone spending money.

"It's peaceful now," Alice said, "but wait 'til they really burn. Wait until the crows eat the bacon off their plates and the eyeballs from their skulls."

She thought of a news article she had read two days ago, about a drunken Russian soldier screaming from a Bakhmut dumpster he'd fallen into, so inebriated he'd not even felt the crows pluck out his soft eyeballs, and it was the sound of his screams that had brought Ukrainian civilians to gaze upon his stricken condition. Alice had wanted to believe that story was true: she'd scrolled through countless uncensored Telegram channels, looking for something to back it up, but ultimately had to content herself with fantasizing belief in it.

"You want to go inside now? It's roasting out here, it's too hot to be dwelling on carrion crows and apocalypse," Jonathan said, and he tapped the back of her shoulder. "Come on, sweetie."

Alice thought about her father sitting with her across from the school principal, when she was a small girl and her confiscated sketches of stick figures getting slaughtered by fire, tornadoes, and tsunami lay on the desk between them. Her father thought the pictures were funny; he explained to the principal that they were *satire* and he was sure his daughter was going to be a literary and artistic genius.

Roasting? Since when did folk worry about roasting in the sun, Alice thought. *They loved tanning and burning, and they loved when women stood in the sun sweating.* More than likely, he was worried that someone in the building across from them would see them or take notice. People in the building across from them had a higher than average likelihood of knowing the actual occupant of this apartment, and might ask questions.

"Well, you're perfectly welcome to kill me," Alice said. "My offer still stands."

"What?" Jonathan exclaimed, taken aback by the shift in conversation and tone. "Will you…"

Alice looked at him. His expression was exasperated in a way one has for a puppy that has just shat the carpet.

"It'll be fun," she said. "You'll see."

She imagined what it might feel like to fall at a survivable height, sitting in the hospital with a dozen breaks all over her body. How had it felt for Jonathan's sister to land on a car from a lethal height? What would it be like to splatter?

"Cut that shit out," Jonathan said. "You're a cute kid and I'm sick of hearing this."

"Come on!" Alice said, her mind swirled with Crayola crayon images of children burning in flames, of men standing with elephant dicks hanging past their knees. "You can throw me off this building and say I tripped. It would be just like your sister. But this time you would have control over it. It could be cathartic!"

Instantly, Jonathan's hands were on her, his fingers digging so hard it felt like he had pierced her and reached her bones. Alice yelped. He lifted her and his nose was nearly touching hers, his eyes burning into hers. "Shut. Up."

"Come on," Alice whispered. The pain his grip inflicted on her was betrayed by the trembling in her voice, and her words stumbled from her lips, rapid-fire and crackling. Cold anxiety bubbled through her blood, despite her bravado. "I can tell a liar when I see one, just as you can, I'm sure, and that story you told me about your sister is only partially true, you're hiding the full story. Purge that bullshit, honey. I'm ready for it. Who got her preg—"

"*Shut up!*" Jonathan pushed her to a sitting position on the balcony, holding her tightly.

"Are you going to throw me?" Alice whispered.

This is fear. This is fear. This is fear.

Her flesh prickled and her mouth went dry and just for one gleaming moment she pondered begging him to stop. She felt like she should apologize. But she could not. Not yet. She wondered if it would hurt when the pavement struck her skull.

"It could happen," Jonathan said, "But I do not seem like anyone other than a nice man with a pretty girl sitting on this balcony right now. They would only see a misguided couple drinking too early in the day, and then oops, the girl loses her balance and falls backwards. So, if your aim is to get me framed for something with your stupid fucking suicide, then you're going about it wrong."

"Push me," Alice whispered.

Jonathan nudged her back so that her little bottom hung off the balcony. Her legs tightened. Clinging. Jonathan could see that, and he knew. He knew that a human body would always fight for life. Here she was fighting for life. If he were to open his fingers right now, she would fall but she wouldn't be a beautiful mermaid in flight. She would be a stupid-ass fucking kid being a stupid-ass fucking idiot.

"Don't…" Alice whispered.

"What was that?" Jonathan asked, "I didn't hear it?"

He pressed his cheek against Alice's. She closed her eyes.

"I…" Alice's voice was scratchy, "I once saw a photo of a woman who threw herself off a building and looked beautiful even though she'd destroyed an entire car with her death."

"Yeah?" Jonathan said.

"I'd want to look like her, but I don't think I would if I fell from this height and landed on a patio table. I don't think the fall would even reliably kill me."

Unbelievable… Jonathan thought. *She doesn't want to die because she isn't Instagram ready.*

"Jonathan?" It was Felix's voice.

Jonathan looked over his shoulder but did not see Felix anywhere. It was Felix's voice as a memory. It was only in Jonathan's head. It brought back the day of his sister's death, and it made him want to wander through the scenario. Their sister had flown off the balcony, Felix huddled on the floor sobbing while it was Jonathan and their mother who screamed.

Jonathan stepped back and took Alice's forearms, holding her firmly and gently. She slid forward. Both of their hands, the fingers entangled. She walked on her tiptoes, past Jonathan, pulling away from him.

"Are you back in your right mind, you crazy girl?" Jonathan said. His voice was warm, as was his smile which was a thing always frighteningly sudden and easy for him. "You seem to be in constant need of…"

"Shh," Alice whispered, gently placing a finger on his lips. Her hair was not so pristine now, because she was sweating, a combination of the direct sunlight and her close brush with death. It was dull and long and twisted in small tendrils, the sort of look women spend a lot of money on expensive salt sprays to achieve.

She tiptoed into the apartment, and Jonathan folded his fingers together and followed her inside. She ended up in the kitchen and Felix stood just at the mouth of the hallway, skinny in an oversize bathrobe, his legs looking like ridiculous pins.

"What happened?" Felix asked.

"She's still trying to kill herself," Jonathan said, coasting through the room into the kitchen where Alice was bent over the sink, splashing cold water on her face. Her legs were trembling. She finally lost all balance and slid to the floor, leaving her face dripping wet as she sat with her knees pulled up to her chest. Jonathan made a point of stepping over her so he could fill a glass with water, which he then very coolly drank.

Felix went to Alice's side, and Jonathan left the kitchen. Felix gingerly touched one of her forearms with a couple of fingers. "Why do you want to die so badly? Is it because of what that man did to you on the beach?"

"If I said yes, would it make it acceptable?"

"I…don't think suicide is ever acceptable, but yes it would be an understandable reason."

"If I said I'm bored and spoiled and I want to die in a way that makes me famous, would that make it a worse reason than any other?" Alice asked.

"Well… that would just make you silly," Felix said.

"So, wanting to die from a rape, that *does* make it acceptable?" Her eyes were large, round, clear and direct. The gaze from her was not weak or sad or even angry. It was just the plain stare one might see on a deer looking through glass.

"I… don't know!" Felix said. This was weird. He was used to comforting women who were lower class survivors, refugees and slaves, women who were desperate for a scrap of affection and validation from someone, anyone who could be empathetic.

"This world is boring," Alice said. "I want to die young and distinctive. And when I die, I want to arrive in what other dimension there is, in this body at this age. I want a world that is nothing but alcohol, drugs, and cocks."

Felix pulled back from her, his fingers curled into a slight fist. "You are… strange."

Alice smiled, her eyes meeting Felix.

"You're a stupid child," Jonathan said. He had a strip of bacon in his fingers, a fresh cup of coffee in the other hand.

Alice's gaze flicked to Jonathan.

"And how am I any more ridiculous than Amy Winehouse or Janis Joplin?" Her voice was cutting and quick. "How am I any more ridiculous than Kurt Cobain, Jimi Hendrix, Robert Johnson, or Jim Morrison? Would my desire to die be more acceptable if I vomited some great piece of art and declared myself The Lizard Queen?"

"Yes," Jonathan replied, his posture a little slouched, mid-section leaning out. "Yes, it would. Because the price of getting into that hell of cocks and booze that you so dearly want to get to, is not only to be young and hot and fearless, but also to provide something that us Earthlings can look upon and gaze at. You have to be an actual poet, a musician, an artist. You have to give us something."

He tossed the bacon strip aside, set the coffee cup down, and then picked up the Brennan Talbot vinyl record that had been floating from room to room in the apartment. He tapped the face on the album cover, and then pointed to Alice with it.

"This is the price The Devil asks. A best-selling album, a painting in the Louvre, a fucking great American novel. You cannot just get into Hell for free. You must make it art, and make some damn good art before you stick your head in the oven. What have you ever contributed to this world, Little Princess? Where is your art?"

Alice smiled tightly, tears sparkled in her eyes, one fell and then she closed her eyes and inhaled deeply. "'You have no idea what I'm responsible for creating. Like my own rare thoughts, a chemistry of stars.'"

Jonathan's smile spread to his eyes; he beamed warmth and recognition at her words, a quote from a novel Felix had never read. "Well, he said, at least you're well read. 'We can't change the world, but we can change the subject, hm? Oh, Gertie, you lamed lamb.'"

Alice half smiled. "I liked Gertie, she was my favorite character."

"Of course, she was," Jonathan replied. "Why wouldn't she be?"

Felix helped Alice to her feet and led her to the kitchen table. He served her some more pancakes and syrup, and she ate and drank a second meal with gusto. He wondered if she would look for a way to puke it all up in a little bit. Since she had so frankly announced her bulimia earlier, Felix found himself wondering what exactly her vomit ritual could be.

Jonathan disappeared into the bedroom and then emerged dressed in a linen shirt and black Givenchy walking shoes, and sunglasses. As he opened the door, Felix asked him where he was going. Jonathan didn't reply directly, just told him to stay and watch Alice.

"You think I'm going to leave?" Alice asked.

"Well, you're certainly not a prisoner," Jonathan said. "If you want to leave, Felix can't stop you, but don't forget your money. I'm more concerned about you killing yourself in our uncle's apartment. It's Felix's job to prevent that."

Alice raised her fresh mimosa in acknowledgment and Jonathan slammed the door behind him.

SEVEN

When Jonathan returned, Felix was dressed in a vintage Teenage Fanclub t-shirt pilfered from their uncle's closet. For much of the '90s, their Uncle Daniel had owned a flat in Glasgow, Scotland, where he'd worked as a guide for established meditation practices, not yet having formed his own brand. He spent his considerable downtime collecting wristbands from countless music festivals all over Scotland; he sold crystals and meditation sessions between acts. Photographs of Dan from that time, fresh from the Teenage Fanclub concert at T in the Park in Glasgow, showed a lanky, auburn-haired, blue-eyed charmer in mud-splattered jeans. Felix very much favored his eccentric uncle, just as clearly as Jonathan took after their father; their deceased sister Alice had resembled Uncle Bertrand.

Felix had paired the t-shirt with jeans. His feet were bare, propped on the coffee table, and he was watching television on the enormous curved flatscreen that boasted a sharpness and definition beyond 4k.

Jonathan deposited some paper shopping bags on the kitchen counter. The bags were Easter-egg-colored, with fiber handles, and they sat upright and stiff. Boutique names were printed on the bags, shops that had trite individual French words as their monikers — *Petit, Vous, Vetements,* and *Sur*. A new pair of Tiffany sunglasses sat on his face; Jonathan pulled them off and flicked them onto the kitchen counter, where they bounced and clattered.

"Get your errands done?" Felix asked.

"Got some things for our guest — that is, if we still have a guest," Jonathan said. He picked up the new sunglasses, realizing that the lenses that had sustained a scratch when he'd tossed them onto the counter. He frowned. *Oh, well.* "Where is our guest?"

"She's cleaning up," Felix said. "She took a shower and then started a bath. She's been in there the entire time you were gone."

Jonathan stared at his brother, his expression an inscrutable sculpture of alabaster. His lips tightened, and he lifted a finger, turned his face, and closed his eyes. Oh, how Felix felt his judgment. He felt it as keenly as if Dad were standing there, about to blow a fuse.

"It's not like we're worrying about a water bill," Felix said, but he sat up straight, his eyes meeting Jonathan's, his scrubbed and smooth face as timid as a spaniel's. "I didn't see the problem with it?"

Jonathan shook his head. "The *problem, Felix,* is that we have a girl who has already been established as unstable and suicidal, in our uncle's apartment — and now she's alone in a *bathroom* with all the hot water she could ever want?"

Felix paled, his auburn hair dark against his skin. He pressed his fingers against his lips, his clunky wrist bones jutting out. "Oh!"

An image flickered through Felix's brain, the possible sight of Alice sprawled in the bathtub, a wrist hanging down, pumping blood all over the floor, the other hand making the water blossom like the aftermath of a shark attack.

"Yeah, '*Oh*'," Jonathan replied. "Now you deal with it. Get in and check on her, and if she's fucking bled out, then you're fucking cleaning it up."

Felix stood up, twisting his fingers together like a frightened child. "Jonathan, I don't want…"

"Felix just…"

The world shook.

Literally shook.

It was a rumble, it was clinking sounds, it was artwork falling off the walls, it was books falling from their shelves, and strange vibrations growling from the piano. It lasted just a handful of seconds, enough to shake but not shatter.

Jonathan and Felix had felt something like it before, in Japan and California — but in Colorado? The brothers looked at each other, surprise lifting their eyebrows high on their foreheads; and then the bathroom door flew open, and Alice emerged, hair long and soaking into the bathrobe she had wrapped around her body. The robe was the same one Felix had used earlier and it enveloped her body all the way to the floor.

"Was that an earthquake?" she asked. Her face beamed with a

childlike combination of excitement and fear.

"Yeah, it fucking was," Jonathan said.

Alice blinked with fast flutters, and then she shook her head, "Wow… in Denver?"

There were voices in the hallway, footsteps everywhere as people ran back and forth from their apartments trying to add up experiences and notes. The balcony door was open, and the voices from the street were palpable. There were people crying out, some even laughing, shouting about what had just happened. There was the sound of cars whistling, alarms triggered from the street parking.

What a terrifying novelty for today, Jonathan thought.

"So, cool!" Alice ran to the balcony and leaned over, staring down at the people swirling like agitated ants below. "EARTHQUAKE!!!!" She screamed in a deep, guttural howl. Her body was folded over the balcony, only her toes touching the ground.

Jonathan shoved his hands into his pockets and went to the French doors leading to the balcony. "You," he said, "dry off. Get presentable. Stop wandering around like a loose sheepdog."

"Remember when that condominium building collapsed in Florida?" Alice asked, turning to face him, crossing her arms. "Was that last year? Two years ago? Remember? It was a luxury condominium building and all of these wealthy Brazilian and Jewish people… I mean, like, the Friedmans were really close with my dad, they were…"

"Who's your dad?" Felix asked.

Alice stopped talking and bit her lip. "I mean, do you think that's gonna happen *here*? A building collapse? Like, right now, should we be… um…?"

Her voice disappeared, her eyes on Jonathan who took command.

"It was an earthquake, and not a big one, so let's not be silly." Jonathan pulled a small plastic baggie from his pocket; it was filled with cocaine. Felix's pulse raced at the sight of it. "I brought some treats home. We can have a little party, but not until you stop wandering around and leaving puddles everywhere."

Felix sucked his lips into his mouth, gnawed on them.

"Holy shit!" Alice exclaimed and she jumped, clapped her hands, squealing. "My very first earthquake and now a real…"

"Go on," Jonathan said. "Shut up. Go."

"Yeah," Felix said, his pulse racing afresh, trying to deepen his voice into something that resembled authority. "Get dressed." He couldn't take his eyes off the cocaine.

"Yes sirs!" Alice said and she saluted, even clicking her bare heels together. "Watch, we gon' *die* of Fentanyl today!"

"Actually," Felix said, his mouth watering, and one of his hands trembling, "I think it's Xylazine that is killing everyone these days. Bu-but Jonathan always gets the good stuff, it'll be clean. You'll see."

Goddamn, Felix thought, his heart racing in anticipation of treats.

He hated himself for it. *You fucking cretin,* he thought to himself, even as he licked his lips. *Just because you want one snort of coke, you're willing to let things get this far? Alcohol should be as far as it goes!*

"Wait!" Jonathan said. He went into the kitchen and picked up one of the shopping bags. He reached inside and then pulled out a garment that shone blue satin, and white linen. It was an Alice in Wonderland costume. "I got you a dress. A couple, in fact." He pulled another dress from the bag. It was a baby doll dress with a Peter Pan collar, a slightly different shade of sky blue. "You're not wearing that same thing from yesterday; I can't stand a girl wearing the same thing two days in a row. We're not fucking animals."

He tossed both dresses and Alice caught them, carrying them into the master bedroom.

"Jonathan what the hell is going on?" Felix asked. He sniffled and scratched at the side of his nose. "I mean… this is too far! Like, I was excited about a minute ago, but I'm really thinking now. Cocaine? To a *kid?* This isn't right!"

Jonathan busied himself with straightening all the skewed art on the walls, his considerable height and heavy steps owning the room.

"Jonathan, I *mean* it! We should probably stop now. Before…"

"Jesus *Christ,* baby brother," Jonathan said, as he righted a toppled snake plant and then brushed the spilled soil into a pile with his hands. He turned to Felix, his eyes bright with rage.

"I have yet to hear one goddamned 'thank you' from you. What the fuck? You've repeatedly asked me to supply debauchery and illicit nakedness; I'm supplying it. It's always my job to let you sample a little booze, a little bit of drugs, keeping you safe yet indulgent, and then delivering you to Mommy and your busy schedule of fundraisers for women's shelters! And all you can do is whimper and whine! You know what? *GROW A FUCKING PAIR*, OKAY? I fucking love you, Felix, but *GROW THE FUCK UP!*"

Felix froze. Although it was Jonathan screaming into his face now, he was in spirit standing before his father. His body was tense and he found himself fervently wanting Mother, or his real little sister, or even just Alice in the other room, to come out and rescue him. He didn't *want* to grow a pair, he just wanted to hide.

"Sorry, I didn't mean to, look," Felix stayed the trembling of his hands and threw himself into Jonathan's body, hugging him tightly, and to his relief his brother hugged him back. "I'm sorry, I really am. I appreciate you."

"Ah," Jonathan sighed, and he patted Felix's soft auburn hair, thinking of all the times he'd watched as their father's temper had boiled and almost bubbled over; their dear mother would absorb his accusations, verbal abuses, and rants with her crystal green eyes opened wide and blank, and a soft, relaxed mouth. When it came turn to speak, she would simply introduce some new subject, and cheerfully turn the conversation towards dinner plans or social gossip, far before the old bastard could ever turn violent. "Sorry kiddo, I've been very…*dad-like* lately. Forget about it. Okay?"

Felix was softly crying, he turned away and blew his nose on a bloodied linen napkin. He cleared his throat and watched as Jonathan left off the conversation and returned to tidying the area. Jonathan found an incense cone and lit it, smiling softly at the wafting smoke.

"I'm not saying stop, I'm just wondering what… the plan here is?" Felix scratched the back of his head, staring down the hallway towards the bedroom, trying to imagine what Alice was going to look like when she re-emerged, wondering if she was eavesdropping on them. What could she think of them now?

"It's cocaine and Wonderland…and apparently earthquakes," Jonathan said. "We'll play it by ear, and if we're lucky, we'll get an aftershock and not die of a Fentanyl-Xylazine contamination."

He reached back into the bag and pulled out a deck of cards and tossed it onto the coffee table. "We can play Go Fish, if you're feeling like that much of a bitch."

"I… where'd you get those cards? They look used up."

The cards were in a torn, smudged box; a few slid loose, and they were creased vertically in half. The deck had to be riddled with every respiratory virus on Earth.

"Some busker tried a sleight of hand game on me out on the street and I sleight of hand stole his cards. You know how much I love stealing.

I'm fucking *good* at it."

Alice emerged from the bedroom; her hair wasn't completely dry. Her legs and feet were still bare, and she was wearing the Wonderland costume. It fit at the waist and hips, but at the tits there were one or two buttons that were straining for their very life. Both men's eyes went straight to those buttons and Alice cringed and loosened the top two. It created a jaw-dropping vision of cleavage, even for the experienced man; Jonathan's mouth watered.

Alice's brain was refreshingly uncluttered at the moment, as undiluted joy pumped through her.

"Fancy as fuck," Alice said, and she spun around on her toes. "Thank you."

"Hm," Jonathan said. He cleared his throat loudly and turned away. Glided into the kitchen and poured himself some sparkling water, which he drank with gusto.

Felix's breaths deepened as Alice passed him. He smelled the city sidewalk on a hot summer morning, car exhaust, and frying onions, and tobacco, but he didn't know why the scent would be so fresh on Alice. He also smelled rosewater and lotion, and shampoo.

"Where did you get this dress?" Alice asked, addressing Jonathan.

"Saw it on a sidewalk mannequin, and I thought why the fuck not? Let's have a party."

Jonathan opened the balcony doors and propped them open, even though the air conditioning was still on full blast. He flicked the bag of cocaine onto the coffee table, reached into one of the shopping bags and pulled out more drugs. It was a combination of pills and powders, and a vial of clear liquid.

"What the hell!" Felix said. "That's…" he finished his sentence with a wolf whistle.

Jonathan cut some lines of cocaine on the Brennan Talbot album cover, using one of the busker's cards.

Felix had never used drugs without Jonathan. Jonathan always knew where to buy the stuff, sometimes within an hour of arriving somewhere new, all jokes about possibly dying of a contamination overdose aside. The first time a reticent Felix had tried cocaine was because Jonathan had insisted that it's always good to at least have a basic experience with street drugs so that one doesn't embarrass oneself by just up and fucking dying the first time one uses at a party.

"Ladies first," Jonathan said.

"Shouldn't you at least explain it to her?" Felix asked. But before he had even finished talking, Alice leaned over and inhaled a monster line straight up. She sat up as the drug took effect, and she pinched her nose shut and giggled, her cleavage jiggled.

"Holy shit, that's amazing," Alice sighed. She pinched her nose one final time and inhaled hard. "That's really good stuff!"

"I think she has the idea," Jonathan said.

Felix looked at the girl with new eyes, and no longer saw a girl, but instead a small, fresh-faced woman. Sadness pierced his heart because he felt lied to, conned; and yet, he also felt a squeeze of relief to imagine they weren't tangling with a little girl.

"You didn't drop any crumbs, little lady," Jonathan said.

Alice, animated on the drug, trembled, her eyelids fluttered, the back of her hand against her nostrils. "Your turn, hombre!"

Jonathan and Felix did a line each. For Felix, what he liked the most about cocaine was that it did not hit him as strongly as it did other people. It just made him confident and happy. He did not have mood swings, he did not have temper tantrums. He just felt… like he fit in. Jonathan had told him several times that that feeling meant Felix was a good candidate for serious cocaine addiction.

Jonathan's reactions to cocaine were always sudden. On the inhale he sat up straight, cursing, his body subtly more animated now, too. He picked at his nose, pinched it.

"So, really do you think this shit doesn't have those weird animal tranquilizer bits in it?" Alice asked, her voice high and girlish. Her eyes were bright and shiny. "Should we have used those, uhh…. like, testing strips?"

"You'd fucking be dead already," Jonathan replied.

"What about this building? Is it gonna fall? I really think it might!"

"No," Jonathan said. "Shut up. We're not gonna end up like your

Daddy's rich Jew friends."

They put a stupid action movie on Netflix and played cards. A few rounds of poker, betting on Alice's cash which she so generously donated to the pot. It was a game no one seemed particularly taken with. They just played the rounds and made the bets, doing more lines in between.

In that time, another small earthquake happened — tremors lighter and shorter than the first rumble — which caused another rush of people in the hallway. The trio listened to the noise, the chattering of human voices, but not a one got up to connect with the outside world, or to check a headline on their phones. They exchanged glances and grins, giggling at the sound of a woman crying in the hallway. Her hysterical chatter indicated that she was convinced that "The Big One" was going to hit soon, even though no such thing had ever been predicted for Denver. She had to be comforted by her husband and another man.

As the woman's sobs turned into howls and became even more shrill and demonstrative, Alice crossed her eyes and twirled one finger at her temple and mouthed, "*Cuckoo.*" Jonathan and Felix's smiles dissolved into laughter.

"I'll make tea," Alice said.

She served it to them, and they sipped at it, a pile of money and cards and drugs on the table.

"What's the rest of the drugs?" she asked Jonathan, pointing at the pile. "Tell us about the candy."

"Ecstasy, more cocaine, and this," he held up the vial of clear liquid, "is GHB."

Alice's eyes widened and she pursed her lips, then lifted her hand as if to say something.

"Why the fuck would you need to get the date rape drug, and who did you get it from?" Felix exclaimed.

Felix stood up so quickly he upset his cup of tea. It rolled and spilled across the carpet. He looked at Alice, wrung his hands together, certain that bandying around the word *rape* around was not the way he wanted to turn the day. Alice, however, seemed calm enough. She scooped up the teacup, placed it back on the table, and then set a linen napkin on top of the tea puddle and stepped on it.

Alice was passively remembering a time when she held her arms protectively around a young boy as they stood in waist-deep water while a bull shark circled them, investigating them like a curious dog before it decided to swim away.

"I don't give out trade secrets," Jonathan said. "Anyway, GHB is pretty nice in low doses. It's actually not *just* for rape. It's even fun for mutually consenting parties."

"Are you guys gonna *mutually consent* and use it on each other?" Alice asked in an awe-struck voice. She continued using her foot to soak up the tea into the linen.

"Ha!" Jonathan said. He held the vial out to her. "Have a peek."

Alice took the vial; she held it up to one eye and tapped it with a finger. "How do you take this? I've never actually seen it in person. I always thought it was like a powder, or crushed pills. Is it injected?"

"You put it in a drink, a shitty drink, and it makes you feel euphoric and horny," Jonathan said. "You're a woman of the world, I gather, you should know everything about guarding your drinks from rich, white cis-males."

"Great White Sharks," Alice replied, and she tapped the vial again. "I want to be euphoric and horny."

"You're not getting fucked, little girl," Jonathan said, reshuffling the deck of cards. "We've already established this."

"What?" Alice sighed, setting the vial onto the coffee table, where it rolled until a bent playing card stopped it. "Why not? Then why did you get this stuff?"

"Because the guy had it," Jonathan replied. "I never pass up a deal, and he offered me a pretty good deal. He fucking threw it in for free."

"Loser," Alice said. She pressed her hands on her breasts and pushed them up.

Felix's attention was acquired, and Alice's eyes met his. Cocaine confidence was still surging in his veins, and he realized that Jonathan was speaking as if Alice were a child. Why could not Jonathan see what Felix saw — that Alice was a vivacious, viable, consenting woman? For once, in their lives, Felix could see it all and Jonathan could not.

"There's three lines left," Alice said, pointing to the cocaine on the table. And then she lifted her arms high and projected her voice as her buzzing cocaine speckled brain fired the words off her tongue, memorized once before off the page of a novel, forgotten very soon after, and now reactivated and violent, "An exquisite dulcet epithalame of most mollificative suadency for juveniles amatory whom the odoriferous flambeaus of the paranymphs have escorted to the quadrupedal proscenium of connubial communion…"

"Only big words for ordinary things on account of the sound," Jonathan shouted, and he laughed heartily and clapped his hands, sounding very much like their dad, "Don't make me fall in love with you!"

"Is this nerd shit?" Felix asked, looking back and forth between Alice and Jonathan's bonded gaze. "You two are quoting something and it's nerd shit and I'm being left out!"

"Yeah, you are…" Alice muttered, her pupils dilated and fixed on Jonathan's equally dilated gaze. "Yes, I said, yes, I will, yes…"

They'd had two lines a piece already, and Felix rubbed his palms together, watching Alice and Jonathan take another line. Felix, whose head was already feeling like a jar full of bumblebees, decided to take that third line despite it, seeing as he was already at a disadvantage because he didn't know what novel Alice and Jonathan were suddenly bonding over. Felix preferred trash television and romantic comedies, the odd trendy show on HBO; but he'd never been a reader like Jonathan. He couldn't discuss their nerd shit, but at the very least he could do his best not to fall behind in the realm of illicit drug dosages.

It was the line that ignited everything. Electricity coursed through every wrinkle and fold in his brain; he knew suddenly — he could *feel* it, as a human being –that he was fucking sparkling.

"I think we've played enough games. Stop babysitting me," Alice said, fixing her eyes on Jonathan. "I am the fire upon the altar, I am the sacrificial butter."

Just… she was looking at Jonathan, not at Felix. Not for an instant was she assuming Felix to be any sort of real player in this.

"Oh, shut up!" Felix yelled and he grabbed a teacup and cracked it against the coffee table. The cup broke into large pieces and Jonathan stood up, holding his hands up at a soft angle, much as one might to soothe a psychotic horse or an irrational female screaming for someone's manager at a register.

"Well, look what you've done, Baby Brother," Jonathan said softly. He pointed to the young woman at the coffee table.

Felix looked at Alice, and she was staring at a cut on her arm that was weeping droplets of blood.

What made this interesting was Jonathan's expression: his face was pale, his hands trembled, and he actually took a step back from the sight in front of him. He *recoiled.* If Felix had learned one thing about Jonathan over the course of their entire life together, it was that his brother feared seeming meek, weak, or anyone's second-in-command, *ever*. Jonathan could afford to be brash and alpha if he was in control of a thing like hiring a whore and then deciding not to fuck her; but once actual violence had been dealt, Jonathan was backing away. At least for now. Caution was key for him when he was not feeling keen.

Alice held her arm up, staring at the blood; she touched the wound with a finger. Her demeanor seemed unreasonably calm, but then her breathing quickened, her bottom lip trembled. Yet, she picked up a dagger of tea cup china and she held it to Jonathan. When she lifted her eyes to him it was with all the liquid desire of a Siren.

"I don't want to touch that," Jonathan said. "I'm not catching rabies."

The blood drops had turned into rivulets that dripped from the tip of her elbow.

Red was Felix's favorite color. He never felt one way or the other about blood in general, but right now it was such a genuinely powerful sight. Against her skin…

With no comprehension of what he was doing, and no care to, Felix snatched Alice's wrist in his hands, squeezed it. Alice made no noise, watching him carefully; perhaps she thought he was going to tend to her. Perhaps Jonathan thought that as well.

Felix pulled her arm gently and he touched his fingertip to the blood, and he looked at it on his finger, smeared, red against his pale flesh, much redder against his skin than hers. He lifted her hand a bit more, thinking of every vampire movie he had ever seen — the lush, romantic ones that he would hate for Jonathan to ever find out about. He pressed his lips to her wound.

She flinched, and he realized that of course it hurt. He moved his lips just beneath the wound and once there he put the tip of his tongue. He would forever tell himself that he'd only licked the blood, not the wound.

"*Jesus . . .*" Jonathan muttered.

The blood was salty and tangy; it made him think of steak tartar. It was not a good flavor. It made his stomach roll with confused betrayal; every fiber of his body rejected this.

It's gross. That's all. It's just gross.

Alice's breathing was short and heavy. He pressed her wrist to his ear and tried to hear her pulse, but the blood in his ears was rushing too heavily.

Felix lifted his eyes to Alice's, wondering if she was finally going to try running away. Her eyes had a dead sort of look.

"I'm sorry… I'm…." Felix didn't know what to say.

Alice pressed her hand to his cheek and Felix met her gaze. Something in her eyes awakened, smoldering now, like melted chocolate. Her lips parted.

Felix kissed her.

Their kiss was slick and warm, their lips parting instantly against each other, their tongues already flicking against each other. It was hungry. It was past the point of shy greeting or curiosity: Felix literally wanted to devour her like a piece of candy, and perhaps he was a dish of ice cream to her.

"Felix, stop it!" Jonathan said. "This isn't fucking right, she's not…"

"I'm not what?" Alice asked, her eyes still on Felix. She was not breaking the gaze because at this point, she felt like a motherfucking cobra, and he was a motherfucking rat.

"You're a child, and you're not mentally well," Jonathan said, and then his voice did the impossible: it cracked. Jonathan paused, and when he spoke again, his voice was awash in grief, "Jesus Christ, kiddo, I'm sorry. You're a fucking nutcase, this doesn't have to…. Felix isn't mentally well, either. You both are sick, you need help, and I…."

Jonathan's voice dissolved. He inhaled roughly, swallowed and choked on it. It was no more sudden or shocking than a small earthquake in Denver. Felix felt a surge of power like nothing he had ever known. He recognized the truth in Jonathan's words: Felix knew he was not well, and he knew Alice was not well. Jonathan, however, with his tears, had perhaps just revealed that at least he was not a full-blown sociopath. One could at least accept small blessings.

Felix kissed Alice again, and she pressed into his body, his pants felt tight, their clothes… he could not breathe… his skin felt tight. *Tight… tight…*

He grabbed Alice, and she peppered frantic kisses on his cheeks and his forehead. This is where Felix discovered that the body just knows what to do. He had worried himself into so much anxiety his entire life around women, even around his own fiancé. When Felicity had reached into his pants, just two weeks ago, he had not for a moment felt the way he did now, with Alice. He had been weak and submissive with Felicity, but… here, with Alice… he was not even afraid.

His hands around Alice's waist, he pushed up the hem of her dress, and he saw her little hand grab her panties. The diamonds on her wrist caught the light and sparkled, and then her fingers went straight for his jeans. Within seconds, her hand held his cock, and for one terrifying moment, Felix thought he was going to come. He grabbed her panties and pulled them over her knees, struggling to get them off; she would not let go of his cock.

He half expected Jonathan to have pulled him off her by now, to try and reassert his dominance in this situation; he glanced at his brother to see him sitting on the couch, his face in his hands. Felix now knew that Jonathan had gambled on the wrong way to teach either Alice or him a lesson.

Alice leaned back onto the hard floor, legs lifted, Felix pressed his torso into the bottoms of her thighs, her calves were against his collar bone, and he slid his fingers down her ass and to the… fuuuuuck…. It was shaved, and it was wet at the slit. His fingers slipped in easily.

Alice cried out.

Did I hurt her? Is she hurt?

"Are you all right?" Felix asked, his voice hoarse.

Alice made a sound in response. Her eyes were closed, her lips parted. He wanted to pull at the top of her dress and rip it open, but his fingers were inside her pussy and…

Jesus Christ. I've never even fingered my own fiancée. Felix was suddenly bubbling over with years of repressed anger. He had never touched anyone; he had never been allowed inside anyone. Jonathan, his older brother who should have been in charge of advice and mentorship for him, had never led Felix to this gorgeous promised land of… Felix pushed his fingers in deeper, and Alice moaned. *Is that a good sound?* He was angry and ashamed at all he did not know.

Am I still supposed to ask for consent? How the fuck does this work? Felix thought amidst violent images in his brain of holding her down and forcing himself on her.

Her hand was still on his cock and the back of her thighs were pressed against his chest with his body weight following. He slipped his fingers out of her cunt and rested them against the cushion of the settee so he could put his weight into following the guide of her hand.

He groaned, his cock slipped halfway in guided by how fucking wet she was, but he could not get in any further. It was like a slippery vise squeezing…

"OH fuck," Alice gasped and with both of her hands she used her fingers to pull the lips of her pussy wider around his cock and he slipped in just a little further.

"You're so fucking…" Felix groaned.

Alice sighed, a sound Felix couldn't discern the feeling behind; but he had, for the moment, lost interest in her feelings. Because now Felix was snug inside a pussy so tight it hurt. He pulled his hips back slightly, but could not bring himself to pull out completely.

"Here…" Alice muttered, and she opened her legs, pulling the one from the other so that her other calf rested against his other shoulder; the movement was just enough to let him inside her to full length. It was one of the most delicious pains Felix had ever felt in his life. The pleasure was drowning his brain at this point, and the unrelenting tightness felt like a challenge, something he wanted to rip to pieces. He hated himself, he fucking hated himself for this very primitive, male need to rip into this girl….

"Oh fuck!" Alice cried out. "You fucking…oh you're fucking huge… you're fucking…"

He knew his cock was rather large. Felix felt smug and powerful and he pulled back and pushed in and pulled back and… *Oh, fuck….*

"Aaaah!" Alice moaned, "not yet, please…"

She was not loosening. The pain was too intense. It was too much pleasure. It was all too much. She slid her little hands in between his ass cheeks and one of her fingers tickled at his…

"Jesus!" Felix gasped. "Jesus Christ!"

He came inside her, pushing harder until he lay emptied and exhausted.

Her mouth was open, her eyes closed, and he wondered how he was supposed to know if she had come or not. Was there a way for him to know that?

"Did you come?" He asked her, and his cock, now limp, slid out of her and he felt awash with how wet and cold and uncomfortable he was. He smelled sperm and a tang of…

Alice's eyes were half open.

"You *fucking idiot!*" Jonathan barked. "No condom. You at least need a condom when you fuck a whore, you stupid suicidal piece of shit!"

"I need to pee," Alice whispered. Felix backed off her and she sat up.

"Are you even on birth control?" Jonathan said.

"I need to pee," Alice said. She stood up and opaque pale fluid trickled down the inside of her skinny leg. It made Felix think of the man who had raped her on the beach, the fluid was on the inside of her ankle now, and she wiped it away with her other foot.

"That doesn't answer my question," Jonathan said as Alice hobbled to the bathroom. "What the fuck happens if you're pregnant?"

Alice slammed the bathroom door.

Jonathan holed himself in his chosen bedroom for the rest of the afternoon. Pants off, shirt open he lay on the bed with his arm over his forehead staring at the shining, small, smart screen of the bedroom television. On the bed with him was a small brass singing bowl, and he tapped it with his fingers as he stared at the television.

Felix remained where he was on the floor, limbs splayed like a broken scarecrow, pants still midway down his thighs. Alice sat next to him, pressing her hand over his. Felix's heart quickened at her touch, and he took her hand in his. He kissed her knuckles, and she touched his cheek, and he pulled her to him, and he kissed her again.

"How do you feel?" she asked.

"I feel… wonderful," Felix said, and he felt like warm maple syrup all through his chest. He kissed her and she hugged him and slid into his lap. His cock hardened, and he thought of how tight, and of how warm, and of how wet… and she grabbed his cock, and he came in her hand, moaning and shuddering until his face fell into her warm cleavage.

"Holy, shit… I'm sorry!" Felix desperately did not want to be laughed at, and he was so glad that Jonathan hadn't seen it. "I… it's so embarrassing!"

"It's ok," Alice said, and she wiped her hands on her dress, then caressed his cheeks and kissed him. "Virgins usually come like that on their first try. So, it's not bad at all that it happened with your second."

Alice was delighted by Felix's musky sex and his coconut-scented hair, the thrill of his beautiful body now smeared with fluids from her own, his sperm still dripping from her cunt. This was the first virgin she had ever fucked, and she found that she felt a protective ownership now for this beautiful boy. *Ah, to eat his meat, to scoop him like pudding, to spread him like butter….*

"How… did I do the first time?" Felix asked. "Was it good? Did… did you come?"

"I don't come," Alice said. "But you were pretty good."

Hollow sadness like hunger, she replayed the juxtaposition of intense pain — the sort she felt whenever *anything* entered her pussy, be it a simple finger or a full-grown cock — and the delight she forced herself to accept from the feeling. Her need to stimulate her clit over a toilet after any sexual encounter, because the blossom of ecstasy just… never fucking came when a man was breathing against her flesh. She'd reached the point where she had started to believe that an actual orgasm during sex was an unattainable lie.

"How can it be good if you didn't come?" Felix asked. He felt elated and disappointed all at the same time. He did not know if he would ever succeed in entertaining this strange girl.

"Women, in general, don't come when they have sex," Alice said. "At least, *I* don't. I'll masturbate and think about it later."

"Really?" Felix said far too eagerly for his taste. He desperately wanted her to like him. "But you come when you masturbate?"

"Of course, I do," Alice said. "I could do it now, if you want. I could use my fingers. I could use the vibrator in my purse…" her voice faltered, and she whispered the last of those words, giggled as she caught Felix's gaze. Already she had told him something about herself that she had never let any man know.

His cheeks reddened.

Alice nodded, "Come on, I liked it, you must have noticed how wet my cunt was."

"I want… I want to be good. I want *you* to come, I mean I don't want to be a disappointment, especially to…"

Alice was nodding as he spoke, the expression of her eyes and lips had a soft, sainted, sweetness to them. Then his phone rang, and he jumped up causing Alice to roll off him. She grunted, but didn't protest or cry out.

"Hello?" Felix said into his phone, "Hi! …. Honey… yeah… I, yeah, we're…. I'm sorry I didn't call you or answer the phone yeah, I… no… no, sorry…. No… Yeah, sorry, no, Jonathan didn't tell me."

Alice rolled her eyes and flicked her hand in a dismissive gesture to Felix. His unfastened pants fell around his ankles as he stood up and he tottered away from her, without his pants, into the kitchen so he could talk to his fiancée. Felicity's voice was loud and tinny; Alice could hear it from where she was sitting, and she could see Felix's future — *a nice boy, always obeying the people around him, never quite pleasing anyone, what a shame…*

"They…they misspelled names on the place settings? Darling, I'm sorry…Yes, I felt the earthquake…no, I'm fine…are you okay? I'm sorry I didn't check in with you, I…oh, that's good…I agree, the place settings *are* more important, yes, it sounds like a *disaster…*" Felix's tone was sincere. "I'm so sorry I left you hanging to deal with that alone . . .

"Mother isn't returning your calls? Well, why was the delivery canceled? Was it the orchid centerpieces, or the peonies that — OK, OK. I know it's a crisis, dear. I'm right there with you . . . I know, I know, I *did* say you should let her be in charge of the flowers . . . Well, darling, it was very important to Mother, and she . . . yes, yes, you're right . . . no, no, darling, no, I've no idea where she is right now . . . you want me to handle the—? Yes, I love flowers, but I'm *not* going to take this from Mother's— yes, darling, I *know* it's *my* wedding too, but . . .

"No, there is *no way* Mother is trying to sabotage the wedding, Felicity, she *loves you!* I know she—

"Wait — who *is* this? …what do you — oh, look, Fauna… put your sister back on the phone. I want to talk to Felicity, I can't have her mad at… *no*, I won't put Jonathan on the phone, Felicity and I were discussing Mother and the flowers…

"*What?* What do you mean, I'm '*giving*' Norman Bates? What does that even *mean?* Fauna, this is…"

About ninety seconds into the exchange, Alice got bored and wandered out of the room, into one of the empty bedrooms, where she picked up the landline and ordered a couple pizzas. Jonathan still had not left the master bedroom, perhaps still sulking about the lack of condom use in this apartment. Felix was still trying to get off the phone when the pizzas arrived.

Alice answered the door and paid with cash, handing the stunned pizza delivery man two fifty dollar bills as tip. Jonathan appeared over her shoulder, grabbing the pizzas and curtly telling the excessively loquacious and grateful pizza delivery man to enjoy his tip.

When the door closed, Jonathan took the pizza, walking heavily to the marble island in the kitchen, tossing the pizzas down and cursing. Alice scampered behind him, pert and unafraid. Noticing her proximity, Jonathan pressed his hand to one of her shoulders and it took only a slight nudge from him to topple her off balance.

"I thought we could all use some food, God!" she said, flailing her arms as she fell against the countertop.

"And you leave him a tip he's going to be talking about, and you answer the door dressed like a slut…"

"Yeah? In the dress *you chose* for me. Whatever, okay? He's a fucking delivery man, who cares what he says."

"This is not acceptable. Everyone talks. When you get to the caliber of me and my brother, and do *not* forget my uncle who lives in this apartment, *everybody* talks. *All* the time. It's relentless."

"Oh. Your *caliber*? Really?

"I see, like most ordinary people, you're under the assumption that you're anyone at all. It's just pizza," Alice replied, grabbing a slice. She bit in with her crooked teeth, the cheese stretching as she pulled it back. "Mmm, it's *delicious*. I am sure a man of your *caliber* will agree. And I won't apologize for needing grease and carbs."

"Pizza is good," Felix said, finally free of Felicity and Fauna's wrath. He tossed his phone onto the couch, and he grabbed a slice, slurping the cheese off. "I don't see a problem with it."

"Boy gets his cherry popped…" Jonathan muttered, rolling his eyes and shaking his head.

Jonathan took an entire pizza to his room and flopped down with it in bed.

In the living room, Alice played with her money on the coffee table while she and Felix together finished off another 8-ball.

As they started doing lines, they agreed that music was necessary.

"Kanye's new album just dropped!" Felix shouted, his smile wide and intense.

Alice, newly energized now from the carbs and the blow, shook her head and squished Felix's cheeks between her palms.

"We are *not* listening to anti-Semites!" she growled, but then dissolved into laughter and rolled back, her hands resting on her tummy.

Ah, bummer, she doesn't like Kanye, Felix thought mournfully, his emotions exaggerated with drugs and the oxytocin flush of post-sex joy.

In response, he stood on the coffee table, his pulse racing, arms aloft, and spoke in an uncharacteristically booming voice, "My child! I think you will find future generations will see Kanye West as a musical force on the same level as Mozart! And this anti-Semite business will be pushed aside! We have to separate the *art* from the *artist*, because most artists are problematic in some way anyhow!"

Alice sat up partially, leaning back on her hands and squinting up at Felix. The drugs had made her voice high and childish, almost like a character from the film *Clueless*. "I dunno, like, Kanye literally said he was going *'death con 3 on Jewish people'* like, that's not shit you come back from, you know?"

Felix ran his thumb over his bottom lip and nodded, "Look, has Kanye said any of that shit since he's been married? He hasn't! He just needs a good wife to keep him in line, you know? And anyway, he *apologized* a few months ago! He's good now!"

Alice squinted, "I missed that?"

Felix nodded eagerly, and picked up his phone, scrolling google to find the old headline, "Yeah right here!" He scrolled the old news article, "Kanye said he's sorry, and he shouldn't have blamed a whole culture for his hate and he thought Jonah Hill was so funny in *'21 Jump Street'* that it changed his mind on…"

Alice groaned loudly, the sound stopping Felix's words, and she covered her face and shook her head. "You know, 2 Chainz is way cooler than Kanye, he's not an anti-Semite, and he's more like Mozart than Kanye is. I mean, I could totally see modern-day Mozart hosting a show called *Most Expensivest*. 2 Chainz is the shit!"

"Know what?" Felix said with a deep sniffle, "Agree to disagree! So what are we listening to then?"

Alice sat upright and scratched her chin, "Uhhhh… put on Young Dolph! He's one hundred percent real!"

"Is he the one who died a couple years back?" Felix asked.

The murder of crows had returned; they were sitting on the balcony and cawing raucously into the cityscape. Since the French doors of the balcony were still wide open, the avian chatter resonated loudly. The afternoon sun was high, and it was scorching hot outside; but the soothing wind from the air conditioning inside kept them safe in their cocoon. Alice picked up a pale pink satin throw pillow and flung it towards the crows, but her aim was bad and the pillow curved in its trajectory and it bounced off one of the doors. The movement sent the crows into a panic, and they flew away in unison.

Alice grinned, watching the crows fly, and she stared at the balcony as she spoke. "See, like, he drove his blue lambo to the local handmade cookie shop and got gunned down holding a box of cookies. The poor dude just wanted some cookies! Like this is America and we can't just have cookies!"

Felix laughed, "But we can!"

He dashed into the kitchen and brought out the glass bowl of the leftover homemade cookies for them to finish off. He put on a 'Best of Young Dolph' playlist.

"To Dolph!" Felix shouted.

Alice held up a cookie, eyes closed. "*Respect!*"

As they munched on the cookies and guzzled down sparkling water, Felix gazed at Alice, awash in the novelty that she was able to talk about hip-hop and rap with him just as easily as she could discuss novels with Jonathan.

This girl is a courtesan! Felix thought. *A creature from* Moulin Rouge *or* La Traviata.

Despite his enchantment with her, the moment came when Felix couldn't take any more of her high-pitched chatter about how tall 2 Chainz was. When that moment arrived, he simply snatched Alice into his arms, and swung her around. She laughed and so did he, and to hold her like this, to kiss her, filled an absolute *void* in his very soul, he was sure of it. He pulled her down onto the floor, and they fucked to the flow of the 2 Chainz album *Pretty Girls Like Trap Music.* They lay in each other's arms afterwards, the French doors open and the sounds of the city traveling into the apartment. One of his thighs was stuck to hers because she had asked him not to come inside her this time, and he had spurted onto her belly and legs.

Her breasts were soft under Felix's cheeks, sitting above the cups of her bra; he'd sucked on her nipples, loving the way it made her breathing ragged.

"Can you unlock your phone so I can change the music?" Alice whispered.

"The password is 'Alice'," Felix whispered back.

"Well," Alice said, "That's… fucking awesome."

He fell asleep and woke to her fingers playing in his hair and her high voice trilling along to a Lana Del Rey song. He gazed into her eyes and their smiles were simultaneous and they kissed, and they kissed, and they kissed, a soft entangling of souls.

"Your fiancée pretty mad at you?" Alice asked, when they came up for air.

Felix sighed, thinking of Felicity's beautiful face. He felt a stone in his gut. "Yeah. I guess I could have at least texted her or something."

"You have your whole life to text her."

Felix peeled himself off the floor, and flopped onto the couch. Alice, a housecat not to be dissuaded, crawled to him, slipping onto the couch and then into his outstretched arm. She rested her ear against his chest and listened to his heartbeat. Delicious prickles of joy in her body, tickling her flesh and her scalp. Alice closed her eyes. Her cunt felt scraped inside, a delicious stretch she felt up to her belly. *Fresh man with a big cock.* She inhaled his scent and then fell asleep.

When Alice woke, she was alone on the couch. It was the height of the day and the sun burned through the French doors. The apartment interior was icy from the air conditioning, and her cheeks and feet were cold because of it; but she had a blanket draped on her body.

She rolled off the couch and got a drink of water from the kitchen, poured a shot of Chivas, downed it, and finally poured another drink which fit comfortably in her hand as she wandered over to pick through the drugs on the coffee table. There was no cocaine left.

She licked her pinkie and ran it inside the bag, sucking the precious grains off her fingertip.

She wandered through the apartment and heard the shower running in the bathroom. Seemed like Felix was scrubbing himself down for the second time that day.

Alice pulled the dress she was wearing off and left it in a soft, satiny, puddle on the floor around her bare feet. She was in her underwear which was a lacey, pale pink demi-cup bra and matching lace thong. She didn't need a mirror to know how she looked. She scrolled through Felix's Spotify, selected Frankie Miller's song, "The Devil Gun," and turned it up to full blast.

Grabbing a bottle of 25-year Macallan's, she took it with her into Jonathan's room along with two tumblers. She lingered in the doorway. He was not asleep; his body lay stretched out on that bed, with his legs all golden and strong.

At the very sight of her, Jonathan let out a long breath through his lips and sat up straight. Goosebumps prickled her flesh as she felt his gaze on her skin, looking her up and down. His quickening heartbeat practically called out to her. She lifted the bottle of scotch and met his gaze; his eyes flicked to the bottle and stayed there.

"Nice choice of music," Jonathan said.

"I heard this on your playlist this morning," Alice replied. "I don't really know who the fuck this is, just that you like it."

"Bring that whisky over here."

She took it to the nightstand and poured them a finger of whisky apiece. He gulped his down almost as fast as she did hers. As she closed her eyes and let that warmth flow through, she wanted to belch but she stopped herself. There should have been a sprinkle of water in each glass, and each drink should be slowly sipped; Alice felt random, sudden pangs of shame for not giving proper respect to the single malt.

"Thank you, sweetie," Jonathan said, and his voice had a strange monotone quality about it. It was odd to Alice that he seemed so subdued, because she had taken his brother's virginity, something she would have thought he would be proud of her for.

She set down her glass on the nightstand, and he set his down on the mattress where it rolled sideways until it tumbled against the singing bowl. The vibrating sound of the glass striking the bowl filled the room and their senses, and she was not pushed away or turned down as she straddled him. Jonathan sighed and he ran his large, warm hands up her lace clothed tits, squeezing and caressing the soft flesh. Alice felt his cock harden underneath her and she struggled to keep her breath from skipping.

"Your brother has a really big cock," Alice said. "That was fucking *painful.*"

"It runs in the family," Jonathan said.

"Good," Alice said.

She took hold of Jonathan's cock, pulling it through his shorts. He hardened even more against the inside of her wrist. It was not as big as Felix's.

She guided the tip of his cock inside her, and she gasped at the pain, which was all the more intense after the way Felix had wrecked her.

"Jesus…" Jonathan groaned.

Alice wanted to cry, and she swallowed it. The pain was an explosion that shattered her brain and her heart. Her hands were on his chest, and she knew she needed to lower herself onto that cock as far as she could go, but she couldn't move any farther.

Oh… fucking GOD! Alice thought.

Jonathan growled, reaching up and grabbing the lacy bra with both hands; in one movement, he ripped it open. Her tits exposed. He squeezed them and aggressively shook them.

Alice moaned.

He sat up, his hands on her lower back moving now to her hips. He pushed her down further onto his cock, causing her to cry out. But, to Alice's surprise, he was most interested in wrapping his lips around her nipples.

Alice closed her eyes and ran her fingers through his thick, soft, golden hair. *This is a prize,* she thought, *having both of these brothers this way.* They were two men that every woman on Earth would want; they would have wives and mistresses and girlfriends, and they would leave every single one of them smashed in the dust.

"Come on," he muttered, and Alice was not entirely sure if he was talking to her.

He bit her nipple, not hard enough to cut but hard enough for her to scream. His hand on her throat cut off the scream, and he let her go.

"Put your weight on me," Alice whispered. "Put it all on."

"I'll crush you," he said.

"Please…"

He obeyed, flipped her onto her back, let his weight engulf her and it buried her into the mattress. She gasped, pressing her hands into his chest and then against the front of his shoulders. She pushed as hard as she could; he didn't budge.

He grinned, "Come on, hit me."

She batted at his chest.

"I wouldn't be able to push you off even if I wanted to," she gasped.

His smile remained stunning. "I could be raping you right now."

"Make it rape," Alice whispered. "Do it. Hurt me."

"You crazy fucking bitch," Jonathan whispered, and he laughed mirthlessly.

"Please…"

Jonathan grunted. With one hand, he pinned both of her wrists above her head, and he drove his cock deep within her body. Alice moaned.

It hurt so much that she almost asked him to stop. Tears filled her eyes, and her face crumpled in a way that revealed both ecstasy and genuine suffering. Jonathan's chiseled body pumped away on top of her, and Alice felt herself at the pleasure of this demon. This kind of pain found the thirst that had nestled deep within her for as long as she could remember.

"Is this what you wanted," he grunted, still pumping into her. "Is this worth my money?"

She wanted to come. She really wanted to, but the pain was just too intense. She felt split, raw. *Is this what childbirth feels like for some women? Does this hurt as much as an actual assault would hurt?*

"Tell me I'm worthless," Alice whispered.

"You're worthless," Jonathan said.

"Tell me I'm trash," Alice whispered.

"You're a fucking piece of trash," Jonathan said.

"Hit me."

"What?"

"Please."

Jonathan would normally be angry, fed up with the ramblings of a stupid goddamned child, but with his cock deep inside this tight little cunt he could not help feeling a wave of attachment. He pressed his hands to her cheeks, and he was not embarrassed by how tender his voice sounded when he asked in a whisper, "Why do you want this?"

"I need you to hate me," Alice whispered.

"You crazy bitch." His words had turned cruel again, but his voice remained tender.

She took his hands to the front of her throat; she pressed her hands over his and applied pressure. Taking the hint, Jonathan squeezed gently; the look of ecstasy on her face was worthy of a renaissance saint. It made Jonathan swell, he squeezed harder, and Alice gasped underneath him, her legs spread wider, but the pleasure quickly turned to pain for Jonathan. Her cunt was like a beak, pinching, biting, squeezing his cock away. As his pain increased, his rhythm slowed; he stopped pumping. Locked in her vice, he briefly worried that he would become stuck inside her; this quickly gave way to the more irrational but also more persistent fear that she actually had a set of teeth down there.

Jonathan groaned.

Alice pressed her hands gently over his ass, then slid two fingers down into his crack, slipping deeper, too far. The release was so intense that he came, fucking *came*, no condom, no protection, he shot his sperm right into her womb.

Once he pulled out afterwards, the crash was intense. It filled him with cold and shock as he looked at her mousy little face, the smug, half-closed eyes. The wave of hatred that flooded his body was so intense that he almost gave Alice her wish: he wanted to hit her.

EIGHT

Jonathan woke shortly after midnight. Alice was asleep, face down on the bed, the remains of her bra wrapped around her waist. He pulled the thick down duvet over her, and she did not stir, drenched as she was in alcohol and drugs.

He groaned and swung his long legs off the bed, feet sinking into the plush carpet. He curled his toes into it. The Macallans bottle was still on the nightstand. He grabbed it and took a swig. The caramel-smooth alcohol burned down his throat, warmed his belly. He carried the bottle out of the room.

He found Felix in the living room, watching television. He was wearing boxers and still in the Teenage Fanclub t-shirt. Jonathan noticed a dark stain on the settee, devil knew what the source was. He saw the tiny, empty plastic bag with the ghost of white powder dusting it. He pointed, "Did you and the little bitch snort up the rest of my cocaine?"

"There's still three ecstasies left," Felix replied. Jonathan realized then that Felix's eyes were overstuffed blueberry pies.

"Ecstasy and Netflix?" Jonathan said. "Is that what you've been doing?"

"You were busy fucking her," Felix said, and his ethereal smile told Jonathan everything about how much ecstasy he was on. "Anyway, I popped it like four hours ago. I was just taking the edge off the *betrayal*."

"What betrayal?" Jonathan asked. "You think me fucking her — the whore *I* paid for both of us to enjoy — is a betrayal?"

"Drugs help me see that," Felix said, slowly waving one hand in a slow arc through the air. "I was mad at first; but then, I realized, of course, she's a whore, so…"

"Good," Jonathan said, and he patted Felix on his warm, hairy knee, "I'm glad."

Ugh I want a fucking line of coke, Jonathan thought, *but am I going to tamper with Felix's high? Of course not! Clearly, I am the more considerate brother. All the money I spent on those fucking drugs, and this greedy fucker just snorted it all.*

He took a swig from the Macallans.

"You were slapping her? I thought I heard that?" Felix asked. "Or was she slapping you?"

Jonathan wiped the back of his wrist over his lips.

"She's a strange girl," he said. "She likes strange things." His cheeks stung and were blotched red because the second time he'd fucked her, she'd repeatedly slapped his face begging him to stop.

The vinyl record album cover was sitting on the coffee table, leftover white powder sprinkled on it. *Fuck yes!* Jonathan used a playing card to scoot the powder around into a passable white line that bisected the face of Brennan Talbot, rich girl, doe-eyed "indie" singer. Jonathan knew that Alice had been right: the only reason Brennan Talbot had gotten her breakout record deal was through her father's money.

It isn't the sort of thing that girls are fond of seeing happen for other girls, Jonathan thought. Another reason he was glad to be a man, goddamn it.

He thought of the last time he had seen Brennan in person — the garden party, last summer. Brennan Talbot was always after everyone's fathers to fuck so that she could write songs about it. Jonathan had seen her fighting with his father away from the mansion, screaming at him while he'd stood tall and unruffled during her hysterics: arms crossed, lips twisted sardonically, ever the superior male. One of Brennan's sisters, a pale, plump starling of a young woman named Mari, had dragged Brennan away.

Jonathan snorted the line, feeling his brain absorb every desperately gathered grain of powder.

"*Fucking shit!*" he barked in electrified exultation, even as the knowledge that he needed to acquire more cocaine very, very soon nipped at his senses, creating a cacophony through his brief euphoria like a marble clattering around a tin can.

On Netflix, Felix had selected some program about depressed young "It Kids." All the Gen-Z characters were being played by Millennials. It was the sort of fare Felix favored, insipid scripts about the young, helpless "in" crowd he always felt left out of.

"Does Alice remind you of anyone?" Jonathan said, watching as some twenty-five-year-old actress playing a fifteen-year-old sucked on some teacher's dick in a high-school bathroom. He thought of Brennan's sister Mari, trying to remember if she were older or younger than Brennan. He'd known Mari longer than Brennan because Brennan had suddenly appeared in Richard Talbot's life as a teenager, filled with fire and ego, a gift from a woman who was decidedly not his wife. Richard Talbot had a habit of collecting daughters, the way some people collected cats. But if memory served, Mari was too fat to be Alice.

"Yes," Felix replied, "I told you when this all started, she reminds me of someone. Probably someone from this show."

The scene on the television progressed to the errant couple having to quickly sneak out of the bathroom. The teacher makes it to class on time, a student points out that his fly is down, and he makes a charming joke and the class laughs. The girl rushes to her class, and sits down clumsily. Both Jonathan and Felix laughed to see the scene unfold with the lady teacher in class noticing a line of semen dangling from the girl's chin. The teacher crossed the classroom and clamped a tissue onto the girl's chin before the rest of the class saw it.

"And they say Girl Code doesn't exist," Jonathan said.

"We should help her," Felix said, eyes locked on the television as the girl on the show found another bathroom stall to sob in, hugged herself while Brennan Talbot's hit song "Pussy Cat Blues" swelled on the soundtrack.

The woman teacher from the previous scene entered the bathroom, found the girl, and hugged her, and they sobbed in each other's arms as the scene abruptly cut.

"We should help her," Felix said just under his breath.

"Alice the Whore?" Jonathan asked, his tone nastier than he'd intended. *Fuck, I need to get more cocaine now.* "What for?"

"Well… I should help her," Felix said.

"And what does she need help with?" Jonathan asked. "Specifically."

At this point, the show had switched scenes: a trio of female characters had begun making out in an aggressive fashion to the swelling, desperate howl of the nouveau indie soundtrack.

"She can't be doing what she does and not need help. I want to help her."

Jonathan wanted to slap Felix.

"Look," he said, "It's too early in the morning to deal with your fake liberal 'helping others' bullshit, ok?"

Felix sniffled and then inhaled hard. He wasn't crying, however; he blew his nose on a linen napkin, dried snot and grains of coke smearing the cloth. "Whatever, Jonathan, ok?"

"And you know what? Yesterday," Jonathan continued, staring at the television, not absorbing anything more of what was on the screen, "she told me about her desire to erase pain and trauma from a person's brain."

"Her trauma? She wants it… erased?" Felix looked away from the television and directly onto his brother.

"Nah," Jonathan said, he took a swig of whisky from the bottle, the caramel fumes of it rose swiftly up his throat and out through his nostrils, "She sounded more interested in the idea of erasing it from another person's brain, as if… someone else's trauma was the thing bothering her."

The sentiment appealed to Jonathan. He thought of their own sister, Alice, in the months before she'd killed herself. In retrospect, it was easy to recognize that there'd been some sort of trauma weighing on her, and that it was more than likely a sexual one — in the way she'd begun to flinch from his hugs, or to pull her skirt down over her knees obsessively, like a nervous tic all the time. A couple times, he could have sworn he'd overheard her crying alone in her bedroom. As she withdrew into herself, she quickly became less and less delighted with his morbid humor and wicked pranks, which made her somewhat tedious. If only they could have erased her trauma… ah.

"You mean like Uncle Bertrand's work? Him and Dr. Lafet?" Felix said. "With the Saint Anne Corporation? Erasing everyone's trauma . . . you know all this shit is proprietary, not even Dad is allowed to know about it, and he's footing the bill. There's no way Alice could know anything about *that*."

"You tell me," Jonathan said, sipping from the bottle now, feeling the alcohol going back to his brain. The idea of a second wave of inebriation, at least, was comforting, if he couldn't have any more cocaine.

I could make the call for some more, but how much more fucking money am I going to spend, goddammit? Jonathan thought, his pulse racing with irritation.

Felix laughed, sat up straight, and looked at Jonathan with his green eyes so dilated they looked black. "What if she's a test rabbit? I know Dad told Uncle Bertrand that he couldn't be experimenting on people, but what if they're experimenting on *people*?"

"Of *course* they're experimenting on people," Jonathan snapped. "Think of what Josef Mengele did, think of Unit 731, think of the fucking Tuskegee Airmen! No advance in medical science happens without some fucking depraved human experimentation." He lowered his voice, realizing that Felix was so high that yelling at him was not going to have any effect. And he didn't want to wake up Alice.

"Well," Felix said, "Do you think she wants…. What could she want? Like, to blackmail us? Or Dad? Or . . . ?"

"Doubt it," Jonathan replied. "There is no way that little girl is any conscious part of something that intense, but… still. I have a feeling that when we find out who she really is, it could really fuck up our day."

Jonathan's gaze was not as clear anymore, his cocaine high already fading, the whisky filling his empty belly hot and nauseating and settling into his paranoid thoughts of Nazi experiments and Southern Gothic medical horrors possibly bubbling into the present day.

"Well…" Felix sat down, picked up the remote control, and backed up the episode, all the way back to the scene where the girl was giving her teacher a blow job. "I still think we should help her, especially now if Uncle Bertrand is fucking with her."

"You're a fucking idiot," Jonathan muttered.

He took the Macallans with him, leaving Felix alone with his Netflix.

In the bedroom, Alice was still sleeping in the same position. He took another swig of whisky and pulled the duvet aside. He thought about sliding the neck of the bottle into her asshole. He imagined turning the bottle backwards and putting the ass end of it into her pussy. He ran his hand over her flanks, tickled his fingers in the crevice where she was still wet. She was cleanly shaved, like most girls her age who took their grooming tips from porn stars. He peeled the halves of her ass cheeks apart like he was opening a piece of fruit, then leaned over and flicked his tongue until she woke up and moaned into her pillow. Soon enough, the juice from her cunt began to coat his chin.

His fingers wrapped around the butt end of the bottle, and before Alice could protest, he clamped his hand over her head, sinking her face into the pillow. She squeaked and struggled, but not enough to stop him, and not enough to alert Felix who still stared at the television in the living room, his eyes round and shining, his pupils dilated…

Alice was still deep in sleep when the morning light woke Jonathan. She was wrapped in the sheets that were rolled around her like a half-shed snake's skin. Smears of blood dotted the fabric around her waist. The room stank of Macallans and piss, both liquids soaked into the mattress. He didn't see any bruising on her throat or cheeks, but her breasts were showing some bruising because at one point he had just held her fucking down and slapped them repeatedly as hard as he could, at which point the little bitch actually came… or, at least, had faked coming. It irritated Jonathan that he couldn't tell which.

He found Felix asleep on the couch, snoring brutally, having gone deep into sleep at the wee hours plummeting and crashing hard from his high of ecstasy and cocaine.

Jonathan turned on the shower, a spacious box with a glass sliding door and a giant rainfall shower head, he scrubbed himself and tried to ignore the swirl of thoughts tearing through his brain. He had come inside that girl three times now. Felix had come inside her at least once. She seemed to have a habit of pissing soon after fucking, like an untrained purse dog. *Any real escort would have insisted on condoms.*

He thought of the diamond bracelet on her arm, and what it would cost him to buy something similar. He just knew he was going to have to pay for a fucking abortion, and all for a girl he'd become weak for when he found out she could quote James Joyce.

"I am caught in this burning scene," Jonathan muttered, "Pan's hour, the faunal noon. Among gumheavy serpentplants, milkoozing fruits, where on the tawny waters leaves lie wide. Pain is far."

The shower door slid open and to Jonathan's surprise it was Felix, skinny as fuck and naked as hell. He hobbled into the shower and picked a side, letting the water pour all over his body. He closed his eyes and groaned, and he pressed his hands over his face, his hair fluffy at first until the water beaded and weighed it down, soaking it so that it looked darker as it flattened over his forehead and face.

Jonathan handed him the shampoo.

They did not say anything to each other as they showered. They had showered together before, in situations where they were both exhausted as fuck and just needed to get clean. Mostly after ice hockey games as teenagers.

It was not long before Alice entered the shower, olive-skinned, huge tits, smooth flesh, skinny body. No diamonds on her wrist. She ignored them as she washed, and both men watched her. No one said anything. Jonathan pulled her back in and he bent her over. He saw smears of blood on her ass that washed away under the shower stream of hot water. He imagined she'd scream if he penetrated her ass again right now.

Felix stepped forward. At first, it was a move intended to rescue her; but she put her hands on his hips, her hands on his cock, that cock over her tongue, and she made sure it touched the back of her throat. Jonathan left Felix to get his blowjob finished in peace.

Jonathan dressed casually for the day, sporting a new pair of Levi's that he had purchased at the boutiques yesterday, and a new Off White brand t-shirt. He fixed his hair in the bedroom mirror.

He looked around the bedroom. Alice's bra was torn beyond repair; he lifted it with his foot and kicked it aside. She still had her dress from the day before, and the one he had bought her for today.

A Himalayan salt lamp glowed peachy and soothing across the room; he moved around the room, clicking on a couple more of the lamps. There was no need for the light, but they were pleasing to look at, and he rather liked pressing his hands against the warmth of them when they'd been on for a few hours. There were crystals and stone specimens glittering all around. The windowsill had a collection of stone and crystal phalluses; he picked up one. But they were small, all of them too small for anything interesting.

Fuck. He wanted her at least another night, but they were already out of cocaine. He had no idea she would be as big a cokehead as his dumbass brother.

Fuck this shit, I'm a babysitter for these dumbass kids.

He sat on the bed and perused his texts and social media. Nothing from his fiancée because despite her temper, that woman knew when to shut up and leave him alone. He already had 10,000 likes on the Instagram post of his half-empty chai cup from Dahlia's café, the one he'd uploaded day before yesterday. He smirked, and then uploaded a picture of the busker's card deck that he'd stolen yesterday. He captioned it with a lyric about sleight of hand, stolen from a Modest Mouse song, and watched the likes flow in.

One of the first comments of approval he received on the picture was from Brennan Talbot. *Hm…* he looked at the little blue checkmark next to her name and then replied, "Met a girl today who hates your music because your daddy paid for your studio time. Hope you're well, girl."

"Like I care about jealous bitches," Brennan immediately commented back. "Let's hang out! I'm in town and my bitches have abandoned me!"

"Maybe later," Jonathan typed, then left the comments section to view his original post.

The likes from strangers on the comment thread was pathetic. The desperation these unwashed peasants had just to be noticed by someone either famous or born rich was why the lower classes would always drown.

Jonathan saw a text arrive from Brennan. It said, *Hey, friend, can you do me a solid and check my TikTok? I'm floating a hashtag that's literally life or death!* Jonathan did not reply to the text. Two more texts arrived from Brennan, so he silenced his phone.

Felix was making coffee and the shower was still going when Jonathan left the bedroom. Jonathan pulled out ingredients to make another big breakfast. Bacon, eggs, pancakes, he did not give a shit if no one ate any of it. He would happily throw it all away, because the making of a meal would always be the best part.

"I haven't had her blow me yet," Jonathan said. "She any good at it?"

Felix was mid-sip of his coffee, looking at Jonathan over the rim of his cup, his eyes widening. He swallowed and put the cup down. "Uh…. Yeah, I guess. She's great. I mean… she's gotta be better than…"

"Your *darling* fiancé, Felicity? Really?" Jonathan said, mockingly. "That's going to be a problem. You'll want your wife to be good at…"

"Felicity is not going to be my wife," Felix said.

Jonathan's flesh prickled and then boiled, and the pent-up aggravation of the past few days twisted him inside out. "What the fuck, Felix, really?"

"I'm being serious," Felix said. "My eyes are open now. I can't marry her."

"Jesus," Jonathan said making eye contact with Felix, his voice was measured into icy, sharp, needles, "This has been a really aggravating set of days for me, do you know that?"

Felix shrugged.

Jonathan aggressively whisked a fork through pancake batter. He watched the batter bubbling and sizzling in the skillet, and he imagined he was burning a child — himself as a child specifically.

"No, listen," Jonathan said, as he continued frying bacon and flipping pancakes, "you're getting married, you're not a virgin anymore,

you're good. Don't let this very necessary action of losing your virginity
mess up the very necessary next action of your marriage."

"You don't even *like* your fiancée!" Felix said. "I adore Felicity, but
you… you *hate* your fiancée!"

"Is that even unusual?" Jonathan said. When Felix looked at him
like he had seven heads, Jonathan shrugged. "You know I hate all women."

Jonathan carried plates of food to the table, deftly as a waiter, and
then back to the stove to crack some fresh eggs.

"You can't understand how I feel," Felix sighed.

The photo-realistic, oversized oil portrait of Barack Obama leered
from the wall. Felix gazed at the cock in the painting, thinking of Alice's
lips.

"You're just excessively grateful for losing your virginity and you
want to savor that freedom a bit more," Jonathan said. "It's a normal
reaction. Fuck, I felt the same for Miss Campion when she took mine. I
get it, but…"

A memory surfaced now for Jonathan: Miss Campion, in tears
because she thought she might be pregnant. Jonathan, hearing the news,
feeling only anger and betrayal. *So this is what it feels like, being used.* He'd
looked her dead in the eye and told her to abort it or his father would
fucking snap her neck and leave her in a dumpster. That was the last time
he ever saw the woman.

Fuck… Jonathan thought, flashing back to present day in the apartment. *How many times have we each come inside her already?*

Jonathan poured himself a cup of coffee, plated the last of the food he was making, and then glared at Felix. "You remember all that idiotic drivel you spouted last night about wanting to help that opportunistic bitch?"

"It's not idiotic. I was meant to meet her. We're connected. I felt it from the first moment I saw her, I just knew something was important between us!" Felix said.

"That 'something' is an amazing pair of young, natural tits," Jonathan sighed. "And how exactly are you wanting to help her?"

"I love her."

"*What?*" Jonathan bit out the "t" at the end of the word, his mouth forming a snarl.

"I'm in love with her, Jonathan," Felix said. "I have never felt anything like this for anyone. I ... not even for Felicity. I even... Jonathan, for the longest time, I thought I might be gay. I always noticed men's bodies. In locker rooms and stuff? I liked looking at their chests, and I liked... I remember looking at you, sometimes, when we were at the beach, and..."

"*Felix!*" Jonathan cut in.

Felix's nose twitched. His lip wiggled at the corner. "I'm sorry, Jonathan. I..."

"*What the fuck!*" Jonathan screamed.

He couldn't help it now: Jonathan thought about all the times he and Felix had been naked in front of each other. As children in the bath, in the gym, locker rooms, skinny dipping. In the shower this morning. All of it flipped upside down. He thought of the first time he had seen a penis in a porn. He thought of the veins on the cock and tugging his own cock and spurting semen with the fantasy that his cock would someday be as big and magnificent as the one he was seeing pound some moaning bitch on a tablet screen.

He knew everything Felix was feeling.

He knew it acutely.

And he knew even more…

He knew what it was like to steal glances down his own mother's blouse, to steal a pair of his sister's panties from her drawer, to glance at the curve of Felix's naked hips, to look… to wonder.

At that moment he really wanted to murder his little brother and throw his body off the side of the building. He did not think he could hate someone so much, someone he thought he would have loved forever. But he simply could not abide idiocy, and yet here was his baby brother, standing in front of him, awash in idiocy.

"Are you… what are you planning on doing? Taking her home to Mother, and showing her off as your new…"

"Wife." Felix said, in a voice that made Jonathan grab a knife from the block on the counter. He didn't lunge at Felix, he just stood there, holding the knife, staring at him with wildly glittering eyes.

"Wife?"

"I'm going to marry her," Felix said. Seeing that his brother was completely serious, Jonathan put down the knife. "I'm going to call Felicity, I'm going to dump her, and then I'm going to take Alice and marry her. She will be my wife, and she will never have to be a whore…"

"I licked out her ass last night," Jonathan said. Felix flinched, and his bottom lip trembled. "I slid the neck of a Macallans bottle up her asshole. She fucking hated it, she fought it, but I made her come anyway. She tastes like a salted piece of steak, I licked out her pussy, did you see the bruises I left on her tits? Do you know how many times I made her come? I came inside her so many times she probably has my sperm swimming up to her throat."

Felix's throat tightened, he swallowed. His eyes betrayed nothing. They were moon pies; his lips twitched. His skin glowed with a sheen as if he had beatified in the moments he'd begun speaking with Jonathan.

Felix thought of Alice's cheek on his bare skin, the sweetness of her tender voice. *She would never be as sweet as that for Jonathan.*

"I'm not mad," Felix said. "I get it. She is really… really good at what she does, and she… and you already know what she is, anyway and… look, we can share her. I'll marry her to take care of her, but if you like her, I mean, the three of us could find time to hang out like this and have fun."

"Felix, have you discussed any of this with her?"

And for a few fleeting moments, Jonathan envisioned a warm,

sienna-filtered future: a hotel room overlooking the fifth arrondissement in Paris, waking up with Alice and Felix, tangled in the same bed, red wine, staggering into the Pigalle district… And then he imagined Felix and Alice without him, touring Tokyo, cherry blossoms falling onto their hair, then perhaps traipsing around the highlands of Scotland, dressed in matching tartans, one of those embarrassing couples that finish each other's sentences. Jonathan knew that it would work for them, as he sat back at the table, unable to resume eating; and he hated them for it.

Felix shook his head. "I was going to call Felicity first and tell her, and then I was going to ask Alice, but I don't see why not. It would be in her best interest, she's smart and she's already shown us that she likes money and comfort and she's reasonably okay with us. I think she likes us. It could be a really cool… *adventure*. Imagine! The three of us in Montreal, or Amsterdam?"

Jonathan blinked quickly, and then shook his head, his blood was cooling, leaving him all over with damp and exhausted defeat, "I… Felix I… I can't even begin to understand you right now, and what's more… I don't want to. I'm out of here."

Jonathan stood up, knocking his chair over in the process. His mind was blank as he put on his shoes, grabbed his wallet and phone.

"Where are you going?" Felix asked.

"To get more money to buy more drugs to stuff down the throat of that gold digger," Jonathan snapped.

None of us are going to see tomorrow, Jonathan thought, his heart and brain filled with doom and apocalypse, *not a fucking one of us are seeing it*. He envisioned the collapsed condominium building Alice had been chirping about yesterday, the bullet that had pierced Saint Cecilia's heart, the ever-expanding war in Europe, the image of a family splattered under a missile's impact. *We're going to die.*

"You can't pay her off!" Felix said.

"Oh, I'm sure I can," Jonathan shouted. "She'll be asking us for pink diamonds soon, just wait!"

He left the room with a slammed door behind him, and soon after that, Alice left the bathroom, wrapped in a towel. She walked with a slight hobble into Jonathan's bedroom. Felix wrung his fingers together, realizing that Alice very well could reject a marriage proposal from him because she preferred his older brother.

Alice emerged from the bedroom wearing the second dress that Jonathan had bought her. It was a simple, Empire waisted thing that disturbingly made her seem fresh and delicate. No bra, breasts jiggling, still no socks or shoes, walking on her toes.

"Breakfast?" she said.

"Mmhmm," Felix said, "help yourself!"

"Yum," Alice replied. Her eyes were on the food Jonathan had made, but not one glance on Felix.

He watched her serving herself. She winced when she lowered her body onto the dining chair, closed her eyes, shook it off and then dug into her food, still no real acknowledgement from her of Felix's presence.

He hated that he was prone to blurting things out, but he could not help it. There was absolutely no way for him to save himself from this.

"Is… is it better having sex with Jonathan?" Felix asked. His pulse raced.

Alice looked at him, her fork in hand, high above her plate, a dripping egg hanging off it, her diamonds shining on her wrist.

"Wow," she said.

"I mean… I felt like… I felt…" Felix said, "Yesterday… that when you… when we… we… I felt like…"

He took another drink of coffee. There was a strange, pleasant look on her face, like… it was not a politely tolerant look, it was the look of someone who was listening to the voice of an adored child. It was welcoming, as if she did not care that he was stuttering.

To feel that from someone, was priceless. All his life, from friends, teachers, from his mother, from Jonathan, from strangers, he was hyper aware of how his fumbling way of speaking elicited at the absolute best times, *patience* and *tolerance*. It made him incredibly anxious.. The only one who had never treated him that way was his dear departed sister, Alice — and now, this young woman, Alice.

"I mean," Felix said, he took a breath, "I mean that I feel like… you really enjoyed it with me."

"I did," Alice replied, "You're so sweet. It's not often I…" She cut herself off, however.

She had been very drunk throughout the night, but not too drunk to be unaware of how Jonathan had sodomized her. She'd begged him to stop, and she hated herself for showing him her limits. She'd peed the bed in fright, and he'd shoved his face between her legs as she did. She'd gone into a stunned shock at that moment, and she felt like a child in a fairy tale, imagining the brilliance of his white teeth, and having vague fear that he might start eating her from the cunt first.

"But Jonathan is better?" Felix asked.

"Eh…" Alice said. She was gazing up at the naked Obama portrait, it suddenly did not seem comical or satirical or gratuitous to her. It looked like a modern statue of David, something pure and safe, and gentle to kneel before and admire.

"That may be the best piece of art I've ever seen," she said, still looking at the painting, her tone the most earnest it had been since Felix had met her. "And, uh… no, I just think that… I think that he's used to sluts."

In the daylight, her fear from the night before felt so trite and embarrassing as she imagined all the older, mature, sturdier, more womanly-women who Jonathan no doubt had experience with. All those women would point at her, and mock her childish weakness, they would be well equipped to take on whatever brutality he could imagine inflicting.

Anyhow, after Jonathan had finished with her, he'd kissed her, stroked her, spoke softly to her about how brave she'd been, asked if she'd ever been sodomized before and told her how strong she was for "taking it" and oddly, through her tears, Alice had felt so loved and important. It would be foolish and silly of her to complain about Jonathan's treatment of her now.

"Oh… So, I could possibly get more experience and make you happy like Jonathan does."

I could marry him, Alice thought, looking at Felix's pretty face, *this beautiful boy who is just as useless as I am, who is just as hungry for love and validation as me.*

"Of course," Alice said, and then she frowned, "I mean, I guess… uh… Like… If theoretically you were a regular. I suppose, of course."

"I mean… you really made me feel good, in the shower," Felix said, "I want to … can I lick your asshole?"

Alice burst into a cough of laughter that she stifled with the back of her hand and then she quickly swallowed it down. Felix, who could not imagine it was in a prostitute's best interest to laugh at a client, felt the sting of insult, which quickly gave way to anger. *What the fuck?*

"I'm sorry I laughed," Alice said pleasantly. Felix was like a dish of creamed peaches compared to the whisky drip that his brother was, and she decided that he was a well-earned reward after last night, and her hands were clasped behind her back as she stood up and circled around the kitchen table. She sat on it, she let out a gasp, her face wincing just enough to betray the pain her ass was in, and then she pulled up her skirt and spread her legs, revealing her bald pussy. "Start with my pussy before you graduate to ass."

"No, I… I would rather get to Jonathan's level first," Felix said.

And his cock hardened as Alice turned around, bent over the table and then spread her cheeks, revealing her pink, abused rosebud, "Come on, cowboy. I'll walk you through it."

When Jonathan arrived, it was to the sound of Alice's moans floating through the locked door and into the hallway. He listened to the sounds, sighed, and patted the small leather satchel he held in which another small fortune in illicit pharmaceuticals was happily residing. Upon entering the room, he saw Alice's eyes were closed, she was wearing the new dress, her face was flushed pink, and her lips were swollen, as she was utterly lost in pleasure. Felix was on his fucking knees, eating out her ass.

"There could be worse ways of having breakfast, I guess," Jonathan said.

"Ohhh, fuuuck," Alice moaned.

Felix came up for air, his eyes closed.

"You like that, huh?" Jonathan asked.

"Yes, I do," Felix breathed, "I do."

"Well, have some more coffee and wash your face, it's my turn," Jonathan said. "And you're supposed to eat her ass, not make her come."

"Ha, fuck you," Alice said, her breasts heaving, her face dewy with lust. "Let the man have some fun."

"Oh, no," Jonathan said. "We're paying to fuck you like a whore, so you're getting fucked like a whore."

He tapped Felix on the shoulder, and his ever-obedient little brother stood up.

Jonathan unzipped his fly as Alice tried to stand up. He pushed her down onto the table on her back, plates clattering and food smashing beneath them. She cried out and slapped him; he held her hands down at the wrists, above her head, smashing them into a pile of pancakes. Jonathan was three times her size, and it finally dawned on Felix that he was witnessing a rape — but he did not want to stop it.

Felix pulled his own cock out; he squeezed it, but did not stroke. Jonathan slipped the head of his into Alice's cunt. She gasped, and he shoved it to the hilt.

She yelped like a wounded animal, her legs kicked out. Felix did nothing.

"Fucking *Jesus*," Alice screamed desperately, "*Stop…*"

"Jonathan," Felix said.

"She's wet as fuck, but that pussy," Jonathan groaned, and he began to pump her hard, causing her to growl in frustrated rage. "Lighten up girl, loosen that…"

Jonathan had let go of her hands to hold onto her hips so he could ram her with more force, her fingers curled against the table and Felix just… kept staring. And then he saw the blood. It was trickling down one of her legs, it made him think of her story about the beach and the man on the beach. The blood was also smeared onto Jonathan, alongside crumbs and food stains.

Why am I not stopping this? Felix's mouth was dry. *Why am I not doing — something?*

Jonathan fucked harder, his ass a perfect marble statue in motion, one of her legs crossed over his butt, and then Felix realized that the tone of Alice's yelps had become moans, deeper, longer, languid, identical to the sounds she was making from Jonathan's bedroom last night. The girl had folded, melted, given in.

Jonathan pumped her a few more times and came inside her, covering her face clumsily with one of his hands. She yelled again for him to stop. Jonathan finished, pulled out and stepped back. Only then did he notice the blood that was smeared all over his cock and the front of his pants.

"Fucking unbelievable," Jonathan said in a breathless voice, pulling off his pants and tossing them across the room. He used a linen napkin to wipe his cock off and threw that across the room as well.

"*Alice.*" Felix jumped in front and grabbed her by the arms; he did not squeeze, he just held her. He gently lifted her off the table, wiping food off her skin. Blood streaked her thighs and the tablecloth; it was not something Felix wanted to touch, in stark contrast to his eagerness lapping from the wound he'd inflicted on her the day before. Her face was dazed, almost sleepy, and Felix spoke into her uncomprehending expression.

"Alice, I… marry us."

"What?" Alice exclaimed. Now she was awake. She turned to and fro, wiping more food off her dress. *I'm going to die today*, she thought. *I've done it, I've orchestrated my murder.*

"Oh, *fuck*, Felix," Jonathan sighed.

"It can be like this every weekend. Imagine how much fun…"

"Oh, *fuck* no," Alice replied immediately. She grabbed the hem of her dress and shook off all remaining crumbs. "Don't be weird."

And then she laughed, half-stifling it with her fingers, but the feel of her laugh was mocking and cruel, as was her tone when she asked, "What the fuck is wrong with you, anyway? Are you 'special,' or something? I've been wondering!"

Is this how a pet dog feels when it bites its beloved human? Is this how fast it happens? Felix felt Alice's skin against his hand, her cheekbone, her soft lips, the snap of it. Just like that, he'd slapped her. He realized that there was something in him that he'd never known had existed. Until now. So, this is what a guy really has to do to get respect? Fine by me.

"*Jesus*," Jonathan yelled, "Felix, you *fucking idiot*. Is there *anything* you can do right? Anything?"

Alice was on the ground, on her side, sitting up. Blood trickled from her lips, and her eyes were fixed on Felix, as wary as a trapped fox.

I've murdered myself, she thought again. *I've done it. It's over.*

Jonathan would have expected, had he been able to foresee this scenario, that he'd cheerfully throw some sort of *I-told-you-so* at Alice — something to rub her face in what a moron she'd been, begging to be hit by them since she'd set foot in the apartment. But his instincts in this moment surprised him, as he moved quickly to her side; he couldn't deny the rush of tenderness he felt for her now. After all, *he* had not been the one to raise a hand to her in anger, not even when he'd wanted to. *Yet again,* he mulled, to his increasing satisfaction, *Felix can talk shit all day long, but it's clear who the more humane — more moral —brother actually is here.*

He wanted to wipe the blood from her lip now, gently place a bit of ice there… something to…

"Come here, sweetie. It's clear that my brother is a maladjusted moron," he murmured, putting an arm around her.

Alice turned her face to Jonathan's, and she spit a spray of blood that speckled his face and shirt.

The entire apartment went silent.

It was a brilliant, crystal clear silence, the sort that chills the bones on a frigid morning. It was the sort of silence that preceded the neck cracking snap at the gallows.

Well… Jonathan thought, already knowing exactly how he wanted to punish her for this, and envisioning *exactly* how she'd scream and squirm and cry, *maybe I am not the better brother, after all.*

Alice remained silent, her eyes locked on Jonathan. His expression was flat at first, their gazes locked on each other just as in their first meeting in the coffee shop. Then, suddenly, he shoved her onto the floor, his arms hooked under her armpits. She screamed at him, kicking and flailing.

Her carefully maintained veneer of arrogant calm had become impossible for her to salvage. Tears in her eyes gave them a lacquered shine; lines of anger and pain creased her face, her lips quivering like jelly.

Now this room was hot with anger, their nerves fried and crackling as it moved through each of them.

"Come on," Jonathan said to Felix, "Get that cock up and shove it into her before you offer her marriage again."

"Fuck you!" Alice snarled as she kicked and squirmed.

Felix's hands trembled as he took hold of her ankles and pulled them apart. The girl's warm body writhed underneath him, it was hot and sweaty, and he was trembling. He grabbed his cock and found it hard trying to get it into her cunt. He realized that every time he had entered her body, it had been with her hand on him, her hand guiding him, soothing him, her hand showing him how, her hand teaching him…

She cried out, her voice deep and angry. There was blood on her now-swollen lip: he had done that. Felix felt shame and terror and he wanted comfort — and he wanted Alice to be the one to give it to him. His anger had faded so fast, and left him merely scared. He pressed his hands over his cock and tried to slip it into… could not find it… fucking…

"Fucking…." He muttered.

"What is it?" Jonathan asked.

Felix heard a sound in the dark. He tasted, smelled, saw…. Something… this was… he looked at Jonathan's hands under Alice's armpits, the tightness of her limbs, the strain on her face… he wanted to cover her face… it would feel more familiar then…

"Jonathan, we've… have we done this?"

Jonathan's face paled and he twisted his lips. "What are you talking about?"

"Have… we've done this before?" Felix said in a deeper, assertive voice.

"No… of course not," Jonathan said, and his gaze on Felix betrayed curiosity, perhaps even worry.

"We have," Felix said, and he felt cold and hot all over, the hot sweat baking his skin and making the sweat upon it cold. He tried to remember something, a mental image of Jonathan's hands under a woman's arms, holding her still… Was it a memory?

"I think I'd remember," Jonathan replied.

But of course, Jonathan did remember. But he'd be damned if he said a thing out loud to validate Felix; he still wasn't sure if the memory was something that had really happened, or if the scene was perhaps from some shitty movie he and Felix had seen as children. It was tiresome being the only reasonable, patient *man* in this goddamned apartment.

"What?" Alice's voice was quivering, her breath shaking, her flesh quivering, her thighs at each side of Felix's waist, "You're trying to remember if you've ever raped a girl before, would that be a correct surmisal of this situation?"

Alice thought of a woman who had escaped death at the hands of the serial killer Richard Ramirez: he'd shot her once, and she'd fled; he'd pursued, but once he'd caught her again, pointed his gun in her face, she'd pointed out quite reasonably that, since he'd already shot her once, couldn't he call it a day for now? The serial killer had seen the sense in her words, and had let her live. Alice often thought of that woman at times when she felt her life was at stake. To be fair, this was the first time her life had ever been in *this* much jeopardy, so she finally felt validated in comparing herself to that woman's harrowing tale.

Felix looked at Jonathan and something about Jonathan's face betrayed the hidden truth as if he were also remembering through the fog.

"You see it, don't you?" Felix said. "We've been here before, haven't we?"

Yes, Jonathan saw it, but he kept his gaze on Felix and shook his head.

"Maybe I have," Jonathan said, "But not you, Felix."

Felix's jaw tightened, and his gaze on Jonathan looked if only for the briefest of moments--venomous.

"I think we all need mental help," Alice said in a much calmer voice, and she laughed.

Felix touched his thumb to her lip. She flinched, but did not pull away. He wanted to kiss her, but he stroked her cheek. Her hand… her beautiful, tiny hand was on him, gripping his cock, tugging it firmly and rhythmically, and Felix hardened.

"The only way out is through," Alice thought, *"the only way forward is back, put the band-aid on the finger before the wound happens…"*

"That's a good girl," Jonathan muttered, his eyes on her hand, on Felix's cock, "Show us you're a pro…"

Alice's legs relaxed and she arched her back and let out a long low groan, "Yesssss…" as she guided Felix into her.

Felix gasped, pushed, felt resistance, and shoved into her. Alice screamed, unable to hide the searing pain she was in. It was as if a blade was slicing through her lungs, her heart, her throat, and her belly, it was more than just the pain between her legs. Felix came, collapsing on top of her, shuddering, resting his cheek on her huge, bruised tits. He wanted to close his eyes and go to sleep. He felt Jonathan's fingers on the back of his hair, stroking him like Mom might.

"You're a fucking moron," Jonathan said. "You know that, Baby Brother?"

"I just want her to marry me," Felix moaned.

Alice sighed.

Felix rolled off her, he saw smears of fluid and blood on himself, as polluted now as Jonathan. He sat up and looked at her cunt, it was smeared in blood. There was blood on the Persian rug, as well. Felix pressed his hand to her thigh; she flinched, and put her hands over her face.

"Are you on your period?" Felix asked.

"Fucking look at this mess," Jonathan muttered.

"No," Alice said. She reached her fingers down to her cunt and spread the lips: they shone with blood and semen. "You've torn me up," Alice said. "Both of you."

"Oh, have we?" Jonathan asked and he pushed Felix aside, knelt at Alice's open legs and with two fingers he stuck them up her slit. The girl screamed like a child would. This was not an act. The girl moved to get away, to get his fingers out of her and Jonathan grabbed her, holding her down easily with one hand, and with the other he spread his fingers open in a scissor-like fashion inside her.

"Does that hurt enough for you?" Jonathan said.

"Fuck!" Alice yelped.

And finally, the tears arrived, the real tears. At the sight of her sobs, Jonathan pulled his fingers out of her. Her entire body shuddered as she curled in a ball, sobbing. Felix wanted to cry as well, but he didn't dare. He looked at Jonathan, who was watching her; Felix saw Jonathan's expression soften.

"Aw, you're just a kid," Jonathan said. "A stupid kid, but still. Just a kid." He pressed his hand to her hair and stroked her, the way he'd done to

Felix earlier. "Do you still want us to hurt you?"

Alice's sobs stopped, but she trembled and sniffled. She made no other reply.

Felix got to his feet, legs trembling and sore. He walked to the kitchen without his pants, smeared in blood from some girl's traumatized pussy. All practical, and empathetic thoughts he had erstwhile entertained about helping women and minorities, being his mother's best helper, saving the world, evaporated into ether. He soaked a towel in cold water and brought over a box of tissues to the girl, pressing the towel gently against her forehead. She mopped up her face with the tissues.

"You know, I can't even remember why we got into this fucked-up situation to begin with," Jonathan said, his original intention of simply trolling Felix lost in the continuing destruction of this girl's will and body. *How does a story like this end?* Jonathan knew a few possible outcomes that could come of this, and each of them ended with their own Netflix true crime documentary. "I seriously don't know whose fault this is, but we're finishing it."

Well, Jonathan thought, *I could now watch the universe perish without shedding a tear.*

NINE

Jonathan was wearing his shirt, no pants, no shorts, the smears of dried blood on his huge thighs. From the remainder of the drugs on the coffee table, he picked up the clear vial of GHB, which was administered orally using a measured dropper. Jonathan took a dose first in a finger of Woodford Reserve, and then he measured it into wine for Felix and then to Alice who had sleepy, puffy eyes. Both accepted their drugs like pious supplicants.

"So, we're all just casually taking the date rape drug together?" Alice said, her voice stuffy from tears, but its sarcastic edge re-discovered.

"I'm putting something on the television," Jonathan replied.

"Make sure it's porn," Alice said. "I like seeing what kind of porn you fucking perverts are into."

"How long will this take to work?" Felix asked, wrinkling his nose and wondering if he could have some more wine to hide that disgusting, salty aftertaste.

"Holy fuuuuuck…" Alice gasped. Her eyelids fluttered and her head rolled back, her hands over her tummy. She pulled her knees up to her chest. "I think it's…. Jesussss…" She sighed.

It was as if a vise of worms had taken hold of her brain and were slipping holes into it, and each hole was alive with pleasure. Throbbing from her belly to her toes, the floor leaving, the world spinning, her organs swelling and vibrating.

"Yeah," Jonathan said, "the smaller the girl, the faster it works; hence, the date rape…."

"Holy shit!" Felix gasped, because he felt something like a hand grabbing his brain and squeezing it and what it was squeezing was liquid pleasure that suddenly dripped down into his body and swelled and throbbed and fuck….. "It's working on me."

Jonathan rolled his eyes. "You skinny piece of shit."

Jonathan only felt something syrupy, calm, and as mean as soured sugar… a nice buzz.

Alice and Felix lay curled on the floor while Jonathan connected the television to the internet so he could play some porn. He set it to a long film, a gang-bang, a petite blonde with huge fake tits and a cherubic face, and muscled men fucking her from every imaginable angle. It was noisy and well-lit and almost too attractive. It was the sort of porn a teenager would find intensely hot, and most adults would consider about as sexy as a department store mannequin or Barbie Doll collection.

Alice kept making little moans and she slid her way back up to the couch, leaving smears on the cushion of fluid and blood. Felix joined her on the couch and she put her arm over his shoulder. He pulled her to his body, and they tangled into a pile of skinny limbs, bruises, and exhausted flesh. Alice giggled and tickled one of Felix's nipples, and he responded by tickling his fingers over her exhausted little clit.

"Is this the porn you like?" Alice asked.

"Do you like it?" Felix asked.

"Sometimes, I guess," Alice muttered. "It's ok. I like the women in it more than the men sometimes."

Jonathan looked at how tangled they were, as natural light spilled into the apartment, highlighting everything. This moment was so *real*. The drug began to take more substantial effects on Jonathan, enveloping him in a warm, bubble-bath high. His drowsy, pleasant brain devoured the naked flesh in front of him.

They were not clean and young and gorgeous; they were a fucking stinking train wreck and yet even the sight of his own brother's bare ass as he fucked Alice gave Jonathan a hard on. He could not help it and he picked up his phone and took a picture.

The sound of the artificial shutter alerted both Alice and Felix. Their dazed faces looked so fucking depraved and drained, the sort of look a photographer like Terry Richardson would die to photograph, and Jonathan took another picture.

"Is there a lot of memory on that?" Alice asked.

"Of course," Jonathan replied, "A man like me has unlimited

everything."

Alice smiled, her eyes half closed, a sleepy sort of snort from her, "Cool."

"Uh!" she suddenly moaned, and Jonathan's mouth watered to see Felix's blood covered fingertips tickling Alice's clit in a way she genuinely seemed to be enjoying and then he came again inside of her. One of her legs wrapped around his waist, her toes pointed, her foot trembling, her moans intense.

God, she must be in so much fucking pain. And still revving herself up to experience, or at least fake, pleasure. What a fucking trooper. Any guilt Jonathan felt about using the girl dissipated as it turned into utter respect for her submissive little ass. She was a fucking treasure.

Of course, that was probably the GHB cocktail speaking.

Felix had a hand on his own cock, when he pulled out of her, tugging at it but it remained spent. Jonathan strutted over to the couch and sat on the other side of Alice, his cock was standing tall, and she glanced at it but did not reach for it. Instead, she pushed Felix's fingers off her and touched herself, lightly moving her fingers in a slow, circular motion.

"You can record it, it's fine," Alice said in an impossible, childish tone that almost made Jonathan come.

Stupid. Fucking. Idea, Jonathan thought, then he caught a quick glance of Felix's grin and lifted his phone and began recording — the camera on her face, on her mouth, her teeth catching her swollen lip, on her soft, huge fucking tits, down her belly, to her fingers and the blood smeared on her pussy lips and the inside of her thighs.

"Are you really enjoying this?" Jonathan asked.

"Yes!" Alice sighed.

"How could you be?" He scoffed. "There isn't anything of you left. You're dripping come and blood everywhere."

Alice slid her hips and spread her lips open. Jonathan brought the camera down, feeling like a creeped-out gynecologist: he could see her pulsing flesh, the blood, the fluid. It was so gloriously disgusting.

"You're a piece of shit," Jonathan laughed.

"Tell me I'm worthless," Alice sighed.

"You're a worthless piece of shit," Jonathan sighed.

Her body shook as she came, jiggling tits, and trembling body. She was a noisy little bitch, and her noisiness was terribly like a porn star's cries. It made him wonder at the theatrical nature of it all. But he let her have her moment, and when her body settled back, the glow on her face, the delicious serenity of her smile — it was the calm, religious superiority of a woman who's just had an orgasm.

"You're a fucking star," Jonathan said. "You dirty bitch."

"Ha!" Alice laughed and she held her hand up as if warding off the paparazzi. "Shut the fucking thing off now."

And Jonathan did.

The porn ran on the television for another couple of hours, in which time the drugs put them into a sleepy stupor, and when it began

wearing off Jonathan administered another dose. It did not hit him quite

like it hit the other two. Alice and Felix insisted on cuddling on the couch,

tangled limbs, snores, and tickles. Jonathan took a few more pictures of

them. There was something edible about them. They looked pure and

serene and peaceful, as he knelt next to them on the couch. Most of the

GHB vial was empty; he wondered if they would survive another dose.

*It might be worth it to kill them… They're feeling good. Drowsy and stupid
and happy. Why not end their lives in this state of bliss? If I had any real love for my
brother — any affection or pity for this stupid girl, come to that — I'd be the better
man for killing them, really.* They had gone too far already, that was the truth

of the matter, and there were bound to be consequences. But it wasn't just

that: Jonathan himself had no intention of sending the girl home right

now, no intention of taking his brother with him to some spa to detox.

Things were bound to get worse, and Jonathan knew it. *Still, I didn't start
this shit — at least, I didn't start it alone. I've been babysitting while they steal my
drugs and make each other bleed. I'll be goddamned if I'm the one who gets saddled with
sweeping in and stitching up all the self-inflicted wounds. Greedy coke-snorting assholes
stole all my fucking coke!* He remained pretty raw about that particular slight.
Force another dose, the last of the vial down their gullets. Watch them die…

He stared at Alice's sleeping face, he pressed his hand against her

soft hair, and he smelled her. She smelled like salt and sperm and sweat

and sunlight, she smelled like roses and lavender and oranges. He smelled the alcohol coming off her breath, and then something else, perhaps

unbrushed teeth or the tang of the drug he was giving them.

She's sweet. She's a good kid. She and Felix could possibly be happy together… but he couldn't imagine Felix keeping her happy for long. *Girls with tight pussies can't come, they just float from man to man, looking for the magic cock that will finally make them come.* Jonathan felt he was too reasonable to really believe that *he* had even made her come, at any point during this entire rendezvous — even if she said otherwise.

Felix must instinctively know that. That's why he offered to share her with me almost immediately. His "wife." He already saw a future where he would have to make do with sharing his favorite thing in the world with his big brother.

Jonathan looked at Felix, his eyes were closed, his reddish lips parted, cherubic and pink and happy. Felix's chest and belly moved with his breath, Jonathan's eyes ran down to his brother's soft, sleeping cock. Jonathan felt his own cock harden and he flicked his eyes away from his brother, back to Alice.

He kissed her forehead and her eyes opened and she smiled.

"I want to see the video you made of me," she whispered.

Jonathan slid onto the couch and Alice stretched over his lap and Felix's. Jonathan let her hold the phone and she smiled as she watched the video which was nearly ten minutes long. Felix stopped snoring at the sound of the moans coming from the video, and his eyes rested on Alice as she watched it. She giggled a few times, and her face was clearly enraptured by what she was watching.

The sight of her enjoying it was arousing to Jonathan. He didn't need to see his cock to know it was angry and awake. He pressed against Alice. Felix's eyes met Jonathan's and both men flushed, embarrassed heat burning under their skin and brightening their cheeks. Both dropped their gazes and Alice, her eyes sparkling like a pair of shiny coals, rolled off their laps, landing on the carpet and sitting up, her slim back arched, her young, enormous tits round and firm as she fiddled with Jonathan's phone, holding it up.

"You two should grab each other's cocks and see what happens."

They both immediately protested as if they were completely shocked and horrified. But both remained hard.

"There's a fucking *line*, girl," Jonathan said.

"Yes," Alice replied. "And you should cross it."

"Ha," Jonathan said, and he looked at Felix. "Can you believe this fucking little…"

"Should we?" Felix said.

Jonathan laughed. His chest felt light, his heart felt… He looked at Alice and grabbed the base of his standing cock and shook it, "Get over here and suck it, you little bitch."

"I wanna see your brother grab it," Alice said in a high, girlish voice, as powerful and insistent as a head cheerleader.

Jonathan grimaced, looked at the beauty that was his cock, and glanced at Felix, "How far would you go?"

Felix's eyes were on Jonathan and his cock. Jonathan could see the curiosity. He had to admit he felt it himself. He felt all of this, and it was weird, but he felt some sort of….

Felix grabbed him, warm, firm.

"Holy fuck," Jonathan groaned.

Nothing is ever going to be OK again. Jonathan grabbed Felix's cock and it was the only thing he could think of to keep himself from coming all over his brother's hand, if he could just concentrate on…

Shit!

Felix came almost immediately after Jonathan grabbed him and he spilled all over Jonathan's hand. Jonathan wanted to be angry, irritated, disgusted — *violated.* Indeed, he felt the shells of these emotions, but they were as thin and hollowed as empty eggs. On a practical level, the hot sperm on his fingers was no different to him than spilling seed onto his own hand. He felt the involuntary buck of his hips and he spurted onto Felix's grip.

Jonathan groaned and he breathed out and pulled Felix to him, cuddling his brother to his throat and chest, kissing the top of his head, and draping his arm over his shoulders. Felix hugged him back.

"We really fucked up this time," Jonathan whispered. *We really, really fucked up this time.* The drug's effects were only flirting with his neurochemistry — swirling his physical sensations and impulses together enough to lower his inhibitions — but he already knew these memories were going to be permanent for him, though he was too high at the moment to hate Alice for it.

Alice scrabbled back onto the couch like a cat. She played the video back, her eyes fixated on it, her lips parted, her breathing shallow and short. Jonathan and Felix watched the video helplessly. It brought tears to Jonathan's eyes.

"What kind of porn do you guys *really* like? Only teenagers like the shit you have playing on the television right now. What do you really like?"

There's no point in trying to understand her thoughts, Jonathan realized. *She isn't worth it.*

He was half right: Alice's brain had fallen into the dysfunctional loop of a GHB blackout. Glutamate production in her brain was down and GABA production in her brain was high. She could feel and respond to all of the experiences she was having right now, but they were not being logged by her brain. Her words, her thoughts, her actions and choices — all of it was meaningless breath into the ether.

Base, reptilian instinct was the only thing driving her needs. She wanted to have an orgasm. She wanted to see Jonathan fuck Felix. She wanted water. She wanted to chew on ice cubes. She wanted a piece of paper. She wanted a pencil or a pen. She wanted to see the porn these two men were going to choose. And there was no way she was going to have a memory of any of it.

And so Jonathan showed her his favorite porn. He loved clips of women being tricked and pressured into sex. Fake taxi sex, landlord sex, creepy gyno sex. He kept his eyes on Alice as she watched, leaning forward, her chin on her hand, her face squinting, taking in the clips. Felix seemed more than eager to show off what he liked: it was a horrifying procession of emaciated young girls in badly lit amateur clips, choking on enormous cocks to the point where some of them puked.

She crawled onto Felix's lap and made out with him. Jonathan pulled her off and pressed her face into Felix's lap, then pushed into her from behind. He thrusted a few times, but quickly went soft. Alice sucked on Felix's cock, but he went soft as well. Jonathan finished the interlude by fucking Alice's pussy with a wine bottle, and when she protested, he sodomized her with it. Felix made a half-hearted attempt at stopping Jonathan, but then ended up taking a turn holding the bottle as Jonathan grabbed Felix's cock again. Afterwards, the brothers lay on the ground breathing heavily, listening to Alice cry.

It was all kind of funny a half hour ago, and now it cut through both the brothers like grief.

I should have killed them both, Jonathan thought.

When it was clear neither cock would stand anymore, and that Alice wasn't going to stop crying, Jonathan fed everyone the rest of the GHB. Eyes glazed over, they stared at a porno clip of a woman sobbing during anal sex and ultimately shitting all over the floor when the man pulled out.

"Bastards," Jonathan muttered.

He ran his large hand over the tabletop and found only empty vials, empty bags, a few ecstasy pills. He ordered Alice and Felix to kneel at his feet, they opened their mouths like good church-going children, and Jonathan placed a pill on each of their tongues.

Jonathan then grabbed his phone and made a call, left a voicemail before taking his pill, and he sprawled on the couch, and closed his eyes and wondered if the three of them would be dead by the time his call was answered.

******

Another night passed and they slept in a drugged haze. It was just after sunrise and Alice was the only one awake when the sound of Jonathan's ringtone filled the room; it was the repetitive emergency broadcast alarm made popular in *The Purge* films. Her eyes were wide, her throat hurt, and her mouth was hanging open. She was sure she had been snoring. She sat up. It felt like her organs were ripping through her skin. Searing, scraping pain filled Alice's senses: her ass, her cunt, the most hidden parts of her felt eviscerated and exposed. Tears filled her eyes, and she wrinkled her nose, trying to remember what had happened in the previous hours. She could only recall a cacophony of pornographic images, men's voices, and the feel of someone's hand striking her cheek.

Jonathan's emergency alert broadcast ringtone continued to scream.

Alice gingerly touched her sore cheek, as she tried to remember who it was that hit her. Could it have been Jonathan? Felix didn't seem like the type to hit a girl in the face.

The French doors were wide open, and the sun was still high, and there were a handful of crows IN the apartment scavenging the breakfast plates. One of the birds, a gorgeous glossy black specimen with a slice of bacon hanging from its beak, made a clucking noise from its throat, meeting Alice's gaze. Alice gasped and the corvids took flight in response.

Jonathan's phone continued to alarm her frayed nerves.

Fuck me, I fucking hate blackouts. Alice couldn't remember the last time she'd blacked out from drinking; but with the number of drugs thrown into this bargain, she supposed it had been inevitable.

Jonathan's phone lit up again with a fresh cycle of its alarming ringtone.

How do I answer that? She found the energy to roll over, and her face met Jonathan's warm, hard thigh. she thought about the feel of his hungry tongue, and she bared her teeth. It had to have been Jonathan who had hit her and made her sore. She opened her mouth against his leg and then she sank her teeth into the bare leg…

Jonathan yelped and sat up straight.

"Fucking bitch!" He grabbed Alice by the throat, squeezing hard. Lights exploded across her field of vision as he cut off her oxygen; one of her hands pawed at his, rather feebly. He let her go when he realized his phone was screaming.

"Your phone," Alice muttered, and she dropped onto her back, one of her slim arms over her tummy.

"Yes," Jonathan said. "I fucking hear that. Thank you."

He staggered when he stood up, but he regained himself and steadied, he blew out a breath and glanced at the wreck of Felix and Alice and the apartment. There were plates of half-scarfed food scattered in the living room, vomit puddles in at least two spots, glasses and mugs filthy and discarded amongst smears of blood. The air conditioning was being wasted out the open French doors, and there was a plate of pancakes and bacon on the balcony. A lone crow pecked at it.

"Fucking losers," Jonathan muttered. He picked up his phone. "Yeah?"

"Yeah!" A voice barked into his ear, "I've got two security guards on my ass, because I've been standing here telling them I have a fucking invitation from you, like an asshole. I have you on speaker, so, if you would please, fucking get these assholes told, will ya?"

"Yeah," Jonathan said, he cleared his throat and closed his eyes as he spoke, "I invited him. Let him up."

The visitor was a slim, short, and sinewy man, with the boyish looks of someone who has been adorable their entire life and is used to it.

"Yo!" The young man said. He had a vibrant, warm voice, and an enthusiastic, smashing-the-pots-and-pans way of speaking that marked him as a New Yorker. "This is lookin' like a match made in heaven, hombre! Reggie never makes a bad connection, never makes a bad one!"

He had a buzzed scalp underneath a black CDG embroidered baseball cap. Black Converse sneakers on his feet were emblazoned with angry red-faced hearts. His shirt was a short-sleeved, forest-green-striped cotton Comme Des Garçons with an angry red heart on the upper left corner. The man's eyes were black, and he was the size of Clyde Barrow or Billy the Kid. He stood at a kind of tilt, one hand on a hip and a backpack slung off one shoulder.

"Candyman is here!" He said. "Third time in three days, pretty good party here?"

"It's just us," Felix said. His eyesight was blurred, his throat dry, his head banging with pain, but he recognized the man as the one Jonathan had purchased drugs from in the alley right before they had met Alice. Even though he had never properly met this man, it somehow felt good to see a familiar face.

Alice pulled her feet onto the couch, tucked her legs to the side, pulled a soft blanket over her body. Her eyes were half open. She imagined her body gluing like Velcro against the fabric of the couch. She imagined having to burn this entire apartment to feel or attain any semblance of clean. She looked at the young man in the foyer, as he dropped his backpack to the ground. He turned a small circle; he had a v-shaped, featherweight boxer's waist and wiry limbs. She imagined he was not that much taller than she; he was certainly much shorter than Felix and Jonathan. He was the type of boy she'd nursed childhood crushes on. The type of boy who liked flirting with her.

She instantly felt ashamed of the battered state of her body, the bruises, the swelling. The sting of being disgusting.

The young man did not look at her. He was all business. His eyes were straight on Jonathan, the man with the cash. He inhaled deeply, closed his eyes.

"Damn, having an orgy, son?" The man said.

"Yes," Jonathan said.

"Smells like it's taking a turn for the worst," the man said. "I'm not above making my money but maybe you all should shower, call housekeeping, and go outside for some sunshine, get some breakfast, and some clean air on your skin. I've smelled bordellos in Mexico that are better than this. Fuck."

The man took stock of his surroundings, his eyes rested on the painting of the naked Obama, and he grinned broadly, "Now *that* is the best fucking art in Denver."

"Oh!" Felix said. He'd pulled his pants on, no shorts. Jonathan had pulled on his boxers, no pants. "We were afraid that maybe the painting was racist?"

"Why you asking *me*?" The young man said, pointing his thumbs to his chest. "Because I am a Black man?"

Felix grimaced and closed one eye. "I guess?"

The man laughed, "Fuck y'all Y.T.s. Save your hand-wringing for helping the starving children and the houseless brethren of this city getting some actual fucking aid. I love me some Rick Dallago art! And sometimes specifically *because* y'all fake liberals don't know how to feel about it."

"Oh…" Felix said, and he turned away, feeling exposed and ashamed.

"You should join us," Jonathan said. "We can talk art shit. Don't mind the smell, the stinking orgies are the best ones. You must know that, kiddo?"

The man grinned, squatting as he unzipped his backpack, his slim legs folded back-of-calf-to-back-of-thigh. He dug through his sack. "I'm probably older than the two of you Adonis-looking motherfuckers."

"I'm twenty-four," Jonathan said.

The young man raised his eyebrows, "Just turned thirty, son. I could be your papa."

"Whatever," Jonathan replied. "Baby faces are baby faces for thirty-five straight years and then one day you'll wake up looking like a misshapen gnome."

The man laughed. "True, true, it happened to my grandpa. Hot Italian flyweight with boyish face until the day he woke up looking like a shovel and a witch's hex."

"Oh yeah?" Jonathan said. "Boxing? Who was your grandpa?"

"Barry Clark Ciccone," The man said, and he pulled out two Ziploc bags full of mysterious treats. "Flyweight champion 1982."

"Fuck!" Jonathan said. "Barry Clark Ciccone is your grandpa? Yeah, I know that man, my grandpa used to pay off his liquor tabs. New York City in the '80's, your grandpa was an awesome piece of Italian shit. I met him a few times when the family would go to New York in the summers. Fucking shame he passed last year!"

"Yeah, fucking Covid," the man named Ciccone said.

"Condolences," Jonathan said, his face as serious as could be. "I can't believe I've been buying from you on street corners for three months now and I grew up knowing your grandpa! What are the odds?"

"Pretty good if Reggie's in charge of the connection, that's probably the detail that was on his mind when he hooked us up," the young man said. His skin was a rich brown color, his features small and delicate, lips full and soft-looking, a perfect picture of African and Italian ancestry.

He stood up and shadowboxed, biting his bottom lip and making *bam!* and *pow!* sounds as he punched at sunlight and dust. "Grandpa even taught me some shit."

"Yeah?" Jonathan said, "You ever fight?"

"Nah," the young man said, and he straightened up; he had a proud and erect little carriage, like a happy Boston terrier. "Grandpa taught me to move, but I never used to fight except in self-defense at school from rich fucks who used to prowl the neighborhood raping our sisters and mothers.

I don't like hurting another human."

"But you'll sell me enough date rape drugs to kill a horse," Jonathan said without a question or irony in his voice.

"That I will," the man named Ciccone said. "I'll be a fucking capitalist until I earn enough money to invest in the socialist commune I'm founding. And then, and ONLY fucking then, will we rise up, take to the streets, kick in your front fucking doors and eat every rich fat fucking one of you that ever dumped money into our starving little throats."

Jonathan scoffed.

"I will eat your warm pumping heart and it's going to taste fucking amazing," Ciccone said. "I like my steak bloody every god damned time." He pointed with his angry finger but stopped shy of touching Jonathan in the chest.

"Is that a threat, little man?" Jonathan said. Even standing in his stained boxers he looked a specimen of perfection.

"It's an *eventuality*," Ciccone said, and his broad smile displayed beautiful white teeth. "Everything is." He clapped his hands together, rubbing his palms. "SO, do you want the usual? Third order in the row?"

"Sure," Jonathan said. "That and whatever you might want to recommend on top of it? Got anything we should know about?"

"Seriously?" Ciccone said. "How much more GHB do you need? I only have three vials left. Where are you even…" At this point, his eyes finally found Alice. "Holy shit."

Alice averted her eyes. She was so very aware of her stink. She became ashamed of the raw shooting pains in her pussy. She became angry at the annoying stickiness gluing her ass cheeks together. Her cheeks reddened.

"Have you been using it all on her? How is she not dead yet?"

Alice met eyes with him. His glittering eyes flicked over her countenance.

"Damn. She's half dead as it is," Ciccone said and the boyishness left his face, he crossed the room to Alice and took her cheeks into his hands.

His hands were rough; Alice flinched more at their calloused, blue-collar squeeze. His thumb brushed over her bottom lip, which was puffed and bruised.

"You hanging in there, honey?" Ciccone said.

Alice pressed her hands over the back of his warm hands. She closed her eyes and felt weightless and blissful. She felt every pain in her body glow, and that glow turned to honey, and that honey bled into the flesh of the man touching her.

"Why don't you have a taste of her," Jonathan offered.

"No!" Felix barked.

Alice kept her eyes closed, not giving a shit if Jonathan was offering her up to this pretty man. She imagined he would hold her to his chest, as gently as her father would. It was only days ago when she had last seen her father; he had asked her if she wanted to do something on the weekend, like go to her favorite oyster restaurant in Cherry Creek. When she'd expressed excitement at the idea, he had hugged her close, and told her that he'd always love her, no matter what, and that he'd always have time for her, and the way he'd been so insistent about saying that had given her a strange feeling.

Ciccone and Jonathan looked at Felix who was wringing his hands together.

"Jonathan… she's *ours*. I don't want… *him* touching her."

Jonathan laughed, "You're fucking amazing, Felix. Now, you're objecting to a Black man near your girl. Remember when you were calling me the racist one?"

"I'm not tasting shit until I know she's okay," Ciccone said, strategically ignoring the comment about race. He snapped his fingers over Alice's face, and back and forth at each ear, "Wake the fuck up, kiddo… Jesus, she's just a *kid*. What's going on, kid?"

Alice opened her eyes and when Ciccone looked into them, he felt a helpless, needy adoration pouring from her, like the feeling he'd first met when he looked into the eyes of his baby daughter. "What's your story, kid?"

Alice touched the tip of her tongue to the tangy wound on her lip, part of her brain was in a loop, seeing her father smile and hearing his laugh when she fumbled an oyster that hadn't been completely separated from its shell.

"You can have a taste," she said, "It's all consensual."

"Why…" Ciccone said, "in the *fuck* would I want a taste? You smell like come, French Onion soup, and blood. You need a break. Are you a hooker?"

"Yes," Alice, Felix, and Jonathan said at the same time.

"Well…" Ciccone said, he stared at the diamond bracelet on Alice's wrist, long enough for her to cover it with her other hand, "Well there's that. I guess. I can't argue with that. I have the regular order for ya," he left Alice's side, kicking over a plate of congealed eggs that had been on the floor, and went back to his backpack, "I have a bunch of oxys, I would recommend giving them to the girl and nothing else. She's going to need them bad after whatever she's on right now wears off. Don't give her anymore GHB, it's a fucking miracle she ain't dead already. I have shrooms and mollies, and crack, some basic weed shit here, but the coke is really the best quality, like everything I've been selling you, it's pure, top quality, not a speck of Fentanyl in it, I test it myself even after Reggie vouches for it, so personally I would recommend you sticking to that. I haven't seen shit that pure come my way in a while."

"Sure, throw it all in, and the shrooms as well," Jonathan said, "We'll take some of that. And hey, anything you might like? Take something from the stash for yourself, on me, Brother."

Ciccone's eyebrows slid up, "You sure? Yeah?"

"Yeah," Jonathan said, "Your grandpa is Barry Clark Ciccone. Fuck yeah. Whatever you want."

"Well," Ciccone said, "I wouldn't mind a little crack myself; I'll light up here if that's cool with you?"

"Sure," Jonathan said, "Park it anywhere you want. But you can snort some of the stuff we're buying, save ya the trouble of lighting up?" He pulled up the cash from the table, counting out bills, finishing the transaction with Ciccone who took the money and tucked it into his backpack.

"Ah, I prefer lighting up," Ciccone replied, rubbing his hands together, "thanks."

Alice watched the proceeding with half closed eyes, she saw Ciccone unfolding a package, flicking a lighter, the sound of aluminum foil crinkling. Jonathan and Felix were snorting cocaine off the coffee table, she wanted water and could not think how to ask for it and then she fell asleep.

"Did we really get magic mushrooms?" Felix asked, his expression shining, buzzing from his latest line of cocaine. "I've always wanted to try magic mushrooms!"

"Yup," Jonathan replied, holding up the reused prescription bottle that held the dried hallucinogenic mushrooms to the light, and then shaking the bottle. "Are these caps or stems?"

"Caps," Ciccone replied, in the midst of tidying up his paraphernalia now that he was done with his smoking session. He flicked his finger over his nose in a jerky, repetitive manner and then ignored the sound of Jonathan's loud voice as he went on and on, telling Felix that they would take some of the shrooms later, when their cocaine high wore off, and that even then he would administer it because Felix would only be able to take a micro-dose to start with.

Ciccone's attention remained on the disgusting piles of human filth collected in the Versailles-esque palace around him. Vomit, blood, shit, and piss, stale food, spilled drinks, and broken glass greeted him at every turn. And then there was the problem of the young girl on the couch. Ciccone wanted to go back over to her to take her pulse again, but he didn't think it was wise to show the brothers that he was feeling any concern.

"Hey!" He finally said, loud enough to interrupt the brother's conversation about what was and wasn't the proper dosage for shrooms. "I'm jonesing for some booze. I can make a pretty mean Sazerac!"

Jonathan set the prescription bottle down and rubbed his hands together, "My man!" He shouted. "Make us some drinks!"

Ciccone grinned, "Coming right up!"

Alice opened her eyes to the synthetic smell of lemon cleaning product. She pulled the blanket around her and groaned at the shooting pains darting through her bones, her knees felt mashed up, her ass and pussy felt ripped to shreds, bruises blotted her breasts, her wrists, her legs.

Every drug that had been coursing through her veins had worn off.

The roar of the vacuum startled her. The way she flinched and sat up, recoiling from the sound, hurt her spine. Jonathan was nowhere to be seen; Felix was on the couch, arm flung over his face, snoring like a dying beast over the sound of the vacuum.

Is there a housekeeping crew in here?

There was not. It was Ciccone. His cap was turned backwards, and he was indeed running a vacuum cleaner over the plush Persian rugs. The entire room now sparkled with the scent of flowery, natural-brand cleaners. Respectability had retaken the apartment — dishes done, soiled linens gone, coffee table immaculate, dining table cleared, kitchen island shining.

Alice felt worse now than she had hours ago, when her injuries were still being inflicted on her; but the sight of the tidied apartment was strangely comforting. The ghosts of blacked-out memories swirled in her brain: she remembered crying, the feel of things up her ass that shouldn't have been there, the sound of Jonathan's laughter.

Ciccone shut the vacuum off when he saw Alice awake. "Hello, Princess," he said. "How you feel, Kiddo?"

"Can I have water?" Alice managed to ask. Her throat was on fire and her mouth tasted like garbage.

Ciccone brought her a full glass of water and some pills to take. She did not ask what they were, just swallowed them.

He took the glass from her and then his hands were on her face. He tilted her face from left to right, up and down, peering at her, his thumbs pulled her lower eyelids down as he checked her pupils. He took her wrist in his fingers, checked her pulse against the digital readout of his Apple watch. Alice met glances with him, and he winked.

"Pulse isn't bad, at least," he said.

"I don't feel too badly," Alice replied.

"You look like a truck hit you," Ciccone said. "And you have a fever." He pressed the back of his hand against her forehead, ran his rough-skinned fingers down the sides of her throat, and then his fingers through her hair. "Even your scalp is on fire. The big guy told me he sodomized you a couple of times. You probably got some sort of infection or perforation. This shit is bad news."

He placed her hand on her lap and leaned close to her throat. There was a gooseflesh-riddled zeal about the closeness, the threat of tenderness, warm breath.

"Why are you cleaning, you weirdo?" Alice said. Her pulse and breathing quickened as she tried to remember through the blacked-out fog what else Jonathan might have done to her. She remembered the first time he had sodomized her with the whisky bottle on the bed, and she legitimately couldn't remember if he'd done it again. She had to agree with Ciccone that she probably wasn't very healthy right now.

"Happens every time I do crack," Ciccone said. "If I see a mess, I clean it. And let me inform you, if you haven't already realized this — you are, my dear, and this entire apartment is, in fact, a hot burning trash fire. I have my mission set."

Felix's snores filled the room, and it made Alice think of a famous actor whose name was in the news because he had died of sleep apnea. Alice was sure she had probably sounded the same when she had been asleep. Jonathan's snores could be heard from the other room, and he had not snored like that the night before. *The drugs are really building up in our bodies.*

"They won't be up for a while," Ciccone said. "I added a little extra stuff to the sazeracs I made for them."

"You drugged them?" She coughed, a sort of half laugh. After all, Jonathan had paid this man a tidy sum to, well… drug them.

"Yup," Ciccone said. "I'm a tough grown man, but both of those boys are pretty strapping specimens. I do not think I could take them both on in a fight, especially not the big one. I know my limits."

"But why would you fight them?" Alice asked.

"Well," Ciccone said, and he placed his rough palms onto her shoulders, her flesh flinching at the feel of this blue-collar boy's shark skin. His pupils dilated like a cartoon character's. "So I can kidnap you."

Oh, of fucking course! Alice thought.

Now that Alice was waking from the fog that had enveloped her over these past hours, she was somewhat losing her fascination for this very polite drug dealer. His kindness would have to come at a price, wouldn't it? And she wasn't particularly curious to know what his angle could be. Alice was so tired. Sleep tugged at her eyelids, her legs were folded and warm; she could not imagine standing on her two feet ever again.

"Why?"

Being kidnapped by a drug dealer had not been part of her plans, despite all of the phantasmagoric scenarios she could have ever imagined getting herself into, fucking older married men, trying to murder her sister over a stupid harp, getting blackmailed by the child she was babysitting. Stereotypical images of trafficked women in motel hovels, strung out on meth and dirty cash flashed through her brain and she realized exactly what kind of an amateur she truly was in the face of the big, wide and wicked world.

"I know you said this is consensual but—" Ciccone began.

"It is," Alice cut in, "I agreed to all of this. It's my own free will."

"It could have started that way," Ciccone said, "and I know with a female it can often start that way, but hey, things could have changed and it's not your fault. But a guy on the scent is not going to hit the brakes when you tell him to, and there is two men full-on in the stink here. So, what is it?"

"Consensual," Alice said.

Ciccone frowned, his forehead creasing, crow's feet and lines forming at the corners of his eyes. Alice noticed now that he had several sunspots and freckles — his brown skin had a leathery sort of look, once you really took the time to observe him.

"What's your story? You a friend of theirs? I doubt it, you're like fourteen or something."

"I'm a call girl," Alice said.

"A…" Ciccone started, and then he laughed revealing his beautiful teeth, all white and crooked, "A call girl?"

"Yes!" Alice said, "That's what I am. They are paying me. I'm an escort."

"You're not a whore," Ciccone said.

"Why couldn't I be?" Alice said.

"Because whores have standards, especially the expensive kind," he answered bluntly. "You're a fucking liar, kiddo. And not a believable one."

"They believed me," Alice snapped, and she flung her arm towards Felix on the couch. "It's good enough for them."

The blanket she had wrapped around her body almost fell, and she caught it but not before Ciccone got a full gaze at the deepening bruises.

"That's because you gave them the free pass for illegal hot young snatch," Ciccone said, leaning back on the plush rabbit fur rug, and squinting at her. "They have a built-in excuse now that you've lied to them, just in case you take it to court or try to blackmail them, or something."

"They believe me," Alice said.

"If they do," Ciccone said, "then it proves you rich fucks are goddamn idiots. Your flesh is going to be like fresh veal when us working-class heroes feast upon it."

"Stop talking about eating people, okay, Alferd Packer?" Alice said. "Anyway, who says I'm rich?"

"Only a hot rich girl would let herself get treated the way you are letting on right now. You're like inbred Siamese Cats. You probably have a daddy who is a rich surgeon or psychiatrist, judging by that bracelet on your wrist. Maybe a politician daughter. Children hate the taste of silver, and that's the only spoon they're given in your social circles."

Alice closed her eyes and found she could not open them again. The burn turned to blackness; her brain was swimming. She felt the couch against her body. She felt the buttery silken blanket fall away from her body. She felt the air on her naked flesh. She felt his gaze on her. She pressed her hands against the soft, cool flesh of her tits, trying to cover the worst of her bruises. She opened her eyes halfway, and he was indeed looking at her. His lips were parted and his eyes studying her as if… well, she could not read what he wanted.

"Kiss me," she said.

He did. His lips were soft, not rough like his hands. They pillowed against hers and then parted, and she felt the soft, moist caress of someone whom she did not want to hurt her. Her eyes were open and so were his, and their breath exchanged. She imagined just a tiny bit of her life transferring into him, something that could stick and follow like a spirit from a Korean horror film.

He then kissed her forehead.

"Come on kiddo, I ain't kidding, you are fucking *burning* up with fever," he said. "Let me take you from here. Put your arms over my shoulders, come on."

Alice obeyed. She slid her hands over his shoulders and then joined them behind his neck. He was muscular and slim. He lifted her easily from the couch and she cried out in pain as he did: it felt like her snatch were ripped in half. Her asshole hurt, too, and suddenly she had a vague flash of memory — *Jonathan's hand on Felix's cock* — and she couldn't understand why she would imagine it. She felt fluid dripping from her body, and when she looked down, she saw bright flowers of blood staining the couch.

Her toes curled. She felt every bruise on her skin, every strain in her ligaments, every creak from her bones.

Alice imagined him carrying her from the apartment, but she couldn't form the words around the thought, only saw the images in her brain like a silent film — an out-of-tune piano playing as he carried her from the apartment, away from the monsters, and into the safety of a hospital bed. But then her mind's eye saw her father's face, his sad dark eyes, his lips tight and his hands in a fist because he thought he was keeping her safe from a million unspoken secrets.

"No," she said.

"Sweetie, it's almost over," Ciccone said.

"It'll all be for nothing," she said. "All of it, if you leave with me."

"What is this?" Ciccone said. "You think that's fucking fair to do to me? You want me hearing the headlines tomorrow about some pretty little girl, missing or butchered, and I could have fucking done something about it but didn't? The beta brother is pretty harmless, I think, but that older one is a fucking Great White Shark, and he is going to cook and eat you soon. Trust me."

Alice leaned her face against his chest. She could hear the rapid beat of his heart, and knew that was the crack at work. She smelled his male stress, the strain trapped in a Comme de Garcons t-shirt that probably had weathered repeated spritzings of a scent she recognized as Yves Saint Laurent.

"I have my own decisions I have to pay for," Alice said. "You're the one who chose to sell drugs in this world, you're the one who decided to live this life. I'm making decisions as valid as yours, I think."

Alice knew she would not be able to fight him if he chose to take her. He turned to the right, the soft sound of the hallway carpeting under his steps. Jonathan's snores became louder, Felix's twice as loud. He swung her sideways and they went into the bathroom.

"What are we doing?" she asked, and she hated the sound of her voice coming out all childlike. She felt as though her mistakes were now unbearable. She could not breathe, she could not understand anything, her chest hurt.

"Well, whatever you're doing now," Ciccone said, "you stink."

She held him tighter as he lowered her into the deep bathtub. The cold porcelain hurt her tailbone. She pulled her knees up to her breasts while he turned on the faucet. He tested the water with his hand the way a seasoned parent would, and then he rummaged through the bath oil selection. Finally choosing one, he poured it into the water.

Alice wanted to fall asleep, but she did not want to miss a moment of this pleasure. The feel of Ciccone's gentle touch as he removed her diamond bracelet and slipped it in his pocket was worth the theft of it. She heard a soft rustling next to the tub and realized that it was Ciccone taking off his clothing: she heard the buckle of his belt and the jingle of a zipper. She heard the clothing falling to soft piles on the tile and she saw his black-furred toes as he dunked his feet into the water.

His knees were bony and darkly furred, his thighs the same. His chest only had a triangle of hair. His arms were furred, however, very much like a proper Italian man. She glimpsed the fur on his crotch, the peek of a cock before it all sank into the water.

The air smelled like tuberose and vanilla, like spices and buttered roses. She let her hands float. She let her legs unfold. Her cheek fell against his chest and she felt his thighs underneath her. She felt his penis, which hardened against her. She wondered if he would jam it up her cunt and knew that if he did, it would probably kill her.

Her bladder let loose and the urine felt like a razor blade escaping her body.

"Ow!" she squeaked.

"Am I hurting you?" Ciccone asked gently, and the softness of his voice hurt her even more. She felt tears and agony, all of it contorting her chest and her breast, ripping her lungs. It made her imagine herself hanging from a ceiling with her ribs shattered and her organs hanging.

Does he feel me pissing into the tub? The warmth of it?

It did not matter.

She fell asleep.

Stars fired in her brain; they fizzled in her blood. She dreamed she'd agreed to Ciccone's offer of escape and that he was taking her somewhere new and soft. She dreamed of pillows and caramels. She dreamed that they were lying in a bed together and that he was touching her hair and then that he was brushing her hair. She dreamed that he was her father and that he was sucking on her breasts. She dreamed that her pussy had turned into chocolate cake, and he was eating it and telling her how good she was and that his bites were bigger and bigger, and that he was eating all the way up to her womb and that she was screaming for him to stop and that the quick of her womb felt like the nerve in a tooth when a dentist had filed off too much enamel and she was screaming…

Alice woke to Ciccone, a hand on each of her shoulders, gently shaking her.

"Last chance, babe. Let me take you out of here. You were having a fucking nightmare."

"What would you do with me? If I left with you? Can I sleep in your bed?"

"I have a girl at home. I have a baby."

"Then leave me here," Alice said.

Ciccone sat her on the bath rug, he rubbed lotion on her, even down to her toes. His hands were rough but gentle, in the way that a man might be if he were used to doting on a woman. He must be good to his girlfriend. She imagined he had women pining for him in different apartments, women who probably only bought drugs off him just so they could see him and suck his cock.

He wrapped her in a fluffy bathrobe that smelled like Jonathan. Their eyes met, his gaze so kind, and Alice wished her face wasn't so swollen and haggard, and that her body wasn't so injured. She wanted him to kiss her and seduce her, she wanted him to fall in love with her and chase her.

"I wish we could kiss," Alice said.

Ciccone leaned in, but stopped short of kissing her.

"Fuck," he muttered, reaching into his pocket and removing her diamond bracelet. He wrapped it back around Alice's wrist, clicking the clasp shut.

Tears filled Alice's eyes, and they fell. "You can keep it. For your baby!"

"It's the only nice thing you fucking own," Ciccone said. "You might as well be buried in it. 'Unknown Girl in a Tennis Bracelet' has a nice ring for a tombstone."

I'll go with you, Alice thought. The base of her throat ached with the urge to shout, to beg him to take her, to tell him that he was correct, and to thank him for rescuing her. She said nothing out loud, however, and settled for imagining the etched marble of her tombstone.

"Can you stand up?" He asked.

"I think so."

If he picks me up and takes me out the front door, Alice thought, *I'll let him.*

When she stood, her legs wobbled. She leaned against him, and he walked her out of the bathroom, directly into Jonathan's broad chest.

"Fuck," Ciccone said.

TEN

"Leaving with her?" Jonathan said.

Jonathan was bare-chested, fit as Achilles and peachy pink. He was barefoot as well, sporting only a pair of low-slung jeans.

"Nope," Ciccone said. "She's your girl."

Ciccone's strong, protective hands left Alice's shoulders, and she felt so exposed and abandoned. She had never known such true fear.

"Good," Jonathan said. "I think you should fucking leave, now."

"Was just helping her to bed," Ciccone said. He stepped away from Alice completely, and she wobbled.

"Oh really?"

Alice screamed. The pull on her scalp was sudden and intense, and she was not feeling so much the pain but the shock and the humiliation of Jonathan gripping her hair and dragging her. Her legs did not work, so she stumbled like a calf being ripped from its stall to slaughter. She jammed her knee against something, she cried out again, and then her body bounced onto the couch, onto Felix who, startled, sat up.

She heard men's voices, a symphony of madness. She let tears fall but she didn't open her eyes, she listened to the voice that could be Ciccone's, he was speaking to her, his voice against his ear, but there were no words she could decipher, it was noise and there was just the feeling of finality.

She heard a door slam.

She heard Jonathan's voice.

She heard Felix's.

She heard words that were not words.

She heard the slap of Jonathan's palm against her cheek, she did not feel it.

She heard Felix yelling and the sound of her body falling hard against the ground as Jonathan hit her again.

She did not feel it.

She knew Ciccone was gone now, and she felt stupid and abandoned.

She heard Jonathan laugh as his fingers slipped with agonizing force up her damaged vagina and pushed her against a wall.

She thought of her conversation with Jonathan on the balcony. She'd heard the whispers and read the forum articles about the possible science that was being worked on to erase the traumas of refugees who had suffered war crimes. She'd never given the idea much beyond surface consideration; she felt apart from — and, if she was being honest, superior to— even the idea of being made vulnerable by proximity to war or needing refuge. She'd been so powerful, in her glass bubble of arrogance.

But here was trauma — pure, happening, unfiltered — engulfing her own brain, swirling with doubt and conjecture, with panic, and clouded with mistakes and shame.

She could not remember how anything felt before this moment. She could only feel how everything hurt now.

"Open your fucking eyes," Jonathan growled.

And Alice did.

What Jonathan saw was the girl's irises black as pitch, round like a cat looking at prey.

Her bottom lip was swollen and split, a steady drip of blood trickling from it; there was a bruise on the side of her cheek, and some swelling. A lump was starting to form on her forehead. This was not a pretty girl in front of them. Just an abused slut. She did not fight him when he jammed his cock up her cunt, but she screamed and he covered her mouth, watched the tears falling over his fingers as he kept her pinned against the wall.

"What are you up to, anyway?" Jonathan said. "I know we've been over this like eleven fucking times. I'm just going to keep asking you and fucking you and asking you until there's nothing left to fuck."

And he raped her with a force she had not thought possible, not even in anything she had ever read — not accounts from victims or cautionary tales, not the fevered imaginings of de Sade's stories. None of it could have prepared Alice for this physical pain that finally sent her body into numbed shock, a tinnitus-like squeal in her ears. She could feel her consciousness slipping, contorting, her sanity draining…

"Jonathan," Felix protested weakly, "just let her…"

Oh, blessed Felix, she thought, *so simple and sweet.*

She regretted every happenstance and decision that had brought her to this moment. She mourned the death of the arrogant young girl who had foolishly assumed she could walk this path, and she thought with fresh longing about how she should have said yes to Felix when he'd asked her to marry him. Her brain transported her to a world where she would feel his heart going like mad and she would say yes, she would, yes… and she began to imagine the fever in her blood cells boiling her body, she imagined holding Felix to her breasts, married to him, reclining with him on linen sheets in some exotic country as they both died from slit wrists…

Jonathan dropped Alice off his cock, and she stayed standing against the wall, bleeding freshly down her leg. He used the hem of the bathrobe she was wearing to wipe himself off. Her eyes were on him, the tears had stopped, and she weakly held the bathrobe closed with one hand.

"Just let me sleep a little," Alice said, and her voice was graveled from thirst and exhaustion. Her lids were low, her eyes pink. "Then we can talk?"

"No," Jonathan said, and he slapped her sore cheek. "No. We are talking now." He slapped her lightly again.

Alice cringed away from the slap, unable to even tolerate an ounce of pain anymore. She whimpered, and the flinch was everything to Jonathan. Everything inside him celebrated, an explosion of fire and fizz, stars of victory. It was like hearing a dying pig scream when finally overcome by dogs. It was like hearing a dying dog whimpering as it looked up to you for validation.

"Listen, darling," he said, and he grabbed one of Alice's soft breasts and squeezed it until she cried out, then he squeezed it harder, and she screamed and struggled against him. Jonathan let her tit go, ignoring Felix who tugged against his shoulder, and he took Alice by the throat and pulled her up. She choked and kicked and wheezed, and Jonathan felt for all the world like a villain in a novel, a villain in her fairy tale. And this angel in his hands, who had just wanted a fucking, was about to get fucked hard.

He let go of her, and she scrambled on her hands and knees away from him, to the couch where Felix joined her. She cried out and inhaled sharply, the wet sound of snot and tears escaping her throat, which she cradled with her hands. Felix's fingers held her cheeks, and she felt his lips on her forehead. He whispered to her, meaningless things, because none of his words had any power to help her.

"You look scared now," Jonathan said.

"Jonathan, stop!" Felix said. He put his arms around Alice and held her to him tightly, only to have Jonathan pull her from his arms and then set her down roughly onto the couch.

Jonathan knelt next to the couch. He smelled fear on the girl, acrid and cutting through the soft scent of the flowered oils from the bathtub. Her hair was still damp. She looked fresh and fucked at the same time. He lifted her chin with his finger.

God, but he felt superior. He was a man. He was a lord. He could buy this child ten times over and sell her twenty. He could kill her and hide her. He was high on victory, and her large Spanish-looking eyes told him that she knew it.

"What are we going to talk about, sweetie?" Jonathan said, and he fought against a weird flash in his gut, because the girl's eyes suddenly looked familiar. He imagined her lips cherry red, and her eyes slathered in black makeup. "Are you high on enough trauma now? Hm? Did our Uncle Bertrand send you to us? Are you going back to him so he can carve it from your brain? Are you one of his lab bunnies, little white rabbit?"

"I…no," Alice said, her gaze unsteady, her lips trembling, "I don't know what you're talking about… no."

"Saint Anne Corporation? Hm? Do you know about it?" Jonathan pressed. "Nothing? It would probably be better for you if that were true, if we could just turn you over to them, back to the madhouse where you came from."

"No," Alice whispered, fresh tears falling down her cheeks. "No, I wish that were true. I would say yes, if I believed you would take me to a hospital. A looney bin? I'll take it. Please… let me go there. I promise I won't say anything, I'm sorry. I'm sorry. Please, let me make this better…

I don't…"

"You don't what?"

Alice thought of the day her father had surprised her with the diamonds that now circled her wrist. His perpetually exasperated eyes softening a bit, the love in his face. She remembered his hug, how good it felt, how it turned into a five-minute father-daughter cuddle. *Safety… warmth… love…* If this was her end, she wanted to remember only that moment.

"I don't want to die!" Alice screamed. "Please!"

Felix was crying. Jonathan filled a glass with sparkling water and let Alice drink it. She enjoyed the burn of the bubbles and the water filling her throat, her tummy. It was so clean that it gave her hope. Jonathan took the glass from her when she was done, and then he stroked her hair.

"Come on," he said gently, and she almost became convinced that his anger was permanently gone and that he was not going to hit her anymore. "Talk to me. Let's talk."

Alice didn't dare look Jonathan in the face. She glanced at Felix, who was rocking back and forth rhythmically, his eyes rolled back. Behind him, the French doors of the balcony remained open, and a flock of crows stared into the apartment. She imagined their eyes were all on her, waiting for Jonathan to snap her neck and leave her body for them to pick apart.

"I like dinner parties," Alice said. She took her attention from the birds, not wanting Jonathan to get the same idea she had. She pulled the bathrobe tighter around her body and groaned as she angled herself away from Jonathan, her eyes pinching shut. Then she opened them. "All of us like dinner parties."

Jonathan sighed, but he did not say anything.

Felix, no longer crying, he slid closer to Alice. He took her hand into his, pressed it into his palms, and at the touch he reacted quickly with concern.

"Jonathan," he gasped, "She's burning up! I think…" he touched her forehead and cheeks, "I think she might be sick!"

He tried to make eye contact with her, offering empathy she could not seem to absorb.

He's dead to me, she thought dully. She no longer bothered to register anything he said. *Useless.*

"She's fine, just fucked up," Jonathan replied, "and, Felix, don't think I didn't see you sneaking more than your fair share of the 'shrooms earlier, even after I told you how fucked up you'd get from a large dose, Felix. You fucking idiot, you don't eat that shit like salad garnish, you're supposed to micro-dose it."

Felix swallowed, noticing his throat becoming tight, and he stared at Jonathan and imagined that Jonathan was flickering like static in a bad video signal…

"Whenever you're at a dinner party, either of you," Alice said, rubbing her palms together, "at your home, do you ever remember the maid with the silver bell, do you ever miss when she would ring it and you could see the fat on her upper arm jiggle, and she used to let you pinch it?"

The memory flashed through Jonathan, like something that burned through his intestines and detonated. It slimed its way through Felix, like cold, mud that filled his belly and twisted his guts. The men did not even need to look at each other to know what they both felt.

"Our sister hated touching her fat, and we made her," Felix said. "Jonathan, remember…"

"Shut up, Felix!" Jonathan said.

"But, Jonathan," Felix said.

"Shut up!"

Alice looked at Felix, a solemn expression, soulful in a way that the romantic painters used to capture. Her hand went to the base of her throat, her fingers tapped the tender flesh in a way Felix remembered his sister doing, the way she STILL did in his dreams.

Felix caught himself up in staring at Alice's wet hair, and he noticed that it was glittering, slithering, twitching like a nest of snakes and he thought of Medusa, a raped woman on her knees at the feet of a Goddess who condemned her for her frailty against a God's cock…

"So, what?" Jonathan said. "I remember that maid. She got caught fucking our butler during working hours, in our pantry, near the food we were supposed to be eating, like a dirty bitch, and she was fired. Are you her daughter, or something? Did she fill you with some sort of revenge fantasy to come after us with?"

"I don't even know that maid's name," Alice said. "She was a woman my mom used to bribe to get entry into your house at odd hours."

"Okay, shut the fuck up!" Jonathan snapped.

Felix dry heaved. He jumped up, stumbling everywhere like a dog on fire, knocking over lamps, falling over furniture. He had indeed taken a large dose of mushrooms when Jonathan's back was turned, and those 'shrooms were now in full bloom within Felix's addled brain. Jonathan had taken a serving seemingly so miniscule that Felix had thought that it would give him a leg up on Jonathan if he could take a larger dose… a considerably larger one.

Jonathan felt red. Red, red, red, he swallowed, and it was red, and he exhaled, and it was red. The girl in front of him looked pink. He inhaled and it was pink. Her eyes were pink, but for Jonathan, he was high on the self-righteous knowledge that he had properly micro-dosed.

Jonathan inhaled slowly. He could hear Felix stumbling onto the balcony, his cries becoming loud. The crows croaked and squawked but did not fly away, they merely hopped onto the balcony railing where they stared curiously, expectantly at Felix.

Jonathan remembered a time when these memories were as raw as soft duck meat sliding down the throat, still twitching and bleeding. He remembered the long months that Mom was gone while pregnant with his baby sister. He never even got to see her belly bulge. She had summered, then autumn'd, then wintered in France; she came back pink-faced and puffy, bringing with her a pink and olive little baby with large Spanish eyes and pink lips.

"I remember the bell!" Felix yelled into the sky, causing the crows to take flight in an explosive movement of feathers and wings. He was covered in sweat, the dry air on the balcony kissing his flesh, and he looked at the crows dotting the clouds and yelled, "I remembered it! I always did!"

"It's true," Jonathan said, "but then again, you could have heard that from any of the help we grew up with."

"When she'd get dessert first," Alice said. "Your mother would give your Alice dessert first."

"Again, any of the fucking help could have…" Jonathan said, and his voice was rising.

His nostrils were aflame with the memory of how his sister smelled like vanilla, and chocolate, like strawberries and wax, like Chapstick and perfume. She often smelled like despair cutting through the soft scents, just like this girl before him smelled like fear… it was a musk that couldn't be captured and safely sold, lest the world turned into a rutting pit of orgies and gangbangs, an eternal rape of an eternal pit of virgins.

"If I did this with my hair," Alice said and she slowly lifted her hands and pulled her fingers through her hair and then pulled half of her hair back, she kept her hand pinched on it as if there were a bow holding it up. The movements seemed so slow and languid to Jonathan that he saw blurred color and double-exposed images. "Didn't she do this with her hair?"

Shit…

Jonathan felt superiority blown away with obviousness, as he looked at Alice's face and knew the inescapable undeniable truth.

"Alice," he said.

"But I'm the unloved one," Alice said.

"You're…" Jonathan said.

Felix stumbled back into the room, "Alice?"

This was their sister on the couch, in the flesh, back from the dead, with actual tits and nutrition, perhaps a little aged…? Perhaps? But, no, she was not. Not aged a day.

"How could you be the same, though?" Jonathan said, he couldn't believe that the first stage of his micro-dose had him talking with his dead fucking sister, "You'd be only a little younger than Felix now, you'd be nearly twenty, you can't have stayed the same."

He thought of the beauty, the silhouette of his sister as she arced in the sky, the sun before her as if she could grab it and hug it, suspended in time and freedom before disappearing past the balcony, before landing on a car, before crushing the top of it. The screams of horrified people from the street below, and not going to the balcony to see it, because why should anyone have that as the last memory of their sister?

Now, Jonathan wished that he'd gone to look, that he had a last image of her corpse, because now, as her doppelgänger sat before him on this couch, he couldn't definitively say a god damn thing. "You couldn't have survived that fall. I watched you jump. I heard you land. Even if you'd survived, you would be scarred as fuck." Jonathan said.

"Alice?" Felix said. He tottered back into the apartment, staring hopefully at Alice's battered face. "Our Alice?"

"Alice," Alice replied. "But not yours."

Jonathan grabbed her cheeks into his hands, and he did not squeeze though he wanted to, did not shake her, although he wanted to. But his voice was low, and it was lethal.

"What. The. Fuck. Is. Going. On."

"Every day," Alice said, "every day since I was young, my mother told me about Alice. Your sister, Alice. She told me about her dark eyes, and her soft skin, like she was a princess in a Grimm's Tale. She told me about her long ebony hair that was soft and fine, she told me about how sweet and trusting she was. She told me about how she adored her brothers, and loved the mother that wasn't hers…"

Now, Jonathan did squeeze her. "What?"

Alice lifted her palms and pressed them over Jonathan's hands, her oxygen was completely cut off, her vision darkening, her palms were cool and soft. The blood was leaving her body. It was staining through her bathrobe, spurting from between her legs. Jonathan released her throat so she could speak.

Alice gasped out, closed her eyes, her hands over her throat but she quickly composed herself, breathing in through her nostrils out through her lips. She was burning with fever, she knew, but her flesh trembled with cold, her hands were trembling, and her body felt like glass. It had to be an infection, from any of the moments her ass and cunt had been desecrated until bleeding. These could be her last breaths, she was sure of it, she could now feel the finality of it, and she thought of her father's hug, her father's love, her father....

"My mom showed me pictures of her every day, she told me the story of how she gave birth to the perfect little nut of a baby, and how the perfect little baby fixed everything from the rape that caused her. Because it was a dinner party where she was raped by your father, and he had his young son help hold her down…"

"Noooooo!" Felix screamed and he staggered out of the room again, back onto the balcony.

This time, Jonathan's eyes darted to the balcony. "Felix," he said, "Get back over here. For one, it is a fucking lie. Felix, you would have been a tiny child, a TODDLER, when Mom got pregnant, even in this little liar's phantasmagoric scenario."

"Mom told me it was only *you*," Alice said, she pointed at Jonathan. "Just a young boy who held her ankles, your father yelled at you to do it, and you just as much a victim as she. She stopped struggling because she didn't want to kick a little boy in the face, but apparently it was a story you used to repeat to Felix when you were…"

An explosion of light as Jonathan slapped Alice again, and she did not even feel pain, just exhilaration; she peeked at Jonathan as he looked towards Felix. His face was red.

"Felix, I'm not fucking kidding!" Jonathan said. "Get the fuck back over here."

"I remember you told me about holding her legs!" Felix cried, he stumbled back into the apartment and fell to his knees, his eyes were wide, the green irises dancing, his skin was mottled pink and red, and his hair seemed darker because it was soaked with sweat, "you told me! We were young and you said once Dad had you help hold down a crazy woman. You said Dad hit her! She was crazy or something! I remember it almost as if I were there helping, but it's because I remember *you* talking about it!"

The crows landed on the balcony behind Felix, staring into the apartment again.

This memory was reemerging like an insect from a board full of holes. And the balcony floor underneath his feet imploded into a million sponge-like holes squirming with grubs and insects, crawling onto his flesh, burrowing into it… A crow behind Felix darted forward and pinched one of his toes with enough force to cause a wail from the young man.

"Mommy gave birth," Alice said, and her voice rose high like a child's would, "Mommy gave birth to a beautiful baby, and she named her Alice. And Daddy hugged them both and then took the baby from her arms and she screamed, and she screamed for days, she wanted her baby back, she wanted her Alice back, but he'd handed her to the woman with pale white skin and red lips. Mommy was never supposed to see her again, but she kept sneaking to your house, she even paid the maid to keep an eye on Alice, and sometimes Mommy snuck to your house to give her Alice gifts, but she could never get her baby back!"

"Fuck…" Jonathan said.

He remembered a wild-eyed, beautiful woman, pushing over the crib and the baby would not stop crying, and Jonathan had dived in to rescue that baby, holding the precious creature to his body. His own mother had run into the room and the women fought like tigers, clawing and screaming until a housekeeper called the police. He was a small kid at the time, but remembered keenly not wanting his baby sister to be harmed by this intruder. And his mother was always tender and loving with his little sister afterwards, but that moment… He remembered all of that now, for the first time in nearly two decades.

Things aren't forgotten, they're just… not thought about, aren't they?

"They found out about Mommy sneaking to the house," Alice said, "and they told the servants not to accept any sort of bribe from her. When she was banned from the house, she cried for weeks."

"Oh *GOD!*" Felix screamed, and he began crying out to the heavens, "GOD, GOD, GOD!" Two more crows had swooped onto him, and he spun around on the balcony, kicking and flailng. The birds stayed just out of reach, cackling and squeaking.

"And then," Alice said, "Daddy realized he had to make Mommy stop crying so he held her down and she got pregnant again. And she gave birth," and she pressed her fingers harder into Jonathan's hands, and then she pressed her palm to her breast, "To me, another Alice!"

Alice flashed a dazzling smile, beautiful if only for a moment.

"It's not true," Jonathan said, and he slid his hands to the sides of Alice's throat. He did not squeeze, just cupped her neck between his palms. He leaned her forehead against his. "You insane little bitch, none of that is true. It would be so easy to fabricate the basics of what you just said, with the most minimal of efforts. You do realize this?"

Alice did not flinch.

Jonathan saw his sister's eyes, he saw his sister's face when she cried, he fucking remembered her scent. He remembered her skin, her flesh, the texture of her hair, the flecks of fur around her cunt. He saw it on this girl who called herself by his sister's name and he knew he was seeing what she wanted him to see.

He was not a fool; he was a man, and a well-evolved one at that. Could he go past it all and admit to at least feeling the things he *should* feel attached to memory? That did not mean this present reality she was peddling was real — this creature in front of him, this imposter.

"If you are, who you say you are," Jonathan said, "that means your father is Richard Talbot. I remember it was Richard's psychotic wife,

Briony, who was harassing our family, appearing uninvited in our home. I remember being a little kid and her giving me some candy, even. She's locked up for good, now, isn't she?"

Alice blinked rapidly. "She has an apartment in Paris."

"That's nice," Jonathan replied, with a sarcastic cut. "So, does she still pine away for my sister Alice?"

"And *my* sister Alice," Alice replied. "She was my half-sister, just as she was half yours. Her mother was my mother, her father, your father."

"It's bullshit," Jonathan said. "Bullshit."

"It's not."

"If it were true," Jonathan said, "like I said, it would mean that our families are close. We would have been at all the same dinner parties, holiday parties, fundraisers, functions. It would mean…" and Jonathan shook his head, with another realization, an obvious one. He picked up the cocaine-dusted album cover from the coffee table and held it up to Alice: "It would *mean* that your sister is Brennan Talbot. And seeing as you *hate* her and her music so much, this definitely *wouldn't* be the first time I'd be hearing that she's your fucking *sister*."

"It isn't," Alice said flatly. "In fact, I specifically *told* you that my sister is a singer. You just don't listen."

Already gaps were filling inside Jonathan's brain, flashes like from an analog camera. Moments captured and oversaturated, his cheeks pressed between both Brennan and Alice as they posed for a selfie. He already knew that if he opened his Instagram right now and scrolled through it, he would see eventually see Alice's photograph, he would see her slathered and caked in too much makeup with an Ariana Grande-style ponytail, with her big sister Brennan and the other sister, that pale chubby dumpling Mari.

"Our fathers have been friends for a couple decades," Jonathan said, defeat dampening his tone. "Dad was the first one to give Richard a chance curating a gallery. He had a crazy psycho wife we sometimes saw at functions, a couple of ex-wives, three daughters. The little one, Alice, always wears her hair in a tight ponytail, wears too much makeup, so much makeup that apparently it's impossible to recognize her without it."

He took a good look at Alice's face now, completely recognizing her. "Little Alice is obsessed with Kate Spade, pop singers, and other shallow shit. Her only real charm is an amazing pair of tits; by the way…" Jonathan shook his head, shook off reality, glared at Alice, "nice touch, you little imposter, for doing your research."

"My older sister *is* Brennan," Alice said, nodding, "and she fucked your dad. Argyll gave her a pink Hermès purse, and she just tossed it at me, said I could have it. Literally the coolest thing she's ever given to me. Brennan is also my half-sister: Dad was fucking her mom while married to my Mommy. Anyway, I interviewed you and Brennan both for *Prodigal Son* magazine. Remember that? The Garden Party at the Cromwell estate?"

Jonathan liked winning. He liked being right. But he was — or, at least, wanted to believe that he was — also an old-school gentleman who could accept when he had lost. Yet, he could not understand how or why this was happening. He felt the beginnings of a bad dream. It was the only explanation for any of this: the drugs, the sex, even fucking grabbing Felix's cock. For all of this.

Because now that he saw Alice, he realized that it was not a trick of memory or mushrooms. As much as she resembled his dead sister, he now saw plainly that she was Richard Talbot's daughter, the same one who had sat across from him surrounded by photographer's lights and microphones, trying to act the part of a charming socialite about to "interview" social-media-famous peers as a gimmick for a trash magazine. *Prodigal Son.* At that time, she'd had cherry-red lipstick and severely plucked brows, like a 1920s flapper; her long hair had been tied back into a severe ponytail. On that day, she had been a "someone" — Richard Talbot's very underage daughter.

Mere hours into the gathering — before it had turned into a highbrow Millennial/Gen Z pandemic orgy — Talbot had taken his underage daughter back home, leaving her elder sisters to their revelry. When Jonathan had thought Alice was some gold-digging, no make-up wearing escort, she had been a "no one" — and he had not recognized a single fucking thing about her.

This mistake… this fucking mistake…

"Why the fuck is this *happening?*" He was genuinely at a loss.

"Because you didn't recognize me," Alice replied.

Jonathan grabbed her ear and twisted it. Alice cried out and slapped at his hand. He let her go.

"What the fuck is this shit?" Jonathan fumed. "You're a little fucking kid, if you are who you say you are." He pointed his finger into her face. "You're *too young* for your big sister's friends, and there's *NO fucking reason* we should have recognized you! You little brat! Whatever you are doing for your psychotic mother is just because she loved *our sister* — whom she was obsessed with — and *not you*.

"Did it ever occur to you that she drilled that fucked-up story into your head for so long, described my sister to you in such complete detail, that you began to take on what you knew of her personality and her looks? Did that ever occur to you? That you might not even be a real person? Not even have a self!"

Alice frowned and she scratched her upper arm, absent-mindedly like a child would.

"Could be," she said, her tone neutral, like a shrug. "I've thought about it that way. I asked Dad about it once and he told me to forget about Mom's crazy stories. I mean, there really is no reason that she couldn't be just a nutcase. I only ever saw your sister Alice at the odd party here or there; Dad had me at a boarding school near Aspen most of the time. I mostly just saw her on Instagram."

"And your mom?" Jonathan asked. "When was the last time you

ever discussed any of this shit with her?"

Alice's eyelids fluttered, and she closed them.

"I haven't spoken to my mom in a while."

The heavy weight of her mother's absence felt renewed on Alice's shoulders. In truth, she had not seen Briony in over a year; she had not been able to speak to her for months. The very thought of her mother's abandonment pushed her down again, now — when she most needed strength.

"And it was *so goddamn important* to play this out?" Jonathan said. He spoke with an aggrieved air, without irony; his tone that of someone who believes they hold the moral high ground. "You have *terrorized* me and my brother these past two days. Do you not understand that?"

"*Terrorized?*" Alice lifted her chin, her eyes closing in pain, and she laughed. Her robe fell a little open, her soft, large tits trembling, her flesh covered in bite marks and bruises. Her joy, her instant amusement almost made the bruise on her lip disappear; and, it made her beautiful.

Jonathan pointed towards the balcony, where Felix was still screaming and flailing, swatting at the air as if it were filled with birds. "What about the state of him? *You're* fucking responsible for that. He's the sweetest boy you — that this Earth — will ever know. He was genuinely *in love* with you! Look what you've *done* to him!" He was shouting now, his finger in her face again.

"Not my fault he's a pussy," Alice replied. "Anyway, you're just mad because now we *both* know that Felix has more cock on him than you could ever—"

And Jonathan slapped her.

Alice did not recover from this slap. She slumped onto the couch, staring at the cushion, a fresh line of blood dribbling from her lips, soaking in, creating a raspberry circle.

"Mom calls it Dark Paradise," Alice said quietly, she wiped the back of her hand over her lips. "This world — *our* world. She's right, you know. You can call her crazy all you want, but this place *is* a dark paradise. She loved Alice… she said I was just like her. That I would be an angel, but when I get fucked…"

Jonathan stared at her. She was leaning on one elbow now, her breast hanging out of her robe, eyes on him like a coyote in a leg trap staring its executioner in the face.

"And is this blackmail?"

Alice frowned. "I don't know. Maybe?"

"And how are you not implicated if it were? Say you decide to blackmail us. Those videos on my phone? They implicate *you* — tricking us, convincing us that you're of age! They show you egging us on, they are as consensual as —" he stumbled over his words for a moment "— as anything."

"I suppose they are," Alice said. "I don't know."

There was no reason to not know at this point. Of course he knew her. Of course he should have known. Of course those videos would never stand up in court, Jonathan remembered her, little wannabe journalist, her obsession with trendy fashion, her hipster culture magazine chasing after interviews of young, hip rich kids. He remembered the Talbot girls, just like any number of other society girls, trying their best to mimic a breezy, kitschy disaffection as if they'd fallen into the world out of a Wes Anderson movie.

"I remember a lavender dress you wore once," Jonathan said. "And I thought to myself how much better you'd look in blue."

Alice closed her eyes.

Jonathan remembered the garden party, after Alice had left with her father — how he'd seen Brennan screaming at his own father, and her other sister, Mari, dragging her away. He remembered asking Brennan what her deal was, later that evening. And Brennnan had only said that his father was a piece of shit, to which, at the time, Jonathan had laughingly agreed.

"What about the box of condoms in your purse? Why were you carrying those around?" Jonathan asked. "And why don't you have a phone? Where's your wallet and ID?"

Alice's eyelids fluttered, her lips slack. "Those were for Brennan. My *sister*. I was supposed to meet her that morning, and she asked me to bring some condoms for her. She just wanted a few, but I got her the biggest box I could find from the bathroom."

"A box of 24?" Jonathan said with a frown.

"Well… she's going on the road soon, she likes sex."

"Runs in the family, apparently," Jonathan muttered. "And no phone? No wallet?"

"Phone's broken," Alice said. "Brennan and I got into a fight on the phone with each other before I left the apartment. She'd been checking out your Instagram, and she told me she was going to fuck you because…" Alice looked away from Jonathan, ". . . because she knew I had a crush on you. And I threw my phone and smashed it."

Alice blew out through her lips.

Jonathan pinched the bridge of his nose. He remembered Alice so keenly now. That little girl with too much makeup who was always staring at him. He'd known for awhile that she had a little crush on him; it was how he'd come, in the first place, to form the habit of ignoring her sometimes. This was not a fact he could deny or escape anymore. He knew… he knew… he'd always known.

"And I usually carry just cash," Alice added, shrugging. "I don't need a wallet, really. I'm not eighteen yet, so I don't see the point of running around with an ID."

"Not eighteen yet," Jonathan muttered. "Not eighteen."

Alice and Jonathan stared at each other.

"So, what now?" Alice asked.

"What now?" Jonathan sighed. "How about welcome to the family.

Hm?"

"*Alice!*" Felix screamed, still flailing. It was a small miracle he hadn't gone over the side of the balcony yet. "Alice, Alice, Alice!"

His screams floated over the balcony, into the sky, reverberating everywhere. They were the sound of something irretrievably broken.

"You know I'm telling the truth," Alice said. "You know it in your bones. I'm telling the *truth*, you useless motherfucker."

"Fucking idiot," Jonathan replied. It was a stock response, a weak insult, and he knew it. He could think of nothing else to say.

"My mom loved you so much," Alice said. "She loved you almost as much as she loved our sister Alice. She was glad that our Alice had you and Felix both as her brothers; despite your shithead rapist father, she thought you boys were the ideal."

"I *did* treasure my baby sister," Jonathan cut in, "because she was everything you're not: a gracious, darling little lady. You see, that girl could come — *you*, however, are a skinny, bitter, frigid little bitch."

"What the fuck ever," Alice replied, her voice growing sharp and aggressive as she drew from her last reservoir of strength. "I'm sure she was faking it, like any woman would with you, you clumsy inbred nephilim!" She attempted to smirk, but her swollen lips refused to take the shape. Her eyes, however, conveyed her contempt. "Am I supposed to be surprised, to find out you're a sister-fucker too? Nothing's too low for a man like you. The only question left at this point is: did we go too far?"

"We may have," Jonathan replied. A grin twitched the corner of his lip, and Alice's expression mirrored it back to him. "We just may have. I think we've broken Felix."

"Alice!" Felix screamed.

"He could be manageable," Alice said. "He could get the same treatment as my mother. They could be roommates in Paris."

Alice's brain sparkled with the images she'd seen of her mom's Instagram feed — a divorced, wealthy woman, finally finding her stride in Paris, living in the Bastille neighborhood, endless photographs of coffee cups, neon signs from the late-night jazz clubs She'd never once invited her daughter to visit, never once responded to Alice's repeated pleas to see her again.

"Don't compare my brother to your stupid-as-shit mother," Jonathan said.

"Do you think there's going to be a wedding now, for either of you??" Alice asked calmly, holding his gaze. "Do you really think Felix is going to go through with it?"

"He sure as shit will," Jonathan said. "After the wedding, we're going to be part owners of some of the most prestigious art galleries in Europe. There is *no way* Dad is going to lose out on…"

Jonathan stopped speaking abruptly, a sudden onslaught of needles pounding his flesh and slicing his veins. He felt sickened. He felt everything someone feels when they have lost a major hand in a card game, a last hand on which they've bet not only every penny, but their dog and car as well.

"You little bitch," Jonathan muttered. He looked out the open French doors at Felix because he could not stomach Alice's large eyes. A crow was standing next to Felix's ankles, pecking at his leg, and there was blood running down the leg. His green eyes were terrified, stretched large and round like glass domes. He was wringing his hands together, in that annoying fucking way he always had when he was being a pussy about something.

"Felix, you're getting married, right? *We're* getting married soon?"

"No!" Felix screamed back. "I will *never* get married! I am *not*! I want *Alice*, I just want Alice! I want Alice!"

Jonathan looked at Alice to see a smug, tickled look on her swollen, bruised face. He stood up, curling his fists as Felix continued to yell unintelligibly.

"Your father is cut from the Forrester Foundation after the wedding," Jonathan said to Alice. "The paperwork, the buyout, everything is in place. Richard Talbot is going to keep one of the galleries here in Denver, and that's it. He's losing control of everything else. It's been discussed with him: he'd asked for a chance to have more individual distinction apart from the Forrester Foundation, and Dad did not take kindly to it. He's cutting your father loose, did you know about this?"

Felix came back into the apartment and slumped down against the wall, covering his face with his hands.

Alice did not blink or make a move to indicate the truth of any of it. "I'm a smart girl. I figure things out."

"My fiancée's mother is the owner of the Solti Art Network. Solti Art and The Forrester Foundation will merge after the wedding, which will very much put our family in control of the global art world," Jonathan sighed and scratched the side of his nose. He inhaled slowly. He'd have to explain this to her like a child — because she fucking was one. "If we don't get these marriages accomplished, and if Brennan fucking Talbot runs around with a new song about how we raped her little sister it would be… problematic. Do you understand that?"

"Brennan will probably be jealous, so I doubt she'll write a song about it," Alice replied.

"So here it is," Jonathan said. "Finally, the truth. All this bullshit about your mother, all this bullshit about your quirky delicate sensibilities, but when it comes down to it, you're just a carnivorous rich kid like my brother and me, and all of this is smoke and mirrors in front of a business coup. You're the dutiful daughter protecting Daddy's tenuous hold on wealth and status."

Two tears fell, one from each of Alice's eyes.

"Really?" Jonathan said.

"My dad is just heartbroken to get dumped like this," Alice replied. "He didn't send me to do any of this. He loves your dad like a brother.

I…"

"And this entire story about your mother?"

"It's probably true," Alice said. "The weirdest stories are, aren't they? When the news broke that your sister killed herself, my mom never recovered. She had her worst nervous breakdown. When she got out she barely talked to me, barely looked at me, wouldn't hug me, wouldn't do anything with me unless Dad made her. She finally just picked up and left us, and she's happier I think. I guess, as long as I leave her alone, I suppose."

"Does it matter to you?" Jonathan asked. "You're a Daddy's girl anyway and she sounds like a dick. I don't buy this as your origin story."

Alice shrugged.

Alice closed her eyes, they burned. She did not want to open them again, ever. She could feel the throbbing, stinging burning between her legs that was like slow, sticky blood and pain. She was injured. Bruised everywhere. *You don't even have a self*, Jonathan had taunted her. Who the fuck was she?

Mom, you fucking left me and I fucking wish you could see me now, Alice thought.

"I don't care what you believe. The fact stands that I am clearly underage. I am the victim, period. I am the one you are legally culpable for hurting — and not only that, even your fucking drug dealer is convinced I'm insane." Alice let out a brittle laugh. "My mother has a history of mental illness. At absolute *best*, you and your brother are using the days before your weddings to take advantage of an underage, mentally ill girl. Congratulations."

"How did you plan that?" Jonathan asked, his forehead burned with his throbbing brain. "How could you plan out all of this? How did you know we would show up in that coffee shop, at that moment…?"

"I didn't," Alice said. "That's the kicker. I was only there to meet up with Brennan, I said that before. None of this would have happened if Brennan hadn't been running late. In fact, Dad is probably going nuts wondering where I am."

The rolling boil in Jonathan's gut continued to churn; he thought of the rapidly increasing number of unanswered text messages clogging his phone. He felt something even worse than being tricked — he felt the complete idiocy of protecting and controlling Felix their entire life, guiding his every move, mocking him for wanting to live it up, and then staring at this girl in the coffee shop and deciding to make a mockery of her, when he should have recognized who the fuck she was to begin with.

Could Alice read that all on his face? She leaned forward and touched his cheek and felt stubble upon it. Tears were beginning to stream continuously down her cheeks.

"I had such a crush on you," Alice said. "My mom had me worshiping everything about you and Felix and our sister Alice. How do I know if she was telling the truth? But I do know that I cared for you —

so much. You saw me sitting at that coffee shop; I watched you and Felix enter, and my heart rose because… I'd said hi to you on the street just a few minutes earlier, and you both ignored me. I thought you'd come into the coffee shop to… make it right! Like, I truly thought you were going to apologize for ignoring me — like it had all been just a joke, or something. And I was so sad that you both were getting married, I wanted at least… I don't know *what* I wanted from you, but I thought I was more important to you than… what you did."

"And… what did I do?" Jonathan said and his pulse was racing so hard he could barely swallow; he could barely breathe.

"YOU *IGNORED* ME!" Alice screamed, her voice cracking and giving out with a squeak, "And *then,* you mistook me for a *whore*. You idiotic boys. WE ARE *FUCKING FRIENDS* ON INSTAGRAM AND TIKTOK, JONATHAN. And you're so stupid, so stupid you didn't recognize me. So stupid you let me, a *little girl,* into your lives and you let me wreck everything important to you, because you're so pathologically focused on your own little problems that you couldn't even recognize me. Your father is right! You're both just *so stupid*!"

Felix burst into a fresh set of sobs and fell onto his knees. He was gibberish, human gibberish, and Jonathan knew he wouldn't be well by tomorrow. It was lost. All of this was lost.

Jesus Christ. Because I couldn't fucking recognize her? Was it that important that this spoiled, shallow, attention-seeking brat be recognized? As what, a human being?

By me? Really? She's a fucking pair of tits. And now Jonathan felt completely justified in not recognizing her. She would have only ever been around Jonathan and Felix in passing; at parties and dinners, she would have had to leave as soon as alcohol was served. She would have been tagging along at her big sister's elbow, ignored by everyone present because she was too young to be there.

Felix continued weeping on the floor. Even if Alice did not want anything from them and all the evidence was deleted from their phones, it would not change the fact that Felix was irretrievably broken. Did she understand that? Did she care? Probably not.

"It's actually kind of funny, when you think…" Alice began saying, but her voice cut into a scream as Jonathan lunged at her and grabbed her by her hair.

The pain was so intense, she felt stars, the floor collapsing beneath her feet as her field of vision went red. Jonathan dragged her across the floor, and she flailed and kicked her legs, trying to keep up with his strides. He dragged her into the bathroom, and she felt the cool tiles on her toes. She saw the water still in the bathtub from her bath with Ciccone earlier; she wondered if Jonathan were going to drown her in it.

Dying now seemed a reality, and Alice did not want to do it. She didn't believe a hell or a heaven was in store for her. The ever-swallowing blackness and permanence of consciousness being extinguished terrified her, and she began to frantically scratch and kick at Jonathan; but he was too big, too made of iron.

"Let go!" she screamed. "Let me go!"

"Fucking bitch," Jonathan hissed. He easily held her with one hand as he fumbled his pants off with the other. His cock pushed against her face, hard as a fucking billy club, pressed against her lips. She clenched her teeth for a moment, but as her bleeding lips began to falter from pain, she found herself opening her mouth, gagging as he shoved his cock so far, she felt it in her throat.

She could meet her teeth together; he could kill her. She coughed as liquid slipped from her throat, slime, and salt, she tasted the tang of his skin, the warmth of his salt and she imagined his cock growing so long that it was going to snake down her esophagus and into her belly and she would be able to digest it and get her revenge that way.

She curled her fingers together. She could not breathe because of the slime and tears slipping from her nose. She slid her palms against his hard ass and pressed into it. She pinched with her fingers and heard him moan, his ass cheeks tightened, and she pushed as if to encourage him to go down deeper and he pulled his cock from her mouth and she gasped, strings of fluid connecting from her lips to his cock, and he took hold of his cock and slapped it against her face.

The moisture touched her eyelids, and she gasped, inhaling deeply, fearing that it was the last breath she would take. He said something she could not understand. She kept her eyes closed and moaned as he took a harder grip of her head, twisting it sideways, and the pain was so great she thought her neck was going to snap. He jerked off with one hand, pulling at his cock and grunting while she pinched her eyes closed, yearning for him to finish because it seemed like he was going to snap her head off her shoulders.

She gagged in disgust. He was coming and the sperm was slapping against her face, stringy and thick, a smell like… she tried to place it but as soon as she felt the smell, she lost her sense of smell. She felt everything about her senses, her taste, her touch, shut off as he finished coming all over her face.

"LET HER GO! STEP AWAY FROM THE GIRL!"

Alice squinted through the gunk on her face and felt a million explosions of pain sparking through her nerves as Jonathan held her tighter, twisted her head just enough for her to anticipate her neck snapping.

She saw two policemen, guns pointed into the bathroom.

It was over.

For everyone.

Silence sparkled between them. Alice could hear her own heartbeat. She saw the policemen's eyes on him and on her, darting back and forth. One of the cops was a stout-looking older man with salt-and-pepper hair, and the other was a young, Hispanic-looking fellow.

"STEP AWAY…" the older cop said.

"I'll fucking kill!" Jonathan yelled, and Alice felt the nerves in her neck and spine scream—

And then the sharp, reverberating BANG of a gunshot, the sound cracking Alice's eardrums, hurting every nerve ending in her body, but the pressure left her neck and she felt blessed freedom.

Alice fell to the floor, catching herself just in time before her face struck it. The sounds of human voices became mush in her brain, and she found herself caught in a feeling like the irresistible urge to fall asleep, consciousness trying to leave her body as her vision darkened but she stared at her hands as they held her weight up on the floor, droplets of blood from her nose or mouth pattering onto them, and then she was feeling the policemen's hands…? Warm, strong, sweaty arms were encircling her body and lifting her to a sitting position.

Felix was screaming in the other room, and it sounded like he was being murdered.

Alice opened her eyes again, after someone began wiping the sperm off her face. She saw Jonathan's body on the ground, his perfect hard ass pointed upwards, his hips, his waist, his arms, his thighs, all looking like a statue of Percy Shelley, sleeping or in a mausoleum. Blood spilled onto the tile from a bullet wound in his shoulder.

Jonathan's eyes opened. He exhaled hard and turned his face to Alice, and their gazes met. Making no move to get up, his lips curled into a smile.

Bang, she thought.

She could hear Felix moaning and crying. Someone was trying to question him, but he sounded like a six-year-old child inhaling tears.

"It's okay, sweetie," the older policeman was saying to Alice, cradling her like a small child. He probably had children.

He probably fancies himself someone who fights tirelessly for women and children — the helpless and weak — but I bet he'd never lift a finger for me if he couldn't see my tits. Alice wanted to bite him, spit blood in his face, flay the hand of any kindness offered to her. Why did her heart feel so molten, so broken? Her anger was helpless: she could make no mark on this world of men who could rape her or protect her or heal her at their whim, sometimes all on the same day.

"You're safe," the older policeman kept saying softly to her, "you're safe…"

"Blessed boy," Alice muttered, she could see Felix just outside the bathroom door being handcuffed. She was carried out of the bathroom, and Felix began calling her name.

Alice knew Felix had not called the police; he wouldn't have. She imagined that it must have been Ciccone who did — the small, scrappy man knew he couldn't physically do a thing to Jonathan, but he must have had a heart to help her. Even if he could be incriminated by making the call.

"Blessed boy," Alice said again.

She was wrapped in a blanket, and another policeman sat with her, then she was handed to paramedics, as was Jonathan, who had been strapped onto a gurney. She was vaguely aware of questions lobbed at her, and that she did not answer them. She dimly noticed the feeling of her robe being taken off her body, her body being examined, someone calling for a gurney because she could not walk properly.

"She's traumatized!" someone said. "They've fucking destroyed this kid!"

An earthquake hit.

The earthquakes the day before had been so alien, and she'd been in such a different state of being that she'd thought it had been a trick of her mind at first — but this one was different. All the furniture shook, glass things broke, and a general panic hit, because Denver was not a city prepared for an earthquake. She clung to someone, feeling like a monkey as she was whisked out of the building, naked and without proper treatment. Everyone was talking about the earthquake, people spilled onto the streets from restaurants and buildings. Alice felt their fear and concern and drank from it, feeling the soothing effervescence of their empathy, until soft, clean arms welcomed her body into an ambulance.

There was a chaotic urgency in the air, a sort of noisy post-earthquake euphoria in a city unused to such phenomena. News crews were already assembling at various locations, and the restaurants at Union Station were dealing with a crisis of exuberant frat-boys, off the Zephyr train, looting the remains of anything ingestible from the bars.

The television screens at the sports bars were silent and black, some of them falling from the wall, some of them dangling by wires; and with their deaths, the silent images of tanks leveling protesting civilians in some far-away European country were extinguished.

This was America. This was Denver. The air was sweet, and the afternoon was passing into evening but the sun was still hot, the baseball field was completely undamaged from the earthquake and the game would go on that evening as scheduled which would make it a conversation starter amongst Coloradans for at least a decade.

It would rain the next day, a chaotic thunderstorm that would normally be marveled at for its deluge of welcoming summer moisture; but the headlines the morning after the storm would be about the tragedy of the young woman who had drowned in a 5.4 earthquake-damaged basement apartment, because she couldn't escape the flood that engulfed the room. She had been babysitting two cats and a boxer named Boris, and the pets drowned with her.

For those first few days after the earthquake, Alice lay in a sterile hospital bed after an exhausting series of procedures to both treat the damage to and to collect evidence from her traumatized genitals and anus. The hospital was a chaotic mess of damaged rooms and equipment, but fortunately the building itself stood strong and sound through the quake, and the staff did their level best with the influx of shaken Denverities bearing injuries to their establishment seeking treatment. Alice's good fortune was thanks to the policemen who had rescued her, as they remained dogged in their efforts to ensure that she was front of the line for priority care, rather than languishing bruised and bleeding in a hospital hallway or an overcrowded room. Unfortunately, the lengths that the officers and hospital staff went to in collecting physical evidence of assault from Alice's body were ultimately for naught, because the rape kit disappeared a few weeks later. Mislabeled, misplaced, accidentally discarded? No one could say for sure.

Felix spent the next week strapped to a bed in the psychiatric ward of the same hospital. The enormous dose of mushrooms he had taken had rendered him trapped for a couple of days in a raving, dissociative state. He'd continued fighting imaginary crows and calling for his dead sister to return, and when he finally came out of it, he was so overtaken with despair that he wished he could have kept his illusions instead.

Jonathan was handcuffed to his hospital bed after being rushed into surgery to treat the gunshot wound that had passed through his rotator cuff. He would heal quickly over the next six months, but his shoulder would never mend entirely. For the rest of his life, he would have to guard against overtaxing that arm, as overexertion resulted in bouts of severe pain. Two armed policemen guarded him as he snarled threats of lawsuits and revenge; he finally fell silent only when his irate, long-suffering mother arrived at his bedside. She did not comment on the conspicuous absence of his father. She did advise Jonathan to keep his fucking mouth shut. He appeared to listen.

The entire Forrester Family was unsure of what they could expect to happen once Alice chose to finally speak. But Alice didn't want to speak. Every time she thought about any of it, her throat felt squeezed shut, glued in place by the memory of Jonathan and Felix's sperm, and she did not tell anyone anything they wanted or needed to hear. She said nothing to her devastated father, Richard, who had been frantically searching for Alice since the first Earthquake struck, holding up pictures of Alice and asking if anyone in Denver remembered seeing her. Brennan Talbot had taken to her TikTok and floated the hashtag #WhereIsAlice. Alice's other sister, Mari, who had some clout as a devoted animal activist, had been using her social media to do the same.

Alice accepted a steady drip of pain medication, and simply refused to answer any question a policeman or doctor, or her father, or her sisters might have for her. She floated in a pink, hazy ether, fantasizing that no one in the hospital knew who she was, and that as a girl of mystery she could leave the building with a new identity and a new future.

There was no hope of anonymity, however; Brennan made such a viral issue of her plight that over the course of the next week, Alice's hospital room filled with bouquets of her favorite flowers — violas, snapdragons, and roses —and cards, letters, and gifts from strangers. All from fans of her sister's. Brennan spent every moment she could at Alice's bedside with a ukulele, writing a song titled "Little Viola" to commemorate her joy that her sister had been found alive.

When Brennan asked Alice's thoughts about the song on a livestream, Alice hoarsely squeaked, in a moment that would be forever commemorated in numerous TikTok and Instagram clips, "It's shit."

Their older sister, Mari, gasped audibly, and could be glimpsed covering her mouth with her hand in the background. Brennan, however, didn't miss a beat, and glibly made a joke about Alice's delirium on painkillers.

The initial headlines about Alice, Felix, and Jonathan read, "Talbot Sister and Forrester Sons Attacked By Looters." The headlines changed considerably over the ensuing days, though the bizarre truth of the situation was only vaguely explained, due to Alice's foggy memory, the blackouts she'd suffered, and her constantly vacillating narrative. The sad fact remained that she just could not —or, as Brennan put it to their father, she *would* not — remember enough relevant details to give law enforcement or the press any real idea as to what happened in the apartment. Brennan remained skeptical after that point of anything Alice said about what had transpired in the apartment. And Alice, for her part, didn't say much.

There was the undeniable fact that Jonathan had been shot down by police while assaulting Alice, but the body-cam footage was lost due to a mysteriously corrupted computer file. Jonathan never wavered from the narrative that the trio had been under the control of a dangerous cocktail of GHB, ecstasy, and magic mushrooms, all served to them without their knowledge or consent, by a supposedly friendly acquaintance who was looking to manufacture a blackmail situation that the Forrester family would not acquiesce to.

Still, Jonathan and Felix were rather publicly dumped by Fauna and Felicity. The Solti Art and Forrester Foundation merger was thus never to happen, and the Forrester parents began the arduous process of rewriting and repackaging the social narrative of their sons. Alice's father was not cut from the Forrester Foundation; rather, he was given four galleries in his own name. Argyll Forrester expected this gift to be accepted by his dear friend Richard Talbot as proof that he, Argyll, was a fair and generous man who valued loyalty. Despite Richard's quiet misgivings about the Forrester patriarch and his boys, he graciously accepted the promotion to spare Alice any further public fallout. He did, however, politely refuse Argyll's offer of personally selected doctors at Alice's bedside, insisting that the hospital's staff was competent to care for her.

Alice's mother, Briony Talbot, traveled from Paris to Alice's bedside, and she poured her tears and kisses over Alice's battered little body. However, Briony dismissed both Brennan's and Mari's insistence that she should speak up against the Forrester brothers. She explained to the young ladies that dwelling on the past was what had harmed Alice in the first place, and that the only way to heal was to never again speak of it.

Briony blossomed in the aftermath of Alice's trauma. Caught up in wanting to nurture and care for the daughter she had tried to abandon, she lost her need for anti-depressant pills and talk therapy. She lavished Alice with precious crystals and singing bowls. She reconnected with her ex-husband, Richard, and declared him, once again, her dearly beloved friend. But somehow, all of Briony's attempts to heal Alice made Alice feel empty and abandoned at the edge of strip-mined holes in her chest, and cunt, and womb — quarries that no amount of celestite, rose quartz, or tourmalines from her mother could heal.

Alice spent several months after that horrific weekend caught in a world of sleep and horrified wakefulness. Her most common daydream was the memory of Jonathan's blood spreading into a bright red pool under his body, over the tiles of the bathroom floor. She often thought of the sounds of Felix screaming gibberish in his own personal hell that she knew he would never be able to outrun.

Sometimes, Alice lay in bed, awake into the wee hours, staring at her phone screen; she'd scroll Reddit and discord threads made by gossipers and conspiracy theorists, many of them speculating that the Forresters were an Illuminati cult and that she, Alice, was a malfunctioning Monarch slave. And sometimes, Alice wondered if that wasn't too far from the truth.

It wasn't until the following spring that she felt energetic enough to take a long walk with Brennan in LoDo. It was a rare moment when she felt well enough to appreciate the cool air and warm spring sun. Brennan had gotten tickets for Opening Day at Coors Field; they had ice cream at Union Station and wandered Wynkoop with iced coffees in their hands.

Both of the young ladies were wearing oversized Colorado Rockies jerseys and baseball caps. Alice's hair was pulled back in a tight ponytail and her makeup was contoured and set to the latest tutorial trend on TikTok. Brennan was wearing a black wig, red heart-shaped glasses, and a press-on Frida Kahlo mustache in a so-far-so-good attempt at anonymity. They were just a couple of young, skinny little rich girls lost in a crowd.

"Do you ever just want to burn the world down?" Brennan asked as she and Alice watched a group of pre-teen girls who were standing on a bench, dancing in unison while their mother filmed them with her smartphone. An emaciated, sun-beaten man watched the girls. He held a pair of safety scissors in his shaking hands, and he was using them to cut tufts of hair from his scalp. The hair lay in scattered clumps on the pavement around his feet.

"We're all food for crows, anyway," Alice said. "It'll be our turn soon enough."

"Yeah," Brennan replied, pointing at the girls, "But I want *them* to go first!"

Alice smirked, "That's your *fanbase*, Brennan."

Brennan grinned, the prickly black hairs of the fake mustache loosening on her damp upper lip. "Made you smile, though? Eh? And you *know* I'm a dick. That's the only reason you don't completely hate me. Admit it."

Alice closed her eyes and tilted her face up to the sun, and she felt hot tears slide down her cheeks as Brennan abruptly hugged her. Neither sister said a word.

Brennan was thinking about how glad she was that she'd been able to get Alice out of the house for such a beautiful day, but she was also thinking of how she was going to go about telling Alice that her new album was titled *The Voluptuaires in the Apartment*, and that Alice was just going to have to deal with it. Brennan didn't know that Alice already knew about the album title because Mari had warned Alice about it; and, Alice didn't mind. Worrying about album titles and song lyrics was just not something Alice had energy for anymore.

Alice saw Jonathan's smiling face in her mind more often than not, even when she closed her eyes in the sunlight. She imagined him staring at the scar the bullet hole must have left on his body and he would smile, because he could always say he'd faced down a policeman who'd then had to clean Jonathan's cum off a girl's face. It would make him a hit in all the circles that mattered, Alice knew that, and he would probably think about her scars, the ones he'd left inside her, and he would laugh.

FIN

ACKNOWLEDGMENTS

I would like to thank Fox Henry Frazier for hearing a portion of this novel read aloud and for her quick work in inquiring about the manuscript's availability!

A million thank yous to Josh for encouraging me to finish the manuscript and reading and responding to it every step of the way.

Thank you to my sister and Stacey for reading and approving of this horrible tale.

Thank you to Hillary Leftwich, Elísabet Ronaldsdóttir, and Mihael Pelin for their blurbs.

Thank you to Sarah Reck for her design work in getting this novel put together, she definitely hit it outta the park.

Thank you National Novel Writing Month for existing and giving me that structure to get this novel finished.

Thank you Leza Cantoral for coming up with a Lana Del Rey-themed anthology, because this novel started out as a Lana Del Rey-inspired short story intended for that anthology—but the manuscript got too long for that!

And most of all thank you to the editors at Agape Editions / Haunted Doll House for being the hardworking force that went above and beyond to create the look and feel for this novel that has blown me away. Getting full creative control is a rare thing for any artist or writer, and that is exactly what this has been for me!

ABOUT THE AUTHOR

Alais Escobar Henri is a Latina author and lifelong resident of Denver, Colorado, who spends all of her money on world travel, collecting crystals, single malt whisky, Kate Spade purses, and John Fluevog shoes. You probably think you know her well, but rest assured she writes about all of the people you don't.

Haunted Doll House is an imprint of Agape Editions. As our name suggests, we aren't afraid of the dark: we live there. We want your horror stories, your mystery novels, your dark sf/f, your genre-resistant writing about the ecstasies, traumas, & terrors that took you to the very edges of yourself.

Agape Editions is a literary micropress created in southern California, now located in upstate New York. We publish visionary literature.

Our name comes from the ancient Greek ἀγάπη (agápē), describing the joyous love that exists universally without seeking or expecting anything in return. Agape can be described as the bond between humans & the Numinous, but we believe it exists everywhere—manifested through the kindness of strangers, felt alone under a sky filled with aurora, made real through a moment of ecstatic meditation or deep connection with another.

A moment of Agape is a moment in which you feel yourself fully—in the broader context of the universe at large.

Agape is about finding the strength & courage to remain open-hearted, in a world that doesn't always encourage or reward an open heart.

Our notions of the sacred & the Numinous span wide swaths of experience—private epiphanies; shared ecstasies; moments of intimacy; sublime revelation; cultural identity; spiritual traditions as conduit for survival. The psychic, the occult, the supernatural. The divinity of the natural world. Wild love. Fascinating scientific discovery. Mind-blowing technological advancement. Fernweh. The thrill of exploration. Sacred feminine rage.

We are profoundly uninterested in attempting to dictate the parameters of spiritual experience. We want to feel through you & your writing what's holy to you & why.

Imagine: awakening, breathless, in the thick of night. You've been dreaming of William Blake's Tyger-burning-bright & all its terrifying beauty. & now, from somewhere in the surrounding darkness, you can hear its quiet breathing.

Welcome to Agape Editions.